BADD KITTY

A BADD BROTHERS NOVEL

Jasinda Wilder

BADD KITTY

ONE

Kitty

"Yo, Kitty—that couple at table six is asking for more mayo, and thirteen needs refills all around." Sebastian Badd—everyone familiar with him called him Bast—my boss, tossed this at me as he passed me on his way back behind the bar. "Also, you've got food up."

I was at the service bar, waiting for Lucian—the second youngest Badd brother—to make my tray of drinks. I had a table I needed to greet still, another table to check on, food up in the window for two different tables, and now the refills to get and the mayo…I was buried. I'd been in the bar serving since eleven this morning, and now it was past nine at night, and

I was exhausted. The tips had been stellar, so it was worth it, but still.

I glanced at Bast as I arranged the drinks on the tray as Lucian finished preparing them. "I'm swamped right now, Bast. Can you run the food and grab the mayo?"

"That sounds hard," he said, in his deep, growly voice, only barely suppressing a smirk. "You gonna split your tips with me if I do?"

I rolled my eyes at him. "Sure—how about a quarter of one percent?"

"Make it two-thirds of a percent and you've got yourself a deal."

I snorted, pulling a wrinkled, crumpled five-dollar bill out of my apron, wadded it into a ball, and threw it at him. "There, that should cover it."

Bast chuckled as he retrieved the wadded money off the floor. "You need a math refresher if you think five bucks is three-quarters of a percent of what you've made today."

I laughed, balancing the tray on my shoulder. "You know, I'm not sure I could figure out three-quarters of one percent. I can do waitress math, but that's about it."

Xavier, the youngest of the eight brothers, was sitting at the booth nearest the entrance to the kitchen; that booth was the permanently reserved as a

"Family Booth," and nearly always had someone sitting in it: an off-duty Badd brother, or one of their wives or girlfriends, and/or kids.

"How much have you made so far?" Xavier asked.

I did a rough estimate. "Umm, probably around four hundred."

Xavier didn't even have to think. "Three-quarters of a percent of four hundred dollars is three dollars."

Sebastian laughed. "Thanks, Professor."

Xavier, as usual, totally missed the sarcasm. "You're welcome. And I'm not a professor, yet. I have three more semesters until I finish my masters, at which point I would be eligible to teach at a university."

Sebastian, Lucian, and I all laughed. I delivered the drinks to the correct tables, greeted the new four-top, and took drink orders, checked on seven and five, and then swung by three and eight, the tables to which Sebastian had delivered food. Shoot—the mayo! But Sebastian had done that too.

Finally, for the first time in over two hours, all my tables were either good or waiting for food—which meant I could pop into the kitchen and take a moment to breathe. Entering the kitchen, I tossed my tray on the silver metal table between me and the line cooks—Jason, Alejandro, and Big D. I allowed myself to collapse forward against the table, resting my head on my forearms. The familiar sounds of a restaurant kitchen washed over me as I closed my eyes and just breathed, shifting my weight from one tired foot to the other.

"La Gatita está muy cansando, creo," Alejandro said, a playful grin cracking his sun-weathered Columbian features.

I nodded, mentally translating his Spanish into *"The kitten is very tired."* "Yeah, you could say that."

Big D—a six-foot-six black man built like an industrial refrigerator, who would be terrifying if he wasn't one of the sweetest, kindest, and most gentle men I'd ever met—pulled two chicken tenders and a small handful of fries from the fryer baskets, tossed them on a plate, and slid the plate to me. "I made extra," he said, in his voice like velvet and syrup. "You oughta eat."

I accepted the food gratefully, scarfing it down with as much lady-like grace as my famished state would allow. "Thanks, Big D," I said, offering him a smile.

He just nodded. "You got someone walkin' you home?"

I shrugged. "It's not far. I'll be fine."

He just frowned at me. "Nah. I'll walk you." He took this job very seriously, never letting me walk home alone after a late shift, even though he had a thirty-minute bus ride and a ten-minute walk to get home himself. "Pretty young thing like you, somebody gon' snap you up if we don't keep an eye on you."

Jason was the newest addition to the Badd Bar and Grill kitchen; he was nineteen, a recent transplant to Ketchikan from way up in Gnome, wore his long brown hair in a loose ponytail, and seldom spoke. "I could walk you home sometime, if you wanted," he said, smiling shyly at me.

Alejandro and Big D both chortled, because Jason was five-ten and weighed maybe a hundred and thirty soaking wet, and was as gentle as a kitten—and just as adorably clueless.

Jason sighed. "I did take three years of Kung Fu, you know."

Big D just clapped a hand the size of a bear's paw on Jason's thin shoulder. "You come by my place sometime, young'un. We'll lift some weights and my lady will feed you—get some meat on those skinny bones of yours."

This was not an idle offer on Big D's part—he was generous to a fault, willing to help anyone out, and had a habit of taking younger guys under his wing. Despite being one of the most genuinely kind people I've ever met, he was not someone you'd even consider crossing, and this was not just due to his size, but his demeanor of calm confidence that somehow contained a veiled hint of past darkness.

Jason grinned. "You mean it? I've always wanted to go to a gym, but I wouldn't know where to start, and I feel like other guys would tease me for it."

Big D grabbed a ticket as it spat out of the printer, reading it over before handing it to Alejandro. "We both open on Friday. You come with me after we're done, and I'll show you some things."

Alejandro spoke while fixing the salad that was the only item on the ticket—a bar food order. "Hey, I like to work out too, Big D. Why you never invite me, huh?"

Big D rumbled a laugh. "I seen your setup, 'Jandro. You got more iron than I do, son."

Alejandro put the finishing touches on the salad. "Then you both come to *my* place and we all lift the weights together, *si*?"

I took the salad from Alejandro after washing my hands. "I'll take it out. I need to check on my tables anyway."

I closed out three tables in the next fifteen minutes, and finally had time to roll some silverware and do some of my other side work while my drinks-only tables worked on their beverages.

Despite needing the money, I was half hoping the bar would die out soon so I could go home; I'd worked doubles the two previous days as well as to-day, but I had tomorrow off. When I'd done as much of my side work as I could do before closing, I went behind the bar and helped Lucian wash glasses and restock, just to keep busy. At this point, I knew if I slowed down or sat down I'd never get back up, so I made sure to keep moving.

I was ten minutes from the official end of my shift when the hair on the back of my neck prickled, and an odd shiver ran down my spine. I was wiping down a table that had just cashed out and left, and slowly straightened and turned to see what had sent that shiver through me.

The front door was propped open, and three men walked through it—although swaggered is the better term for how they moved. Heads high, shoulders back, arms swinging loosely, their gaits slow and lazy. I gaped at them as they spread out in the entrance of the bar, eyeing the interior for a good place to sit.

They were identical triplets, and each of them was utterly jaw-dropping. Six feet four, easily, if not six-five. It's easy to talk about solid muscle, but these men took the concept to a whole new level. I was the head waitress for Badd's Bar and Grill, and I was close enough to the eight Badd brothers after a year and a half of working for them that I thought of them as almost like family; my point here is that the Badd brothers—especially the older four—were some of the biggest, most powerfully built, and, honestly, sexiest men I'd ever met in person. Each of the brothers was fit to the point of absurdity, and Bast, Zane, and Bax, especially, were built like professional athletes. So monster physiques didn't faze me very much, until now.

These three triplets…

I was fazed.

Very, very fazed.

Bast was six-four and I knew from overhearing his conversations with Bax that he weighed somewhere around two-forty. These men had to be packing at least twenty pounds more than that of solid, lean muscle. It was mind-boggling. Yet despite their insane muscle mass, none of them lumbered around like a muscle-bound juice-head. They moved with lithe, easy, catlike grace. Like Zane, in some ways. They had a similar look in their eyes as the combat-hardened former Navy SEAL, and moved with the same intimidating assurance of their own prowess and power.

They were blond-haired and blue-eyed, with square-jawed, hard-hewn features. The first through the door had his hair cut short enough that it stuck up in natural spikes, and was clean-shaven. The second was similar, though his hair was longer on top and slicked straight back, also clean-shaven. The third had hair long enough to sweep over his head and drape in front of his face, with a short, neat blond beard. Each wore faded, well-worn blue jeans over battered, scuffed, dirty, square-toed cowboy boots, plain black leather belts, and T-shirts printed with various logos—the first through the door wore a shirt featuring a parachute with wings that said "California Smokejumpers," the second bore the logo of the US Forest Service, and the third, worn by the triplet with the beard, wore a baseball T-shirt with a professional rodeo logo on it.

They stood together for several moments, three pairs of mammoth arms crossed over enormous chests, surveying the bar, and then swaggered as a unit toward the table in the back nearest the currently empty stage. They sat down so they could all put their backs to the wall and face the bar. They didn't speak to each other as they waited, seemingly content to just sit in silence.

I hesitated, wishing, oddly, that there was someone else to pass the table off to. I'd cut both the other waitresses already, though, so it was just me in the bar, and the guys, but I wasn't about to look weak or scared in front of the Badd brothers. I'd worked my butt off to win their respect and affection, and I wasn't about to lose it by wimping out just because

I felt a weird frisson of unease in the presence of the newcomers. The Badd brothers—and their significant others—were not easily impressed, and their respect was definitely hard-won.

Why was I being such a wuss? It was just a few guys. After waitressing for years in bars, restaurants, and clubs, I'd dealt with pretty much every kind of clientele there is: burly, loud-mouthed bikers, grouchy but lovable regulars, handsy frat boys, sloppy club lushes, and everything in between. These three were nothing I couldn't handle.

I'd hesitated too long at the service bar, though.

"Problem, Kitty?" Lucian asked, as sharply observant as ever.

I shook my head and shouldered my tray of drinks. "Nope. I'm good. Just spacing, I guess—I've had a long few days."

Lucian glanced at me, and then the table of muscular blond gods, and then back at me. "I can take eleven if you want."

"And miss out on the *amazing* tip I'm sure I'll get from them?" I rolled my eyes with a sarcastic huff. "Not on your life, pal."

"You wouldn't be stereotyping our customers, now, would you, Kitty Quinn?" Lucian teased.

"Me? Stereotype someone? Why, I *never*!"

Lucian just quirked an eyebrow in that expressive

way all the Badd brothers had. "You called me Legolas for the first three months you worked here." With exotic features, long brown hair, and a mysterious aura to him, Lucian definitely resembled, in my mind, the character from the JRR Tolkien novels.

I laughed. "I still think of you as Legolas in my own head."

He tossed an ice cube at me, bouncing it off my tray and into my apron pocket. "Go serve those meatheads."

I walked away, tossing over my shoulder, "Now who's stereotyping?"

I dropped off the round of beers and shots to thirteen and then, with a deep, fortifying breath, headed to table eleven.

"Hi, I'm Kitty. You boys want to see some menus, or are you just drinking?" I said this with my best, brightest, and fakest smile, and a pleasant lilt in my voice.

All three pairs of vivid, intense blue eyes locked on me. I was immediately struck by a sensation of being a deer trapped in a clearing surrounded by hungry wolves. I clutched my tray in front of me, arms crossed over it, waiting for one of them to answer me.

"Just drinking," said the one in the rodeo shirt.

"Speak for yourself, dick," the smokejumper shirt said. "I'm eating."

"Yeah, I'm hungry too," said the US Forest Service shirt.

The first to speak rolled his eyes. "Fine. Menus then. What-the-fuck-ever."

"What's good here?" asked Smokejumper.

"Everything is good, but we're pretty famous locally for our burgers and our fish and chips."

"What kinda fries you serve?" he asked. "Those stupid little stringy ones, or the real fries, the thick ones?"

"Actually, we have both," I answered. "Shoestring or steak cut."

He nodded. "Killer. Are the burgers actually any good, or are you just trying to sell me on them?"

I only partially suppressed a frown. "Well, it *is* my job to sell the food here. I eat here sometimes myself on my days off because the food is actually good. The burgers are hand-pressed fresh every morning. The specialty, and what I'd recommend, is the Get In Here burger. It's two, one-third pound patties pressed together around a slice of aged cheddar, topped with bacon and house-made jalapeño mayo. After it's grilled, the cheese is melting out the sides of the burger, and if you like spicy stuff, the mayo packs quite a punch. It's amazing. Created by our very own Xavier Badd," I said, pointing at Xavier, who was still sitting at the family booth with a laptop and a stack of textbooks.

"That sounds pretty tits, actually," Smokejumper said. "I'll have that."

Sounds pretty tits? What kind of chauvinistic horse crap was that? I stomped down the urge to sigh and roll my eyes at him, and instead forced a smile on my face. "And to drink?" I asked. "All Alaskan Brewing Company draft pours are three dollars between ten and close."

He nodded. "The Alaskan Amber, then."

I went through the same rigmarole all over again with the other two, because they weren't paying attention—their gaze was focused firmly on a pair of barely twenty-one girls who'd come in dressed—or rather *undressed*—to attract maximum male attention. The entire time I was giving my spiel to the other two brothers, however, the first had his eyes on me, following my every move.

I tried to ignore him, but he made it hard. He had a ghost of a grin on his face, and his eyes were—like his brothers'—a shade of intense, neon cerulean that was so bright they were almost hypnotic. And he wasn't subtle with his gaze, either—as I spoke to his brothers, I felt him eyeing me up and down, felt his eyes watching my face, my expressions, my lips. I saw him out of the corner of my eyes the whole time, blatantly staring at me.

When I was done taking their order, I glanced back at him. "Didn't your mother teach you it's rude to stare?" I asked, trying for a careful balance that was neither rude nor flirtatious.

He did the thing with his eyebrow that all the Badd brothers do, and it sent my stomach tumbling in weird flips. "No, actually. She left when we were seven."

I could only blink at him for a moment, waiting, I suppose, for the *just kidding*; it never came. "Oh, I— um. I'm sorry about that, then. But this can be your lesson: it's rude to stare at people."

He just kept smirking, his expression amused. "Is it? People stare at me all the time." He winked at me. "And I bet they stare at you, too, beautiful. You'd think you'd be used to it by now."

He just complimented himself and me in the same breath? Full of himself, much? Jeez.

Flustered, I just let out a little sigh as I turned away. "I'll be back with your drinks in a minute."

"Take your time, sweetheart," Smokejumper said. "I'll just be enjoying the view from here."

And yes, I felt his gaze on my butt the entire way from the table to the point-of-sale computer where I rang in their order. Lucian poured their beers and I dropped them off, promising their food would be out soon, and then left to make the rounds of my other tables. I did my best to ignore table eleven, and the one man in particular, but it was difficult. He would catch my eye every now and then, and he would grin at me in a confident, suggestive way that implied he knew exactly how charming and heart-stopping that grin was.

I brought their food, made sure they enjoyed it and that their beers were never empty, and pretended to stop noticing Smokejumper.

Except...I couldn't help but notice him. Outside of his sheer imposing size, his presence somehow dominated the bar. Everywhere I went, I *felt* him. And every time I found myself helplessly drawn to glance at him, he had that grin for me, with those white straight teeth and the suggestive gleam in his cerulean eyes. The other two brothers seemed more interested in the two barely legal girls, who had also very definitely noticed the triplets. Heck, it was impossible *not* to notice them. But this one?

He had eyes only for me.

Was I flattered, or creeped out? A little of both.

I mean, I was in my Badd's Bar and Grill women's V-neck, which was flattering for a work shirt but definitely not sexy, and I was wearing what I thought of as my "work jeans," which were my most comfortable and most worn pair, but not my most-flattering, fit-wise. The girls, his brothers were staring at, for example, were ten years younger than me, wearing roughly 80 percent less clothing which they filled out way better with their nubile little bodies. Plus, they seem interested, and I'm not.

I'm *not* interested.

Not at all.

Sure, he resembles John Cena, except bigger and better looking.

Yet it's *me* he's looking at. Weirdo.

Okay, don't get me wrong—I'm not self-conscious, I don't have body image issues...at least not any more than any other modern American woman. But why ogle the slightly above average-looking at best waitress when there are at least ten single women in here with bigger assets and nothing to do but angle for his attention?

I shook the thoughts away, resolved to be better at ignoring his attention, and went back to doing my job. Thankfully, there was a bit of a drink rush at eleven, just after our kitchen closed, so I was slammed enough that I had no time for anything except to make sure the triplets were good on drinks.

Maybe I was stereotyping them, but I expected them to pound their food down and then get to work putting away as much booze as possible, as fast as possible. Instead, once they finished their food they kicked back in their chairs and sipped, slowly nursing their beers. They still managed to down half a dozen beers each in the next hour, but they seemed as steady and sober as when they'd walked in.

There were a few odd things about them, though: they were barely conversing with each other, just sitting there, watching the crowd, me, Sebastian, and Lucian behind the bar, occasionally glancing at Xavier, who was oblivious to the entire world outside of his textbooks and laptop. They weren't on their phones, either; in fact, I'm not sure I saw a single cell phone between the three of them. They seemed content, literally, to just sit, drink, and watch the bar. Which was odd for men so obviously fit and active.

Finally, the rush slowed around midnight and I had a chance to catch my breath. Big D was still hanging around in the kitchen, prepping for dinner the next day and making the occasional basket of fried food: after the kitchen officially closed at eleven, the fryers remained on and someone was always around to drop a basket as needed—having fries, cheese sticks, chicken tenders, sweet potato tots, and other greasy fried food available all the way to closing time was a huge draw for us, as we were one of the few places that served alcohol *and* had food besides pretzels and nuts available past eleven. The food was served in paper baskets, too, so there was minimal cleanup.

I sagged a hip against the salad line in the kitchen,

grabbed a handful of carrots Big D had just chopped, and snacked on them while watching him dice chicken for the next day's special: chicken pot pie.

"Are you still walking me home tonight, Big D?" I asked.

He didn't look up from dicing, his knife working at lightning speed. "Sure am, baby girl."

I nodded, not quite sighing in relief. "Cool. Thank you."

He looked up then, hearing the not-quite-sigh. "Whassup, Kitty-cat? Somebody creepin' on you out there?"

I wobbled my head side to side. "I'm not quite ready to say he's creeping on me, but he's been watching me all night. I'm not, like, *scared* of him—I don't get that feeling from him, I just…" I shrugged. "I don't know."

D just kept dicing, sliding piles of chicken aside as he finished one breast and started on the next. "I got you, boo."

"Thanks, D."

He raised his knife in response, and went back to dicing while I left the kitchen to check on my tables and hit more side work while waiting for Bast to announce last call.

As I swung past table eleven and the three imposing figures hunched over it, a particular pair of ultramarine eyes found mine, and then slid down to watch my hips as I approached.

I had to consciously stop myself from popping them as I walked. Which was utterly stupid of me, because I'm not that girl. I'm a professional server, and I do *not* flirt with customers. Ever.

And I'm not about to start now, and not with this guy.

"How are you guys doing?" I asked. "Another round?"

The triplet with the beard and the longer hair flicked the late-night mini-menu stapled to the side of the cardboard Corona Light six-pack holder that held the salt, pepper, ketchup, mustard, silverware rolls, and extra napkins. "You really serve food till close?"

I nodded. "We're certainly not in the business of trolling our customers with fake menus," I said, smiling a little to take the sting out of my snark—something about these three brought out the sass in me, which was quite rare for me.

The bearded triplet just stared at me balefully, seriously, his gaze intense and lacking any trace of humor. "Funny." He drained his beer. "An order of tenders, fries, and cheese sticks. Another beer, too. And a shot of Jameson."

The other two brothers eyed him.

"You on the rag or something today, Ram? You're

eating nonstop and you're acting like a cranky little bitch." This was from the Fish and Game brother.

"Fuck you. I'm hungry." This was the response from the brother who was, it seemed, named Ram.

"Fuck you back," came the reply. "Stop being a bitch-ass punk bitch about it, at least."

"Shut the fuck up, Rem. I'll drag your dumb ass outside and knock your block off, you nosy-ass cock-nugget," Ram snapped, not seeming in the least as if he was kidding.

"Yeah? I'd like to see you try," the brother named Rem said. "Which one of us failed his black belt test and had to retake it? Oh yeah, that'd be you. And which one of us passed his black belt test with highest marks? Oh *yeah*, that'd be me."

I was waiting for the others to order drinks or food, but instead I seemed to be held captive to a trip-let squabble. And a very offensive and foul-mouthed one at that.

The obsessed-with-me brother glanced at me with an amused grin and apologetic head shake. "Don't mind these dicks, Kitty. They fight like bitches literally nonstop."

"I wonder if any of you could go a whole sentence without cursing?" I mused out loud, without meaning to.

"Well, we fucking could, but we choose to

fucking not, because cursing is a lot of fucking fun,"
Smokejumper said. "Besides, don't you know a pro-
pensity for swearing is a sign of intelligence?"

I rolled my eyes. "At least your brothers were
somewhat creative about being offensive."

"You're offended by us foul-mouthed rough-
necks, princess?" he purred.

I ignored this. "Can I get anyone else more food
or drinks?"

"Double the food order, another round of beers
all around, and three shots of Jameson," he said. His
eyes slid to mine, and he grinned wolfishly. "And your
phone number."

I stared at him in surprise. "Wow. Um…How
about no?" I shook my head. "I'll be back with the
round in a minute."

As I walked away, I heard the bearded brother
murmur, "Way to be subtle, Rome."

Rome, Rem, and Ram? Were those their given
names, or short for something?

Why did I care?

I didn't care. Not even a little.

I sent in the ticket for their orders and fumed
while waiting.

Princess?

"And your phone number." Jeez. Who does that?
Who asks for a waitress's number by phrasing it as an

order? How rude can he get?

The cursing, and the staring? Ugh. What a caveman.

He was getting under my skin, and I disliked it more every time I interacted with him. It'd be so much easier to just ignore him if he wasn't so darned good-looking. It was kind of ridiculous and unfair, really. No one person should be blessed with that amount of sexiness—and there were *three* of them.

I dropped their drinks off and managed to get away without interaction, but only because they were locked in some kind of childish and complicated three-way arm wrestling/thumb wrestling competition.

When their food was ready, I brought it to them and set the various baskets on the table, hoping to get away again without any more nonsense.

Instead, as I walked away, I felt a hand latch onto my wrist, halting me. "Hold on, beautiful."

I glared at him. "Excuse me. Take your hand off me, please."

He let go immediately, holding his hands up palms out. "Sorry, I was just hoping you'd stick around to chat for a second."

"Well, calling me a demeaning and inappropri-ately familiar term of endearment and grabbing me aren't the way to get that," I said.

"Sorry." His grin said he wasn't sorry at all,

though. "How about this: Hey, Kitty—you got a minute to chat?"

I sighed. "Chat about what?"

He reached out a long leg, hooked a nearby chair with his toe, and dragged it over next to his. "Sit, and I'll tell you."

I glanced around at the bar, but it was for show—I knew without having to look that my other tables were all fine. So, I perched on the edge of the chair, my tray balanced on the edge on my knees as a shield between us. Sitting bolt upright, a wary and impatient expression on my face I said, "Okay. How can I help you?"

He snorted. "You're just all business, ain'tcha?"

"I *am* at work…"

He just waved a hand. "Relax a second. You've been busting your ass all night. Just chill for a minute."

I rolled my eyes. "I have other customers and I'm on the clock, so I can't just *chill*. Thanks for your concern, however."

He plucked a tender from the basket, his gaze speculative. "You worked here long?"

"A year and a half. Why?"

"Just curious." One bite, and the tender was half-gone. "You like it here?"

I nodded. "I do. Very much."

"What are your bosses like?"

I frowned. "The Badd brothers? I mean, they're basically minor celebrities, now. They were all raised here, so they're local legends, too. But they're all super cool. Why?"

He shrugged. "Like I said, just curious. I've heard about them, wondered what they were like."

"Well, they're great to work for." I shot him a meaningful glance. "But they do expect their employees to *work*, and not dillydally while still on the clock."

He nodded. "I would, too." His eyes slid to mine. "Got a boyfriend? A lovely girl like you *has* to be spoken for."

I gaped at him. "That is absolutely none of your business."

Lovely girl like me? Deep down, I wanted to appreciate the statement. But such was his delivery that I just couldn't.

"I—you—"

He just smirked. "You don't, then." He waved a hand. "I'm being nosy, sorry. I'm just curious."

That got words out of me. "You're asking an awful lot of very personal and probing questions for being just curious."

He chuckled. "Personal and probing? I asked if you were dating anyone. That's hardly personal or probing. It's more...the kind of question a guy asks a girl if he thinks she's hot."

I struggled for a reply, appropriate or rude or anything. "I—you think I'm—?" I stood up. "I have to check my tables."

I bolted, but I felt his eyes on me. Speculative. Interested. Intelligent. And...appreciative? I didn't know.

Fortunately, one of my tables needed refills, and a young couple came in and sat in my section, so I was busy for a while.

Not long enough, though.

My brain was racing, jumping, darting. What did he want? He was more than just curious—but about me, or the bar, or the brothers who owned this bar? I couldn't tell.

He thought I was lovely? Hot?

What did he want?

I swung back by their table like a fly drawn to a zapper light. Once again, those eyes were following me, unreadable and deep.

"We're getting close to last call," I said. "You want anything else?"

He nodded. "Yeah." He shot me a grin that was a million percent too charming for his or anyone's good. "You."

I choked on a reply. "You are so—ugh!" I didn't have to fake the surprise or the ire. "What is *with* you?"

He just laughed. "You didn't let me finish." He pulled a thrice-folded stack of papers from his back pocket, set them on the table, and tapped them with a thick forefinger. "This is the deed to a place a few blocks away. My brothers and I are opening a bar."

I glared even harder. "Good for you."

He leaned toward me, powerful forearms crossed on the table. "I want you to be our manager."

The brother named Rem frowned. "We do? I don't remember discussing this."

"Executive decision," he murmured to his brother. "Trust me on this one."

I shook my head, baffled at his hubris. "I told you I *like* working here. What part of that makes you think I would leave a job I like, working for bosses I like, to come work for you, whom I've just met?"

"Because you like me," he said, grinning. "And because you'd be managing, not waitressing, which would mean a nice steady salary. Benefits, too."

"We don't *have* a benefits package, Roman," Rem hissed. "We don't even have a fucking *name* for the place."

"Shut up, tool," Roman, my admirer, snapped back. Turning back to me, he deepened the intense charm of his grin, making it megawatt bright, dizzying, breathtakingly perfect. "Just think about it. Okay, beautiful?"

I was dumbfounded. "You are something else, you know that?" I was still trying to formulate a response, but everything that was coming to mind was a jumbled, confusing mixture of anger and attraction, neither of which was helpful.

He just shrugged a heavy shoulder. "So they say." He popped a whole mozzarella stick in his mouth, chewed, swallowed, washed it down, and then glanced at me. "So you'll think about it?"

I groaned in aggravation. "No, I'm not thinking about it!"

"You really should. You'd love working for us."

I was so flabbergasted I couldn't formulate a reply. He had a way of leaving me speechless. "I—you—you're just—"

He just laughed. "Take your time, sweetheart. I've got all night. Although, I can think of a few things for you to do with that pretty little mouth besides talk."

Dumbfounded, flabbergasted, shocked speechless—I was running out of ways to describe it. I made an inarticulate sound of disbelieving rage, whirled on my heel, and stormed away.

I had to leave the dining room entirely and hide in the kitchen to regain something like equilibrium. Sebastian, unfortunately, was leaning back against the line, eating a giant salad out of a takeout container.

His eyes latched onto me, assessing, and he lowered his fork without taking another bite. "Problem, Kitty?"

I shook my head. "Nah. Just a difficult table."

He narrowed his eyes. "Eleven?"

I sighed. "I can handle it, Bast."

"What's he doing?"

"Who?" I asked, aiming for innocent and missing by a wide margin.

"Don't play dumb," he growled. "It don't fit on you."

"Bast," I said, "I can handle it. I'm a grown-up, and I can handle annoying, pushy, overly masculine customers." I quirked an eyebrow at him. "I *do* work for you...and Zane...and Brock...*and* Bax...and all the others, for that matter, but you four are the worst."

Sebastian merely leveled a steady gaze at me. "The big blond douchebag. What's he doing to piss you off? You're usually the most laid-back person I've ever met."

"He just gets under my skin," I said. "I don't know. A couple of words from him and I'm steaming."

"Well, he's got you unbalanced, and as my best server, and the girl I've got my eye on to take over as manager, I need you balanced."

At that moment, Lucian popped into the kitchen, a napkin in his hand, which he handed to me. "The big guy at eleven asked me to give you this."

I took it gingerly, warily, as if it were a snake or an unexploded bomb. "Did they leave? They haven't paid their tab yet."

Lucian shook his head. "No, they're still there. They're counting cash, though, so I think they're getting ready to leave."

I unfolded the napkin. His handwriting was a messy angular, all-caps scrawl—*Kitty: when you decide to work for me instead, call me. You'll be...pleased*. And he included his phone number. No signature, because clearly none was needed.

Bast stared at the note over my shoulder. "The fuck? You're quitting?"

I whirled, horrified. "No!" I had to gasp for air for a moment. "Apparently he and his brothers are opening a bar in town, and he...propositioned me, I guess is the best term. I told him no, unequivocally, and in no uncertain terms. He's just a relentless jerk."

"I do *not* fuckin' think so," Bast snarled, and prowled out of the kitchen.

Ohhhhh boy. Two enormous, territorial, masculine men facing off? This could get messy, fast.

I trotted after Sebastian, with Lucian on my heels sending a flurry of texts—presumably for backup. I arrived just as Sebastian was crowding up to table eleven, massive arms crossed, glowering impressively.

Roman didn't seem intimidated, however. He just ignored Sebastian and continued counting out cash for their bill.

"Hear you're trying to poach my waitress." Sebastian said this in a bass snarl. "And being a general pain in the ass."

"Just checking out the local scene," Roman said, setting the cash on the table. "And damn, son, have you got some fine-ass scenery around here, man." He said this with a lewd smirk at me.

"It's not appreciated."

Roman just laughed. "I ain't too concerned about what you do or don't appreciate, big fella."

"I think it's time for you to leave," Sebastian growled.

Roman's eyes glinted with humor. "Aww, Sebastian, you wouldn't be trying to kick out your own cousins, now, would you?"

TWO

Roman

I COULD TELL HE WAS STUNNED SPEECHLESS. NOW, I know I have that effect on women, but it's not often I can make another man flap his jaw like that.

"The *fuck* are you talking about, asshole?" My admittedly imposing cousin said in a snarl Dad would have appreciated. In fact, everything Sebastian had said so far was in either a growl or a snarl.

I just winked. "Didn't you know? You have cousins." I gestured at my brothers, who were silent, letting me handle this, seeing as it was me getting us into this. "Three of us."

"Knowing how Dad's sleazy ass is, odds are there are more out there we don't know about,"

Ramsey added.

"Cousins?" Sebastian was eyeing us, arms at his sides, fists clenching, as if contemplating just swinging first and asking questions later.

I nodded. "My name is Roman. Roman *Badd*." I gestured to my right. "Next to me is my brother, Remington, and next to him is Ramsey. And yeah, we're identical triplets."

Behind my cousin, Kitty was staring at me with those pretty brown eyes wide and confused. I just winked at her, and turned my attention to Sebastian.

"You got anything to say?" I asked.

"Yeah—get the fuck out with your bullshit."

I stood up slowly, and he backed up, visibly tensing. I just laughed. "Hey, easy now. We ain't here for that kinda trouble." I reached into my back pocket and withdrew the photo Dad had given me—I extended it to Sebastian. "Take a look, if you don't believe me."

Sebastian took the photo from me and glanced down at it. First glance was enough, I could tell, but he looked back up at me, more critically now, and then back at the photo.

"What…the…*fuck*…is this?" he whispered.

"Yeah, it was a shock to me, too." I leaned forward and tapped one of the men in the photo. "That's our dad, Lucas Badd." I tapped the other. "That's your dad, Liam Badd." I tapped the woman in the photo.

"And *that*, my friend, is Lena Dunfield. Your mother. And the reason we never knew about each other."

His fist smashed into my jaw, a lightning fast hook that took me utterly by surprise. Even more surprising was his hands, both of them, wrapping around my throat. He slammed me back up against the wall and lifted me—and the motherfucker was *powerful*, because he got me up on my toes, and I ain't light.

I extended a hand to stop my brothers from jumping in; I could handle this, and him. "Hey—ease up," I rasped.

The long-haired guy—who I assumed was one of my other cousins—was at Sebastian's side, pulling at him. "Let him go, Bast."

Kitty was there, too, pleading with "Bast" to let me go. As if I couldn't wreck him on my own, if I wanted to. Although, considering the grip he had on me, and the fact that I was still reeling from his hook, I wouldn't necessarily want to try unless I had to.

Finally, his grip loosened and I sagged to my feet, coughing for air.

"You don't get to talk about my goddamn mother," Bast snarled. "Her name was Lena Badd. And you don't know the first fucking thing about her."

I held up both hands palms out. "Hey, chill, man. I wasn't talking shit about her," I grated, my throat on fire. "She's passed on, God rest her, and I may be an asshole but I don't speak ill of the dead—especially not my own aunt."

Sebastian or Bast or whatever his name was pivoted, pacing away, the photo in his fingers. The younger brother was right there with him, murmuring to him in low tones. Bast shook his head like a bear shaking off bee stings, glancing at the photo.

We had an audience, at this point. As in, the whole bar was watching, taking photos, whispering to each other.

"Can I make a suggestion?" I said. "This is a private conversation, and this ain't exactly a private location."

"Yeah, well, you brought this shit here to *our* fucking bar," Bast snarled. "We have customers. We can't just shut down for some asshole claiming to be cousins we didn't know we fucking had."

Kitty touched his arm. "I can handle things here. This isn't something you can just ignore, Bast."

"Fuck that, this place is slammed. You can't run the entire bar by yourself." He sighed heavily, tapping his palm with the edge of the photograph. "And by the time we got anyone here to help, it'd be time to close. Fuck." He glared at me. "You had to bring this shit here, now?"

I just shrugged. "Oops?"

Bast shook his head again, and then seemed

to make a decision. He paced across to the bar and hopped up onto it with an ease belied by his bulk and size. He cupped his hands around his mouth and spoke in a booming, authoritative voice. "Hey, listen up! We've got a family situation going on. We're closing a little early. See Lucian on your way out for a ten-dollar voucher as an apology from the Badd brothers for the inconvenience."

Lucian, the younger, long-haired brother, stared at Bast. "You know how much that's going to cost us?"

For the first time, the youngest brother, whom I'd seen on TV appeared. "What's going on?"

Bast just laughed. "Welcome to the party, little brother." He gestured at me, Rem, and Ram, and then handed the youngest brother the photograph. "Meet our cousins, Roman, Remington, and Ramsey. Identical triplets. And oh, by the way, they're apparently opening a bar here in Ketchikan."

Lucian had vanished after asking about the cost, and then reappeared with a stack of vouchers in his hand. He stood by the door handing a voucher to each person as they exited. I winced, doing some quick math—there were at least a hundred people in the bar, if not more. Which means this little thing was costing them a thousand dollars, if not more.

Not my intention, but hey, I'm an asshole, and that's what assholes do.

Rem and Ram stayed seated at the table, waiting, as the crowd slowly dispersed. I stood, watching my cousin count the heads as they exited. Just as the last few people were leaving and Lucian was locking the door, footsteps echoed from the kitchen, along with voices. Quite a few of them.

A group of people whom I assumed were the Badd family members trooped into the main bar area; a pair of twins came through first, both dressed like rock stars—our cousins, judging by the Badd brown hair and eyes—followed by two stunning blondes, one of whom was carrying a baby on each hip. Behind the two sets of twins was a scary-as-fuck looking dude, swaggering, massive, with a Navy SEAL tat on his arm, wearing gym shorts, a tank top, and a pissed-off expression. Next was another Badd cousin, even more bulked out than Bast or the Navy SEAL, and with him, her hand tucked around his bulging bicep, was a stunningly gorgeous woman with jet-black hair. Behind them was a tall, Hollywood-handsome Badd brother with a tiny but sexy little blonde with a pix-ie cut. From a doorway between the kitchen and the stage came a beautiful redhead and an equally beau-tiful, exotic-looking girl with long black dreadlocks.

I surveyed the crowd, specifically the wom-en. "Seriously, what the *fuck* is in the water up here, man?" I said to no one in particular. "I haven't seen this many gorgeous women in one place since I went to that Victoria's Secret show."

No one answered, and my brothers and I found ourselves surrounded by a ring of pissed-off, tired, confused people—half of whom were our cousins, each of whom was fit, ripped, and intensely capable-looking. Hopefully this hadn't been a massive miscalculation on my part.

"Hope to fuck you know what you're doing, Rome," Remington muttered to me. "I don't like our odds of getting out of this in one piece."

"No shit," Ramsey added. "The SEAL and the bodybuilder are making me nervous."

"Chill," I shot back at them. "I've got this."

Rem just snorted. "The fuck you do. You're winging this, like you wing everything."

"Sure as fuck better be a good goddamn explanation for dragging me out of my fucking bed," the SEAL growled. His eyes flicked to me, my brothers, and then the photograph in Bast's hand. "The fuck is this?"

"Think you could squeeze a few more 'fucks' into that sentence, Zane?" This was from the diminutive blonde with a pixie cut. "I don't think there were enough."

Zane—the SEAL—didn't seem to catch the sarcasm. "There sure as fuck better be a good fucking expla-fucking-nation for dragging me the fuck out of my fucking bed," he growled. "Is that fucking better, Claire?"

Claire, the blonde, just nodded primly. "Yes, thank you, Zane. Much better."

"Glad I could fucking help."

"You'd think an ex-Navy SEAL would be better at being woken up unexpectedly," said one of the male twins—he had long brown hair in a loose topknot/manbun hipster-douche thing.

"Shut the fuck up, Cane." Zane, clearly, didn't appreciate being woken up.

The other twin, with an even more hipster-douche undercut, snorted derisively. "Someone's on the rag, obviously."

Zane growled deep in his chest, sounding like the bear he resembled. "I will knock you the fuck out, Corin."

Lucian, the longest-haired, second-to-youngest cousin, stepped forward. "Enough. Quit baiting Zane, you two. I would very much like to hear how we have three cousins we knew nothing about."

Several people spoke in unison: "Cousins?"

Bast indicated the three of us with a sweep of the photograph. "Them. They're our cousins."

"Like, third cousins twice removed or something, right?" This was—god, it was hard to keep them straight—the youngest. Xander? Javier? Xavier? Something like that. "As far as I've ever been aware, we have no family except each other."

Bast handed him the photograph. "Nope. First cousins. Dad's twin brother's kids."

"Dad did *not* have a twin brother," Hollywood snapped. "He'd have mentioned that at least once in our lives."

"Apparently Dad had a secret, then, because you can't fake that shit," Bast said, reaching out to tap the photo as Xander-or-whatever handed it to Hollywood. "That is a real, undoctored photograph, right, Xavier?"

Xavier, the youngest, nodded. "As far as I can tell, yes. I am not an expert in photography manipulation or alteration, but all of the available evidence supports Roman's claim." He indicated the photograph. "That is very obviously an old photograph. It is faded, the paper is wrinkled and stained on the back, and the corners are dog-eared. It is possible to doctor a photograph this old, but it requires a very specific set of skills, and I do not see the benefit of going to that kind of lengths in this scenario." He gestured at me. "Furthermore, and more apropos to the root conundrum, these three individuals very clearly and very strongly resemble both our father, and, thus, us." He paused, glancing distractedly at the ceiling. "The odds of this being a dupe, ruse, or some kind of scam are… slim. I could calculate the precise ratio, if you'd like."

I stared at him. "*Okay*, then, Stephen Hawking."

"There is no resemblance whatsoever between myself and the late Stephen Hawking," he answered, "whether physically, emotionally, medically, or intellectually, except insofar as that we are both—or rather, I *am* and he *was*—possessed of somewhat higher intelligence than most." He blinked a few times, staring toward me but not looking *at* me. "I am uncertain whether you meant that comment as an insult or not, but I choose to take it as a compliment, as Mr. Hawking is one of my greatest heroes."

"Does he speak normal American?" I asked, addressing this to Bast.

My comment—admittedly somewhat dickish— earned me growls, glares, and threatening stances.

Bast stepped toward me, muscles bunching, eyes blazing. "You really want to watch what you say, motherfucker. Maybe you don't count so good, but you three are seriously outnumbered right now. So fucking watch it."

Xavier put himself between me and his oldest brother—a bold, ballsy move considering the amount of muscle he was putting his skinny body between. "Thank you for your willingness to defend me, Bast, but I can handle such commentary myself." To me, then. "I am high-functioning autistic, with savant tendencies. This is an extremely uncomfortable social situation for me, and I tend to retreat into highly formal speech patterns when nervous. To that end, if you find yourself unable to translate what I'm saying into boorish barbarian or whichever pidgin dialect of English you speak, I'm sure my brother Bax is more than capable of providing such a service."

Silence followed, and then Baxter glanced at me, laughing openly. "I think we both just got burned, cousin."

"Yeah, I think you're right," I said, laughing good-naturedly, and turned to the youngest Badd. "Dude, if you can insult me to my face in such a way that I don't follow the insult, you kinda get that one for free."

"Can we get to the part where this dick explains what the hell is going on?" This was from the more hipster twin—Corin, I think his name was. "Because I'm seriously confused."

"That sounds like a good idea," I said. I withdrew my wallet and pulled out two one-hundred-dollar bills and tossed them on the table. We're not flush with cash, but we've done all right. "But how about a round for everyone first, on me."

Bast took the bills, rounded the bar, and pulled several pitchers of beer, grabbed a bottle of whiskey from off the back shelf, and snagged a stack of pint glasses and shot glasses, carrying the entire load back to the table with the practiced ease of someone who has spent a lifetime behind a bar. He poured a round of shots, and we all raised our shot glasses.

"To figuring out what the fuck is going on," Bast said.

"Hear, hear," Zane replied, and everyone clinked glasses, drained their shot, and set their glasses back on the table.

Everyone got a beer, and then all eyes were on me. I pulled up a chair, and glanced at my cousins and their women. "Are ya'll gonna stand around trying to intimidate me, or could you take seats?"

Reluctantly, everyone pulled up a chair, and I gestured at my brothers. "So, our dad is a pretty hard-to-communicate-with fella. He's been a drunk longer than any of us have been alive, for one thing, and when he's at the bottom of the bottle, he don't care too much for talk or company. So, we never knew much about him. Our ma took off when we were seven. I guess raisin' a set of crazy triplets she never wanted was just too much for her dumb skank-ass. So, we sorta raised ourselves, you might say. Dad worked and kept food on the table, but he didn't care a single good goddamn about what we did." I heard my Oklahoma accent creeping out, and tried to correct it. "Point of all this is, he never talked about his past. We knew he grew up in Alaska, Ketchikan or somewhere around here, but that he left when he was pretty young. And, literally, that's all we knew. All we still know, for the most part."

"Where do we come into this?" Bax asked.

"Gettin' there," I said. "We left Oklahoma soon as we graduated, became wildfire fighters, hotshots first and then smokejumpers. Kept us busy, kept us away from the barren shithole wasteland where we grew up. Well, a life of hard livin' caught up to him and he had a heart attack. Brought all three of us back to Oklahoma sooner'n we expected. I was sittin' in the same tiny, stinky, ugly-ass trailer we grew up in, watching TV, one of those celebrity gossip shows. They had—what's her name—Harlow Grace on there. With her, was this kid." I gestured at Xavier. "And fuck me if he didn't look a hell of a lot like an old photograph of Dad I'd seen a few times, one of him with our ma from when we was first born. Triggered somethin' in me, got me askin' questions. Dad didn't appreciate the questions, but he answered them. To an extent, at least."

"What'd he say?" Bast asked, sounding curious despite his ire.

"He said, and I quote, 'the fucker had *eight* kids? Thought for sure I'd have beaten him there, at least.'"

"What does that mean?" Bast pressed.

"He had me grab his old trunk, found a stack of old photos, and showed me that." I tapped the photo in Corin's hand—it had been making its way around the group. "Coulda knocked me over with a feather when I saw that shit."

"So you didn't know either?" Lucian asked.

I shook my head. "Hell, no. We grew up thinking we were one funeral away from being orphans, with not even a great aunt or someone to take us in." I sighed. "So the story, as told to us by our dad is this: Our dads grew up kinda like I imagine all of us did— wild, mostly unsupervised, and a little crazy. Twins, in the Alaskan countryside. I guess our grandparents raised them way out in the country, in the real deep bush, you know?"

Bast frowned at me. "Dad never spoke much about his childhood. I asked once, and he said there wasn't much to tell, and I knew enough to leave it at that."

I laughed. "Sounds about right. All our dad would say was that they grew up in the ass-end of nowhere, and the only reason they had plumbing or electricity was because our grandpa had run the pipes and lines himself back in the early fifties, usin' a backhoe and country bumpkin know-how." The photo had made the rounds back to me, and I gazed down at it as I spoke. "This is where it gets interesting. I guess Dad and Uncle Liam were real hell-raisers in their day. Moved here to Ketchikan, which I guess to them then was like movin' to the big city, and raised all sorts of Cain. And then, one day, they were both at a pool hall and met a girl. 'Most beautiful girl we'd ever seen,' Dad says. Lena Dunfield."

"Mom," Zane breathed.

I nodded. "They both fell for her right then and there. At first I guess it was innocent brotherly competition, see who could get the girl. She was the talk of the town, to hear Dad tell it. Every single guy under the age of fifty had his eye on Lena Dunfield, and more than one married man had made passes at her, he said. She'd been turning down marriage proposals from the age of sixteen, and never seemed to give half a shit for any of the local Ketchikan boys. Until she saw Liam and Lucas Badd. I guess she fell head over heels right off the bat, too, but couldn't make up her mind which of 'em she liked more. Turned into a real ugly pickle, sounds like. She started favoring Liam, which, obviously got under Dad's skin. Brotherly competition for a girl they both liked turned into two brothers gone heart and soul for the same woman, and then, at some point, Lena chose Liam, and Dad got the shaft. When it became clear she'd chosen his brother, Dad got pissed at them both." I shrugged. "I dunno if your dad was like ours, but I know Dad had a hell of a temper when he got riled."

Both Bast and Zane nodded. "He had a temper, all right. Mom could usually settle him down, but if he got well and truly pissed, it just took time and space for him to calm down," Bast said.

"Sounds like Dad," I said, "only he never had anyone to settle him, so he'd just stew in his own juices. I'm not sure he ever learned how to really get over anything, truth be told."

"So after Mom chose Dad instead of Lucas, it turned into a fight?" Zane asked.

I nodded. "What it sounds like. Turned really ugly too. Dad wouldn't talk about that, only that their fight over Lena damn near tore down the city."

"Jesus, you mean like an actual physical fight?" Corin asked.

I nodded again. "What it sounds like. Dad said Lena tried to stop 'em, but couldn't. Seems they both walked away from that fight half-dead and bitter as hell, 'specially Dad, since he walked away alone, without his brother *or* the girl he was in love with."

"And they never spoke again?" This was from the redhead, who was sitting on Bast's lap, toying absently with his hair.

I nodded. "Never saw each other again, never spoke again. I think at first Dad was too pissed and too hurt, and then after a while too much time had gone by and both of their stupid stubborn-ass pride wouldn't let them reconnect. And then Dad met our mother, and that went to shit after like eight years, and then Lena died." I stared down at the photo again. "Looking back, I can mark the exact date when he found out Lena had died."

"Callahan's," Ramsey muttered.

"He was never the same after that," Remington added.

I blew out a breath. "He went up to a dive bar outside of town, got obliterated, started a fight, nearly killed a coupla local farmers with his bare hands, and then wrecked his truck and nearly died himself. We were what...eight? Ten? We found him passed out in front of the trailer in a pool of his own puke, covered in blood, with several busted bones and a punctured lung. I called 911, and they barely saved his life. After that, he was...different."

"Shit," Bast murmured. "That sounds rough."

I nodded. "It makes sense why he's been a drunk his whole life. I don't think he ever got over Lena."

"And he lost not only her, but his twin, and then his wife divorced him, and he was stuck raising triplets on his own," Hollywood said.

"They weren't ever married," Ram said. "Just shacked up on account of us kids. We were the accidental results of a one-night stand, and they tried to make it work for our sake, but our mother couldn't handle us. We *were* pretty difficult kids."

Corin and the other twin, Cane, exchanged looks. "I can't imagine a fight so bad we'd stopped talking for the rest of our lives," Corin said.

"I'd rather die," Canaan agreed.

The redhead spoke up again. "What I don't understand is why you're here in Ketchikan."

"We wanted to meet our cousins," I said, with a flirty grin. "The fact that all'a ya'll managed to land seriously fine-ass honeys is just a bonus."

"Wait, hold on a second," Kitty said.

I'd nearly forgotten about her in all the drama with my cousins, as she'd sat quietly up until now, listening and watching.

God, what a woman. Not flashy, oh no. Not my usual fare by a long shot.

Five feet seven, slender, with long, fine hair that was somewhere between blonde and light brunette. It was her eyes, man. Brown, the sweet warm shade of mocha and hot chocolate and little wide-eyed puppies. In this case, however, her eyes were snapping and blazing with fire, which was hot as fuck; I like a woman with attitude. She was wearing minimal makeup, if any, and she didn't need it to be beautiful.

And when I say beautiful, I mean...not average

hot, or slutty sexy, but legit beautiful. Lovely. Her nose was kind of crooked, her cheekbones high, her chin delicate. Her lips were plump and kissable and had the faintest sheen of lip gloss. No layers of eye shadow, no caked-on foundation. No smoky eye or bright red lipstick. Just unadorned beauty. It was refreshing, honestly. And alluring in a way I was unfamiliar with.

And her body? It was hard to tell, considering she was in a waitress outfit—somewhat ill-fitting jeans and a black V-neck at least two sizes too big to be sexy. But even with that outfit, it was easy to see the girl had curves. I mean, the jeans didn't do her any favors, but her ass was still mesmerizing in its sway and bounce and roundness, and the way she filled out that baggy work shirt told me she was rocking some serious cleavage under there.

God, I wanted her naked. I was trying to imagine what her body would look like when she spoke again, and her words snapped me out of my reverie.

"You told me you guys were opening a bar," she said, her eyes hard and her voice harder.

I had been hoping to avoid that particular tidbit for a few more minutes at least. "Yeah, well…we wanted a change of pace from smokejumping, and running a bar seemed like a decent challenge," I said, breezily.

Bast's eyes narrowed. "And then you try to poach

my waitress. For a competing bar, in the city where *we* live." He stood up, crossing his arms over his chest. "Kind of a dick move, if you ask me."

I shrugged nonchalantly. "Yeah, well, from what I saw, there's plenty of business to go around." I gazed levelly at Kitty. "And, as far as Kitty goes…fair game is fair game, know what I'm sayin'?"

Kitty's already hard, pissed-off gaze blazed with renewed fury, and good god*damn* was she sexy when she's pissed. "I'm *not* fair game, jerk. Not for you, not for anyone."

I just smiled at her. "Yeah, well, we'll see about that, won't we, Kitten?"

"Don't *call* me that," she hissed.

Bast took a threatening step toward me, and the three largest brothers followed suit.

"I think it's time you left," Bast growled. "Now."

Rem, the more cautious of the three of us, shoved me roughly for the door. "Let's fucking go, you reckless tool."

Ramsey, the quickest tempered of us, and the one most likely to spoil for a fight, just laughed as the three of us trooped out onto the sidewalk. "What, Rem, you scared to tangle with our Alaskan cousins?"

Rem shot him the finger. "Fuck off. I don't mind a fight, but only when the odds are something like fair." He jerked a thumb at the bar we'd just left. "And those boys seem more than capable of giving even *us* a fight we won't forget."

"Exactly!" Ram exclaimed. "It'd have been fun."

"I don't find fistfights as fun as you do, Ram," Remington said.

We had booked a nearby extended stay hotel for a month, just so we could get our feet planted here in Ketchikan, and fortunately our hotel was within walking distance. We didn't say much as we walked the quiet sidewalks; streetlamps flickered and buzzed orange, an occasional car slid past, headlights stabbing bright spears of illumination.

"That waitress shut you down, Rome," Ramsey said, eventually, glancing at me to gauge my reaction.

"First time for everything, I guess," I said.

Ramsey laughed. "You know, my gut tells me you may just have met your match with that one. She didn't seem at all susceptible to your charms, bro."

I growled. "Yeah, don't fuckin' remind me." I had her face in my mind, those blazing, fiery, intelligent brown eyes. "But make no mistake, Ram—she will. She just doesn't know it yet."

THREE

Kitty

IT WAS A RARE DAY OFF FOR ME. I WORKED FOUR DOUBLES in a row, including one the day after the bizarre and intense confrontation with the newly arrived Badd triplets. After the fourth double, Sebastian told me in no uncertain terms to go away and not come back for at least twenty-four hours. He pretended to be kicking me out, and I pretended to be ungrateful, and it was funny.

Sebastian wasn't an overtly humorous sort of man; his humor was very dry, sarcastic, and you had to know him pretty well to know when he was joking. The first few times he insulted me, I took it literally and nearly quit. And then his dear sweet wife, Dru, pulled me aside and explained that Bast only insulted people like that when he liked them, and to not take it seriously, and that if I wanted to really earn his respect and affection, I should insult him back. Play his game. So, I watched how he was with his brothers, and realized they were constantly insulting each other, making a game of who could come up with the harshest burn, so to speak, and that the harder they teased each other, the more fun they were having. There was very clearly an enormous amount of love and respect between the eight men, and I appreciated that. And I wanted to be a part of that. So I learned to trade insults, which is way outside my comfort zone—as the daughter of a kindergarten teacher mother and a philosophy professor father, I was raised to be kind, sweet, polite, accepting, open-minded, and generous. To a fault, quite honestly. I had to learn the hard way that sometimes a little distrust and suspicion is necessary to keep your heart intact.

Such as, for example, in the case of Roman Badd.

The man is walking, talking trouble. Or rather, more accurately, swaggering, blustering heartbreak. Everything about him screams trouble, from his dirty, foul mouth, to those big blue eyes sparking with humor and cunning, to that enormous, breathtaking, predatory body, to that cocky assurance of his own indomitable supremacy in all situations. He's the living embodiment of a red flag.

Stay away, that's what my gut, heart, and mind are all telling me.

Annoyingly, my body seems to have a different viewpoint.

WANT, WANT, WANT! That's the refrain my traitorous, weak, ridiculous body is chanting.

I managed to overrule my body's desire to flirt back with Roman last night, but it was a hard-won battle, and I was kind of bitchy about it, which, somewhat absurdly, I feel guilty about. But if I have to be a little bitchy to keep my heart intact, does that make me a bitch, or just prudent?

Ugh.

Currently, I'm at the grocery store. Most of my food spoiled since I was working so much, and the rest didn't amount to anything I could make a real meal out of, so my day off has been spent doing laundry, paying bills, and now buying groceries. Woohoo! Adulting is fun!

Not.

I hate laundry day, though. I get so few days off that when I do laundry, I literally end up having to wash all my clothes, which means I spend the day wearing a less than amazing outfit. I mean, it's not like I wore evening gowns on my days off or anything, and I'm not a fashionista like my roommate Izzy, but

I try to look like I didn't just crawl out of bed. Which is what I look like today.

Seafoam green cotton daisy dukes so small and so tight that I get front *and* back wedgies *at the same time*, with a white cotton V-neck undershirt so thin and old you could probably see my nipples if I didn't wear a bra. And speaking of bras, the one I was wearing was a plain-Jane white granny bra, with plain-Jane white granny panties to match.

So sexy.

Not.

Of course, I wasn't trying to be sexy, not for myself or anyone else. Which was fine. I didn't need to be sexy. Chore day isn't a sexy day anyway, so if I was going to be all scrubby and sloppy, with my hair in a messy bun, no makeup—not even lip gloss—and my feet in two-dollar Old Navy flip-flops, then it might as well be today.

Once I had all my groceries paid for and in my zippered reusable bags, I had to figure out how to get all these bags home. I only brought my keys, wallet, and phone which, when empty-handed, is fine because it's only a three-block walk from my apartment to the store. But now that I had five reusable grocery bags full of food, getting my groceries home became a juggling act. I removed my sunglasses from where they were shoved in my hair—ripping out a tangle of hair strands in the process—put them on, hooked my keyring on an index finger, shoved my phone in a bra cup so the bottom end of the phone stuck up out of my shirt, and then hung two bags from my elbows, three in one hand and two in the other.

And suddenly, a little three-block walk seemed a lot farther.

A block and half later, I had to stop and set the bags down to give my burning, trembling arms a rest. With a tired sigh, I heaved the bags back up and resumed my slog. Another block and a half—almost two full blocks, really—and I was within sight of my apartment building. And, of course, Paulie the mailman was standing half-in-half-out of the apartment building door, sorting mail in his bag.

Paulie was in his late forties with a thin, graying ponytail and a straggly graying goatee, fond of wearing wraparound Oakleys even on rainy days and inside. He was a little overweight and super friendly, always happy, always ready with a warm smile and a dumb joke.

He looked up from his mail sorting. "Hey-ya, Kitty, how are ya?" He flipped through the stacks of mail, found a particular section, and withdrew the mail, extending it to me. "So…what do you do with a sick boat, Kitty?"

I was already laughing in anticipation of

the cringe-worthy punch line. "I don't know, Paulie—what?"

"Take it to the doc, of course." He laughed at his own joke, and flapped the handful of envelopes. "You want these, or should I stick 'em in your mailbox? Looks like you've got your hands full."

Yeah, and it wasn't getting any lighter.

I tried to shift things so I could take them, but I was out of hands. "Um…" I clacked my teeth together. "Just put them in my mouth."

Paulie's eyes widened, and he halfway restrained a snicker. "Oh man, Kitty, I've got so many jokes right now, but I'll be a good boy and keep 'em to myself."

I rolled my eyes at him. "I suppose I walked right into that one."

He stuffed the envelopes between my teeth and left the apartment building—letting the door close as he did so. "See ya, Kitty!"

I watched the door close, standing on the sidewalk, helpless to stop it. With my hands full and the mail in my mouth, I couldn't even call out to stop him, other than make unintelligible grunts.

If I put all these bags down now, I was worried I'd never get them all upstairs. My arms were jelly, I was sweating, and clutching the bags for dear life. I tried to scrabble at the knob with the hand I had the fewest bags clutched in, but it was a losing battle.

I should just put them down and make a few trips, but I refused. I knew once I got upstairs, I would collapse on my couch in front of the A/C, drinking an iced tea, and watching my DVR'd backlog of Bachelor in Paradise, one of my guilty pleasures.

I shifted the handle of the bag to my wrist, let it slide backward to catch against my elbow with the other two heavy bags, and reached for the door-knob—but the angle sent all three bags sliding down my forearm suddenly, forcing me to lift my arm to arrest their motion.

"Darn it!" I hissed.

Just then, a huge, tan, strong-looking hand reached past me and opened the door.

I felt him before I knew it was him. He smelled like dust and sweat and deodorant, and radiated body heat.

"Let me help you, Kitty," he murmured in his basso rumble.

"I gah ih," I said around the envelopes.

He just chuckled, and suddenly all three bags in my right hand were gone, and then the two in my left. He had all five heavy bags in one hand, and it didn't appear like he found them heavy at all. He grinned at me, his empty hand closing around mine and sliding the keyring off my index finger.

I was stunned stupid by his sudden appearance,

clearly, because I made no move to stop him. Nor did I have the presence of mind to take the mail out of my mouth. Nor did I attempt to stop him when he glanced down at my chest, his grin widening, when he reached down, bold as you please, to withdraw my phone from my bra.

I stopped breathing when he did that.

And then, finally, he plucked my mail from my teeth.

Everything I'd been struggling to carry for the last three blocks he balanced easily. And still had the facility to kick open the door, tromp up the stairs, and head right for my apartment door.

Finally, my brain caught up, and I trotted after him. "Hey, wait!" I flounced up the stairs after him.

And, of course, he had stopped to let me catch up, so he saw every, erm, *bounce* of my flight up the stairs. "Can you go back down and do that again?" he asked, deadpan. "I think I missed some of it."

I just glared at him. "Don't be a pig."

He oinked, a surprisingly accurate impression, and continued down the hallway. He stopped at my door, whirled the key ring around his finger to catch the keys, unerringly picked the right one, and stuck it in the lock.

Unlocked my door.

Opened it.

And let himself in.

I stared after him, stunned at his sheer gall.

And then I remembered to go in after him, catching up as he set the bags down, along with my mail and my keys. My phone, for some reason, he still had in his hands.

"How—" I blinked at him, summoning words. "You—"

He just grinned. "Take your time, sweetheart. I've got all day."

Anger barreled through me, knocking loose the tirade. "How did you know which apartment is mine? How did you know which key was the right one? How dare you go into my apartment without asking, without permission, and without me? Why are you here? What do you want?"

He was utterly unfazed by my outburst, leaning back against the kitchen counter. "Whoa, darlin', one question at a time."

"Quit calling me stupid, condescending, chauvinistic names," I snapped, and immediately felt guilty for snapping at him even though I was proud for sticking up for myself. Which was confusing.

He twirled my phone between his finger and thumb. "First, your address is on your mail. Second, you have three keys on here—one for your mailbox and two for doors. The silver one is almost definitely for the back door of Badd's Bar and Grill which means the bronze one is for your door." He shrugged. "Logic. Where was I? Oh yeah, third—I had all your stuff in my hands, so where did you want me to go? Somewhere else? Fourth, I'm here because I was passing by and saw you, a damsel clearly in distress and in need of my brave assistance. And as for what I want…"

He pushed off of the counter and towered over me, his gaze blatantly tripping down to my cleavage, and remaining there. "Simple, babe—I want *you*."

"Me?"

Stupid, stupid, stupid. I sounded breathless—which I was—and baffled as to why *he* of all people would want *me*. Not like I had self-esteem issues or anything; I knew I was pretty, had a decent body, and that I had something real to offer the right kind of man. The doubt came in when I looked at Roman. He was the kind of man who picked up horny supermodels and ditzy sorority bimbos and slutty bar bunnies. Not people like me.

Roman sidled closer, his gaze fixing on mine and not wavering as he reached up and stuffed my phone back into my bra—his knuckles seared against my skin as he tugged the cup away and tucked the device further in.

"Yeah, Kitty. *You*." His hand drifted up, his eyes

skating over my face, down to my cleavage, and then upward again. With a single jerk, he yanked the ponytail holder out of my hair, letting my hair spill free of the messy bun and drape around my shoulders. "That's better. You're hot with your hair up, but you're drop-dead fucking stunning with it down like this."

He stepped closer, and now his chest was pushing against mine; I stood my ground, but barely. My breasts pressed against his chest, flattening—a fact his wandering gaze did not miss. He gathered my hair in his hand, wrapping it around his palm twice—I've been growing my hair out my whole life, only trimming a few inches off the bottom now and again, so it's down to my mid-spine, which seems to be its terminal length. He tugged my head back on my neck so I was forced to stare up at him—my breath whooshed out of my lungs, and my thighs clenched shut tight.

Fear and arousal warred inside me.

He was so huge, towering over me, his broad chest blocking out the apartment beyond him. His shoulders were like mountains, stretching the cotton of his black T-shirt, and his arms were as thick as my thighs, round and hard and veiny. His eyes were so blue they stole my breath. He had a forest green US Forest Service hat on backward, a tuft of his fine blond hair peeking out the opening of the snapback.

I'd almost forgotten his grip on my hair, so lost was I in his eyes, his perfect cheekbones, his carved-from-granite jawline. He reminded me of this salient fact by tightening his grip, so my hair pulled at my scalp, and then brought me closer to him. Now my breasts were smashed flat, and I was up on my tiptoes, barely breathing, utterly and helplessly hypnotized by his primal, magnetic perfection, his captivating dominance.

His lips brushed against mine, and my mouth tingled, my lips parted and my tongue fluttered against his, an automatic reaction to the tease of his kiss.

"There she is," he murmured, with a cocky chuckle of assurance.

That broke the spell.

I shoved at him, hard, heedless of his grip on my hair. Slapped him across the face as hard as I could, so hard the *crack* echoed in my small apartment. To my credit, his head snapped to the side from the force of my blow, and he actually staggered back a step.

"Get *out*," I hissed. "Get out!"

He was rubbing his cheek with one hand, looking dazed. "Damn, girl, you can *hit*." He said this with no small amount of awe—and, unfortunately, amusement.

He was also very clearly NOT leaving. Instead, he was grinning at me. "You know, you're sexy as hell when you're pissed. I mean, you're sexy as hell regardless, but when you're pissed?" He shivered in delight. "Mmmm-mmm-*mmm*."

"I told you to leave, Roman."

"But I just got here." He faked a pout, making a pathetic moue with his lips, batting those big blue eyes at me.

I put my face up close to his, kept my voice low and hard. "I *said* leave, Roman. *Now.*"

He held up his hands and backed away. "All right, all right. I'm going."

I watched him head for the door, hating the way my body was still shell-shocked. Hating, as well, the fact that his compliments and flattery, as arrogant and crude as they were, had sunk a little deeper than I'd like to admit. He paused halfway through the door, just looking back at me.

I narrowed my eyes and crossed my arms over my chest. "What now?"

He shrugged. "Nothing, I just wanted to get one last look at you." He swept a finger up and down, gesturing at me. "I suspected the other night that you were probably hiding a pretty damn amazing body under those frumpy work clothes, but god*damn*, girl, I had no idea how amazing."

Half of me wanted to shiver at his words and preen and ask what else he thought, and the other half was disgusted and angry. "You're a pig."

"You said that already." He shoved a hand in the pocket of his khaki cut-off shorts. "But if appreciating a glorious female body makes me a pig, then oink oink, sweetheart."

"Don't call me—"

He held up a hand, forestalling me. "Sorry, sorry. Forgot." He waved, pivoting out the door. "I'll be seeing you around, Kitten."

"My name is—" The door shut between us, cutting me off. "Kitty, not Kitten," I declared to the empty apartment. "And I hope not."

That wasn't quite true, though. Some part of me *did* want to see him again. If I could lock that silly, horny, hormonal, weak part of me in the basement, I would. Because that part of me kept betraying me at the worst possible times.

I'd almost *kissed* him, for crap's sake.

Why did that stupid part of me find the way he'd wrapped his hand around my hair and tilted my face up to his so darn hot? Why did that part of me want him to do it again?

Stupid, that's why.

The door opened again right then, and I half expected it to be Roman again, but it was my roommates, Juneau and Izzy.

"Oh—*my*—*GOD*," Izzy said, trouncing through

the door, her arms full of bags from The Plaza. "Kitty, you will not *believe* the guy we just saw. Seriously. He was, I kid you not, *the* hottest man I've ever seen in real life."

"She's not kidding," Juneau added. "He *was* pretty gorgeous."

I sighed. "Let me guess. Six-four, built like the Incredible Hulk, with eyes like Paul Newman's and a face so perfect you either want to smack him or kiss him?"

"Smack him?" Izzy stared at me, incredulous. "*Kiss* him? Shit, woman, I'd take him to bed and never let him leave—assuming I could get him even look at me. And you know what? Forget the bed, I'd take him on the floor, or up against the wall—shit, I'd fuck that man in a public bathroom."

"Izzy!" I said with a groan of reproach. "Don't be nasty!"

"Well, I would." She narrowed her eyes at me. "Wait. How did you know who we were talking about?"

I sighed. "His name is Roman Badd, he's the cousin of my bosses, and he's as much of an arrogant jerk as he is pretty."

Isadora Styles, Izzy to anyone who actually knew her, was a true strawberry blonde—heavy on the strawberry, light on the blonde—with the creamy skin and adorable freckles to go with it. She had long, thick, wavy hair she almost always wore down and loose, hazel eyes that leaned toward green, and a body I suspected most men would happily kill for. At least, I knew I would. I mean, she was an inch taller than me, had a slimmer waist, a tighter butt, bigger boobs, and most of her height was leg. She was also a successful fashion blogger who paid the bills by managing an on-line couture-clothing store. She had impeccable taste in fashion and a flair for drama. And a potty mouth, and a sex drive that left me boggling, *and* few inhibi-tions…not to mention a trail of broken-hearted men that led all the way back to her childhood crush back in Memphis, Tennessee, which also explained her hint of a southern accent.

Juneau Isaac was the opposite in every way. Short, curvy enough to be just this side of plus-size in most stores, with raven-black hair she almost always wore in a thick braid, and dark brown eyes. One hun-dred percent Inuit, Juneau was shy, quiet, careful, and hard to read. She'd had one serious boyfriend that I knew of, and she'd broken up with him when he had pushed her for things she hadn't wanted to do, sex-ually, something I suspected, but wasn't sure of. She rarely brought anyone home, and only went on occa-sional dates which almost never turned into a second date. Juneau was the sweetest girl I'd ever known, and

I was, in some ways, closer to her than to Izzy, simply because I was more like Juneau than Izzy.

Izzy put a hand on her waist and popped her hip. "Katerina Maureen Quinn. What aren't you telling us?"

I rolled my eyes at her. "Not even my mother uses my full name, Izz."

"Well I do, especially when you have dirt on a hot guy and aren't sharing." She smirked at me, taking in my appearance. "Must be laundry day, huh?"

"Yeah, and Roman saw me in this too."

Izzy raised her eyes, knowing I tend to be pretty modest under most circumstances—I prefer one-piece bathing suits, rarely spring for low-cut tops or dresses, and keep most skirts mid-thigh or lower. This outfit, then, is something I never wear outside the house unless I have to, and today, I had to. I *only* wear it at home with Juneau and Izzy. Today was the first and only time I'd ever gone outside the house in it, and I felt naked and self-conscious the whole time. I was really regretting my error in judgment.

I'd been too focused on the insane rollercoaster of feelings Roman instilled in me to think about it then, but him seeing me in this outfit...I was mortified.

The full magnitude of it was just then hitting me.

My eyes widened and I put my hand over my mouth. "He *saw* me in this," I whispered. "Not even my own father has seen me in this."

"He'd tell you to go put on real clothes if he did," Juneau said. "Even if you were home alone, he'd tell you to put on real clothes."

"Shoot me now," I moaned. "I can't believe he saw me in *this*. In fact, I can't believe *anyone* saw me in this."

Izzy was unsuccessfully stifling laughter. "Oh my god, Kitty. You're seriously panicking about this?"

"Yes!" I cried. "I met him once, the night before last, at the bar. And he was an arrogant jerk then just like he was an even more arrogant jerk today. And he saw me in this outfit, which is the single sluttiest thing I own."

Izzy snorted. "Yeah, well, your idea of slutty is a lacy push-up bra."

I glared at her. "Not all of us feel comfortable wearing cupless bras and crotchless panties, *Isadora*."

She just shrugged. "I'm not going to apologize for being confident in my body, nor for wanting to flaunt it."

"I'm not asking you to apologize, just don't make fun of me for not being the same way."

Juneau, ever the peacemaker and reasonable one, chimed in. "She wasn't making fun you, Kitty. Just pointing out your differences."

Izzy lifted a finger. "Actually, I kind of was making

fun of her. Just a little bit, though."

"Izzy, don't be mean," Juneau said.

"I wasn't being mean. Just teasing." Izzy wrapped an arm around my shoulders. "So tell us about this Roman Badd of yours."

"There's not much to say except he certainly isn't mine." I drew out the silence, knowing there was plenty. "Apart from having an overinflated opinion of himself and acting like a macho jerk all the time, he's one of a set of identical triplets."

Izzy drifted, as if in a daze across the small apartment, and sank slowly down to sit on the couch, and put a hand over her mouth. After a moment, she stared at me, wide-eyed. "There are *more*? That look like *that*?" She shook her head in disbelief. "That's not possible. It's just not possible."

"I've met all three. Roman, Ramsey, and Remington." I sighed, hopping up to plop my butt on the counter, kicking my feet. "And yes, they all look like him. And, from what I can tell, the other two have just as much cocky arrogance as their obnoxious jerk of a brother."

Juneau frowned at me. "Wow, he *really* rubbed you the wrong way, didn't he? I don't think I've ever seen you this fired up before."

"Or, more accurately, you want him to rub you the *right* way, and you don't know how to handle that." Izzy grinned at me. "That's it, isn't it? You're scared of big bad Roman Badd, aren't you? You want him, but he scares your sweet innocent little pussy into hiding."

"Izzy!" I scolded. "You are *so* crude!"

She just snorted. "You need to loosen up, Kitty. There's nothing crude about the word 'pussy.' There just isn't. It's not like I'm saying cunt. *That's* a little crude, and it's a term I reserve only for the bitchiest of bitches. Like my evil stepmother." She shuddered, and we all shuddered with her, having met Tracey—who was, legitimately, the source of inspiration for the evil stepmother in *Cinderella*, and possibly the witch queen in *Snow White*. "But for real, what would *you* call your lady parts? A vagina? That may not be crude, but it's so…formal, and archaic, and…*boring*."

I sniffed primly. "I wouldn't refer to myself in that manner at all."

She just stared at me. "So…how do you talk dirty, then?" She faked a breathy moan, speaking in an overly dramatic fake-sex voice. "Oh, *Roman*! Put your manhood into my womanhood! Yes, right there in my womanhood, you handsome gentleman, you!"

"You're such an idiot, Isadora," I said, rolling my eyes at her even as I had trouble stifling a laugh. "Dirty talk isn't necessary for a meaningful and intimate sexual experience."

"No, but it sure is a lot of fucking fun." She shook her head. "Seriously. You need to get with a guy like Roman just to see what else is out there."

I knew where she was going with this. "Izz, don't. Please don't."

"I'm just saying—Tom was a great guy. You were good together. You cared about him, he cared about you. I'm not knocking your relationship with him at all. But honey, he was your first serious boyfriend, you were with him for eight years, and you haven't really done much by the way of dating since you and Tom broke up." She lifted her eyebrow, and I knew the real doozy was coming in her next statement. "And knowing what I know of Tom Holbrook I have to admit that I doubt you guys were very…erm…adventurous, sexually."

"What if we liked it that way? What if I don't need sex to be some crazy adventure? What if I like it to be meaningful, and intimate?"

"And boring, and predictable?" She shrugged. "I'm not saying break out the handcuffs and anal beads, Kit-Kat, just…get outside your comfort zone a little."

Juneau spoke while staring at her toes. "It *has* been almost a year since you and Tom broke up, Kitty. It might do you good to…I don't know, look beyond the average fish in the sea, I guess."

I frowned at her. "You're turning on me too? You've been on, what, seven dates in the last year?"

She lifted a shoulder, offering a shy smile. "Seven that you know of. I went on several more dates with one of the guys I brought over, but I just kept it quiet and met him after work." Her shy smile shifted into a mischievous smirk. "And then we met a few more times, but I wouldn't exactly call what we did dating."

"Juneau!" Izzy shrieked. "You little minx! You never told us this!"

"Who was it?" I asked. "Wait, don't tell me—it was that one with the long hair. Chris?"

She nodded. "Yeah, Chris."

"You slept with Chris?" Izzy asked, leaping up off the couch to join us in the kitchen. "What was he like?"

Juneau shrugged, glancing at the floor again. "Sweet, at first. And then, once we'd been together a couple times, he got pretty—well, he liked stuff that I know *you* wouldn't call kinky, but for me were pretty out there."

"Like what?" Izzy demanded. "Anal?"

Juneau looked suitably horrified. "Oh god no! That's virgin and staying that way. Yuck." She shook her head, shuddering. "Just...different positions and stuff."

"Don't knock anal till you try it," Izzy said. "So

are you still seeing him?"

Juneau shook her head. "I'll leave that to you, Izz. And no, I'm not."

"Why?" I asked. "Seems like you liked him and had fun with him."

"It was a lot of fun, and I did really like him. But he…we were at his place, hanging out. We got a little tipsy and, unbeknownst to me, he invited a friend over. A girl." She hesitated, still gazing at the floor. "She walked in without knocking, took one look at me, and started taking off her clothes. I asked Chris what was going on, and he said he figured I'd be down for a threesome. I guess because I'd been willing to try pretty much everything he'd wanted up to that point, he figured I'd just go along with a threesome."

Izzy stared expectantly. "So? Did you? Was she hot?"

Juneau and I exchanged looks. "No, I didn't have a threesome!" Juneau exclaimed. "That's gross. No way. And yeah, I suppose she was pretty, but I'm not into girls, or sex with more than one person."

"And don't say 'don't knock it till you try it,'" I put in.

Izzy just laughed. "Actually, that's one thing I haven't done myself. But if I were going to, it would be with two guys, not another girl. I kissed a girl once, and I didn't like it."

Juneau and I stared at each other with matching looks of revulsion.

"Oh my god, no!" I said, shaking my hands. "No way! *Two* guys? God no."

"Same," Juneau said.

Izzy shrugged. "It sounds hot, but I feel like it would be a lot more work than it's worth. I mean, guys aren't hard to please, but they do get jealous."

I glanced at my phone, sitting on the counter. "In unrelated news, I have to go switch my laundry. Who's going to come with me to keep me company?"

"I should probably do a load or two," Juneau said.

"Me too, actually," Izzy said.

So we all three headed for the laundromat, and while our conversation wandered to other places, part of my mind kept wandering back to Izzy's advice that I needed to get out of my comfort zone a little.

Problem was, Roman Badd wasn't just a little outside my comfort zone, he was in an entirely different universe.

Which was, most likely, a large part of the appeal of the man.

That, and the fact that he could pick me up like I was a feather. And those devilishly blue eyes. And those muscles. And his rough, strong hands. And the unbelievably soft brush of his lips...

Argh. If only he wasn't such an arrogant jerk.

FOUR

Roman

D AMN THE GIRL. I JUST COULD *NOT* GET HER OUT OF MY fucking head.

I shouldn't be this attracted to her. I mean, I've hooked up with not one, not two, but *three* Laker girls. Not at the same time, mind you, but still. I've hooked up with more than a few actresses, a backup dancer for some pop star…all of them insanely hot.

But this girl, man. What the hell was it about her? I don't know how to put it without sounding like a dick, so I'll just sound like a dick. Put her on stage with some of those other girls I've banged, and she wouldn't measure up, not in the kind of hotness those girls embodied.

But Kitty is her own kind of hot. I don't think she realizes exactly how sexy she is, either, which is maybe part of it. She's not stuck on herself. She clearly has confidence, because it takes confidence to stand up to a guy like me the way she has. Twice now. But she just…god, I don't know.

The other girls I've hooked up with, when you put them in casual clothes, their persona changes. I've noticed this. Get 'em all dressed up, made up, shaking their booties in the club, hunting for a guy to take 'em home, they have a kind of swagger about them, an attitude. Not confidence, exactly, but a put-on sultriness borne of the fact that they know how to lure a man with their assets. But remove the fancy outfits, the four-inch heels, the updo, the layers of makeup, take away their posse of girlfriends and the dim lighting of the club—put them in ratty sweatpants, a messy bun, and no makeup, and they just…I don't know. They lose some part of their appeal.

And before you go getting your panties all in a bunch about me being a shallow, chauvinistic douchebag—which, admittedly, I am, most of the time—that observation is not about my opinion of their appearance, but about their behavior. They don't have that same predatory confidence from the night before. It's like when they get ready to go out, they put on armor, piece by piece. Which I totally get: when we get ready to jump into a wildfire, we gear up. Piece by piece, we put on our firefighting gear, and with each piece we're putting on a kind of mental armor. We're not the guy you'd meet in the bar anymore, and we're not the guy you'd sleep with or have coffee with—we're the firefighter, the warrior. So for some women, I think, it's similar. Take away the armor, you take away some integral part of their public persona.

Kitty is different. She was exactly the same in what clearly was an outfit not meant for going out in public as she was in work clothes, with her apron and tray as her armor. She had the same energy about her, the same attitude, the same confidence.

Her beauty was the same. It's a bone-deep beauty.

An essential loveliness in who she is, and in what she looks like. She doesn't need fancy clothes or layers of makeup to be sexy and alluring.

The pajamas she was wearing when I ran into her on the street, though? Holy motherfucking shit. Those work jeans and the Badd's tee were hiding a siren's body.

Long, strong, sleek, smooth legs. A delicate waist that curved down to bell-like hips. A tight, firm, bubble of a heart-shaped ass that was busting out of those tease-tiny pale green booty shorts. God, that ass. The moment I saw it as she whirled around in her apartment I wanted, so badly, to just take a double handful of it and *squeeze* until she squeaked. Jesus, so fucking perfect. Her hair was long, fine, silky smooth and glossy, with the barest hint of waviness to it, although that may have been from being tied up in a bun. Her face was perfectly proportioned, heart-shaped to match her ass. And those *eyes*. Holy mother, those eyes. To call them brown wouldn't be doing them justice. The brown of a freshly crafted mocha latte, with just as much sweetness and heat. But piss her off, and god, those eyes could blaze and spark like a territorial she-wolf's—and I, obviously, was an expert at pissing her off. Last, but certainly not least...her tits. Even tragically hidden behind the world's most boring plain white bra, her tits were epic. Not silicone injection huge—not the largest I'd ever seen, but great breasts are about a lot more than just size. It's about shape, firmness, lift, bounce...I could give a dissertation on what makes boobs great, but I'll restrain myself. Suffice it to say, hers were perfect. Big enough to be more than a handful, and I've got big hands. Obviously natural, firm, but jiggly enough that each movement sent my dick twitching in my shorts.

She wasn't self-conscious in that outfit, but neither was she rocking it like she knew every guy who saw her would want her—the latter being the truth, seemingly unbeknownst to her.

"Roman?" Ramsey's voice sliced through my

daze, and I felt his hand smack into the back of my head. "You're daydreaming, asshat. Get with it."

I shook my head, trying to clear it of the image of Kitty in those shorts and that barely holding-to-gether T-shirt. "Sorry. Sorry. Just—"

"Daydreaming about that waitress who shut you down," Remington said. "We know."

"She didn't shut me down," I snapped.

"Oh, bullshit!" Ramsey laughed. "Yes, she did! She shut you down *twice*. You came back talking about her nonstop and acting like a total bear. Which can only mean she shut you down, *again*."

"She's just playing hard to get," I muttered, shak-ing my head. "It's sexy."

Remington laughed. "Hate to break it to you, bro, but I don't think she's playin'. I think you finally found a woman who is actually just immune to your, uhhh, *charms*. She don't like you, Rome!"

Ram laughed with him. "The man has met his match."

"We almost kissed, I'll have you know," I groused.

"Coming from someone who can get girls to fuck him without saying a word, *we almost kissed* counts as losing." Ramsey moved up beside me, grabbed my hand, and lifted it, then brought it down so the ham-mer in my hand connected with the wall we were de-molishing. "Now, get to work you damned lovesick puppy. This place won't demo itself."

We were in our newly acquired bar, ripping out the outdated decor. The place had obviously been decorated in the '70s, and hadn't been updated since. The boys and I had done our share of off-season construction work, so we knew our way around a renovation. We figured the kitchen was good enough as is, since we didn't plan on doing much by way of food service, which meant all we really had to do was rip out the ugly-ass wood paneling and ripped vinyl booths, build some new booths, find some old tables, throw up some antique saws and old rifles and deer heads on the walls, and we'd have ourselves a nice little rustic cabin bar. Suitable for Alaska, right?

So, we went back to work. And I did attempt to keep my head in the game, because I really did want this venture to work. I loved the rush and thrill and challenge of being a smokejumper, but after our friend Kevin's death I'm finding it hard to go back to that work, and I know my brothers are, too.

Plus, Dad isn't getting any younger, and he can't keep living on his own in the bass-ackwards end of Oklahoma, drinking himself to death. We pulled rank on the old coot before we left to come up here— meaning, we went and sold the Oklahoma property, trailer and all, out from underneath him. He was fit to be tied, but it got him off his ass and out of the countryside. He's currently "driving across the country to find himself again," whatever the fuck that means. We used the funds from the sale of all those acres he owned to buy him a nice new pickup with a fancy little Airstream to go with it. Figured, he'd have to get out of Oklahoma, and maybe this way he'd eventually find his way up here.

Maybe not, but it was worth a try.

He'd been sober ninety days before we left, and seemed a hell of a lot healthier than when we'd first showed up. Small win, right? And, honestly, he seemed pretty excited about his new truck and trailer, and the prospect of being a vagabond again, like he used to be. Selling the property felt kinda ugly to us boys, especially since weren't even on the deed, but we knew if Dad stayed in that trailer on that property, he'd end up relapsing, have another heart attack, and he'd be gone. He may not have been much of a father, but he's all we've got and we want to keep his grumpy ass around a bit longer. Why? We're not always sure, but it is the right thing to do, and while it may not seem like it most days, the three of us *do* have something resembling a moral compass. It might be cracked, but we've definitely got one.

We spent the next two weeks demoing the bar, building the new booths and tables, stripping and restaining the hardwood floor, putting in the new bar and stools, and a dozen other minor improvements, until the basic renovation was mostly finished. At which point the three of us had been together without a break for over three months, and we all knew we needed a little time apart before we killed each other. So, Remington called up a buddy and headed out for a couple weeks of hiking and fishing. Ramsey headed for Seattle to hook up with some drinking buddies from our hotshot days and I, of course, stayed in Ketchikan, because I was a sucker for punishment.

Over the past two weeks I've been working my ass off, and I've been so busy I haven't done anything except work, eat, and sleep, much less have time to go to Badd's Bar in the hopes of seeing Kitty. But that hasn't stopped me from trying to figure out how to get Kitty to sleep with me.

But I think I've finally figured it out. I've been approaching her all wrong—she just needs a little... finesse.

I wasn't nervous. I don't get nervous. Even when I'm three seconds from jumping out of a perfectly good airplane into the heart of a blazing wildfire, I don't get nervous.

Yet, for some odd reason, my heart was thumping

a little, and my palms were clammy. And I'd been practicing all afternoon what I was going to say to her when she opened the door.

I was standing outside her apartment building, hesitating like a teenage dweeb.

Why would I be nervous? She's just a girl, and I just wanted to get her naked and make her scream my name a few dozen times, that's all.

"Fuck it," I muttered. "Fuck it."

I jabbed the button to ring her unit, holding it down for a few seconds. There was a long moment of silence, and I started to wonder if she wasn't home. Maybe she'd gone out somewhere while I was busy grabbing the items in my hands—I'd figured out that she usually had Mondays off, so I'd timed my arrival to coincide with when I thought she'd be home alone.

I knew she had roommates, and I had no plans to let my brothers get wind of either of them or this situation could real messy real fast.

I was about to assume she was gone when a voice burst from the little speaker, tinny and irritated. "Yes? Who is it?"

"It's Roman Badd."

Another silence. "Really?"

I laughed. "No, not really. My name is Herbert, and I'm an accountant from Omaha."

"What do you want?" I heard a tinge of humor

in her voice, and I knew my comeback had gotten to her. But I also heard very real irritation and confusion in her voice.

"I told you what I want, Kitty."

Another long silence. "You're wasting your time, Roman."

"I have wine and pizza."

Yet another long silence. I could almost hear her cursing me in her head. "You're *so* annoying."

This was accompanied by the buzz and click of the door unlocking. I yanked the door open before it could lock again—and before she could change her mind—and headed up to her unit. I balanced the bottles on the flat box of pizza, holding the flowers I'd also purchased in the other hand.

Yes, flowers.

Actual flowers, fresh ones, arranged by a professional. Not roses, because I had a feeling we weren't quite to the roses portion of the seduction just yet.

I stood outside her door, grinning like a fool. She opened the door a crack, peering through the tiny opening, just a slice of her face and one eye showing. "I'm not dressed."

I grinned even wider. "Awesome. My kinda pizza party."

Her eye narrowed, hardened. "Don't be an ass. Just…wait there for two minutes, and then come in."

She hid behind the door and flipped the latch so it wouldn't close. "Promise me."

I rolled my eyes. "I promise I'll wait here for two minutes." Play nice, I reminded myself.

I heard bare feet on the floor, and mentally started counting backward from one-twenty...even as I edged up to the door and peeked through the crack, because I'd promised to wait, not that I wouldn't peek.

Sadly, all I managed to see was a pale blue bath towel and a hint of wet hair as she vanished around a corner. But I also caught a whiff of that powerful female smell—shampoo, body lotion, wet hair. And that is a sexy smell. I don't know why, but it is. An instant turn-on.

I did wait the full one hundred and twenty seconds before toeing the door open and entering. All I could smell was her, and I had to work hard to not picture her in nothing but a towel, gazing up at me as she all but begged me to—

I stopped myself. No, no, no—don't be a dumbass. Slow it down or you're going to blow this.

I slowly let out a breath, setting the pizza box on the counter. I wasn't sure what to do with the flowers, so I just held them and waited.

Five minutes later, I heard a door open. A second later I felt a hike in my heart rate. It must be an abnormality--something I should get checked out by a doctor. I'm in perfect shape, the kind of shape elite Olympian athletes would be jealous of, so erratic jumps in heart rate shouldn't happen. Nor should my palms sweat. I had my whole spiel practiced until it sounded natural, some saccharine pile of bullshit about starting with friendship and seeing where it led. I was ready to deliver.

She rounded the corner from the hallway, saw me standing by the refrigerator with a bright, colorful bouquet of flowers in my hand, wearing an actual polo shirt and nice jeans, and she stopped in her tracks.

And all my mental preparation went straight out of my head.

Her hair was still damp, but she'd brushed it out and left it loose, so it hung in a dark golden wave down her back, a few strands drifting in front of her eyes. She was wearing a dress, but she managed to make it look casual, somehow. White and filmy and clinging, with flowers in shades of blue and purple, thin straps that bared her shoulders, and a modest but sexy neckline. The hem came to mid-thigh, and she was barefoot. Simple, beautiful, modest, and incredible. My cock was ramrod stiff, and she was showing less skin now than when I'd seen her last. No makeup, or very little. Maybe some lip gloss, or a little color on her eyes. I don't know, I know shit-all about makeup, only that I don't really like too much of it and she was wearing just enough.

"Jesus, Kitty," I murmured.

She frowned at me. "What?" Offended, almost. Or ready to be.

"You. Fuckin' gorgeous." Wow, super eloquent and not caveman at all. Way to go, Roman.

She snorted softly. "Thank you." Her eyes went to the flowers. "What are those for?"

I had to force myself into motion. "You. They're for you."

She held her ground as I took a few steps toward her. "Why?"

"Because beautiful women deserve beautiful things." I remembered part of what I'd intended to say. "And, um, because I know I come on a little strong sometimes. It's just—it's the only way I know, you know? I guess this is me trying to, uh, not come on quite so strongly."

"A huge bouquet of flowers, two bottles of wine, and a box of pizza—out of the blue, after two weeks without a word—is you trying to not come on so strongly?"

I shrugged. "Yeah. I guess."

She blinked. "Roman, I—"

I held up my hand. "Pizza. Wine. Conversation. Can we just start there?"

She hesitated, gazing at me as if trying to divine my intentions just by sheer eye contact and force of will. "Okay. But you'll have to behave yourself, or you're out of here."

"I'll do my best," I answered.

But I was really thinking, *I'll do my best to make you give in to the fact that you fucking want me.* But I didn't say that, and I barely let myself think it for fear she'd somehow read my mind. But I doubt my intentions are unclear, seeing as I'm here with wine, flowers, and pizza. That's not the action of a man interested in a casual friendship.

She shook her head at me, but only swept past leaving a swirl of woman smell behind. "I'll get some plates. The corkscrew is in the drawer by the stove, wine glasses right above."

I found the opener and the glasses, worked open the bottle, poured us each a glass, and carried them to the living room, setting them on the low glass coffee table along with the box of pizza. She joined me with two large ceramic plates and a bottle of ranch dressing.

I laughed. "Ranch? And real plates? Paper would have been fine."

She frowned. "You don't dip your pizza in ranch?" She shook her head. "You haven't lived, then, my friend. And we don't do paper plates. They're bad for the environment."

We helped ourselves to the food and dug in; I wolfed down three pieces before I remembered that I was supposed to act like I've been around other humans before, instead of the wolves I was clearly raised by. I glanced at Kitty sheepishly, watching her daintily munching on her first slice.

"Sorry," I mumbled. "Used to eating with the guys."

She just laughed, a musical, lilting sound that punched me somewhere in my chest. "You eat like the Beast from *Beauty and the Beast*."

I realized I had tomato sauce on the side of my mouth, a piece of cheese on my thumb, and grease on my hands. And I couldn't help but laugh. "Yeah, well, I've never seen that movie, but I have seen actual wolves eat pizza, and I'm guessing that's kind of what I looked like."

She glanced at me curiously. "You've fed pizza to wolves?"

"We were fighting a big ol' bitch of a fire in Montana, and after we got it under control, Ram, Rem, Kev, Jameson, and I all headed out to this ranch Kev had heard about. They did horseback hunting rides, and the guy also raised wolves. Why, I dunno, but folks that live out in places like that do some weird shit, you know? So we naturally wanted to see the wolves, right? I mean, they're fuckin' wolves. While we were watching them fight over a bone, the rancher's wife brings over a bunch of pizzas, figuring it'd be nice and hospitable. Only, the rancher takes an entire pizza and tosses it over the fence. Those things went *nuts*. Snarling, snapping, biting each other…made me glad we had a ten-foot-high electrified fence between us, because those things are *scary*."

"That does sound scary." She eyed me. "What is it you and your brothers do, exactly?"

"Well, up until recently we were smokejumpers."

She nodded, finishing her first piece. "I heard you say that. But what is that?"

"You know what a hotshot is?"

"A firefighter, right? But for wildfires."

"Basically. So, in places like California, Idaho, Montana, they get a lot of wildfires, right? Well, the US Forest Service is responsible for fighting those fires. There are the regular wild firefighters with the US Forest Service as well as with the Bureau of Land Management, and then there are specialty crews— hotshots and smokejumpers. Hotshots hike up to the fire and fight it on the front lines. Smokejumpers parachute down into the fire and fight it from the inside, basically."

"So, is one harder than the other?"

I shook my head. "No, not really. My brothers

and I have done both. We started as hotshots, but our personalities and style didn't really mesh with the other hotshots, so we transferred to a smokejumper crew out of Redding."

"Didn't mesh how?"

I shrugged. "Well, the hotshots are more tightly organized, more regimented. The smokejumpers are a looser bunch. I guess because you've gotta be a little crazy to be willing to jump out of an airplane into a wildfire. As you can probably imagine, my brothers and I are a little cuckoo for Cocoa Puffs." I took a bite, and spoke after chewing a few times. "I have a lot of respect for the hotshots. That shit is fucking *hard*. It just wasn't for us."

"And now you're in Ketchikan, opening a bar?"

Abort, abort, abort. "Yup, that's the plan." I needed to change the subject. "What about you? Have you always been a waitress?"

"No." She sipped wine, shrugging. "I waited tables in high school and all throughout college, but I entered the workforce, or whatever you want to call it, after I graduated."

"What's your degree in?"

"Graphic design with an emphasis on marketing."

"No shit, really?" I eyed her with renewed respect. "And you had a job in that field?"

She nodded. "Sure did. A good one, too. I

interned the last few semesters of my senior year, and ended up getting hired at that firm. I was an account supervisor by the time I left." She hesitated. "I—well, I actually really loved that job."

I want to ask, but if I did, it'd open me up to questions, which could be dangerous. But shit, I'm curious about the girl. "Mind if I ask why you left?"

She laughed, a rueful chuckle. "A breakup."

"You left a job you loved over a breakup?"

She nodded. "Yep."

"Ugly, huh?"

She shook her head. "No, not particularly. I mean, I've seen friends go through ugly breakups, and this wasn't like that. But when it was over, it was just hard to be there at all. Everything I did, everywhere I went, all I saw was just…Tom. I knew I needed a change if I was going to move on, and my roommate from college had moved here so I figured, why not. Fresh start and all that, right? Only, I couldn't find a job in graphic design here, so I ended up waiting tables to pay the bills, and just haven't…I guess I've been putting off looking for a real job or whatever you want to call it."

"You like waiting tables, then?"

She tilted her head side to side. "Eh, yes…ish. It's good money, for the most part, but it's stressful, and the hours suck. And it's kind of a dead end, you know? Unless I want to be a server my whole life, which I don't. But keeping up with bills and work and all that makes it hard to put job hunting on the front burner, you know?"

I shrugged. "Uh, well, not really. If something is a priority to me, I get it done. That's the only way to get anywhere is to put yourself first. Do what you gotta do. If I was in a job going nowhere and I wanted a change, I'd do what I had to do make it happen." I glanced at her, worried I'd offended her. "But that's just me. I'm a Type-A, hard-charging sort of guy, if you haven't noticed."

She laughed. "Yeah, I've noticed." She was quiet a moment. "You know, if I'm being honest with myself, I guess leaving the firm back in Anchorage was about more than the breakup, now that I really think about it. I was born and raised in Anchorage, went to college there, and had a good job that promised steady promotions, but I think I was afraid I'd be there forever, you know? Like, suddenly I'd be fifty and living in the same city my whole life. And it's not like I chose Anchorage, my parents did. I think part of it was wanting to—I don't know how to put it without sounding stupid."

"Strike out on your own?" I suggested.

She laughed, shrugging and nodding. "That was what I was trying to avoid saying. Because I was twenty-eight when I left, and striking out on your own at twenty-eight just sounds kind of lame, doesn't it?"

I shook my head. "Not at all. I get it. Rem and Ram and I couldn't wait to get out of Oklahoma, and the podunk town our dad had settled in. I think he picked it just because it was remote, and small, and quiet, and away from everything he'd known. He could hide there, I guess. The second we could, we left. Moved to California, joined the US Forest Service, and started fighting wildfires. It sounded challenging and exciting, and California was as far from Oklahoma as we could imagine."

The conversation wandered after that, to stuff like favorite movies and bands. We shared an affinity for nineties country, a dislike of eighties pop, and a love for classic eighties films like *E.T.*, *Karate Kid*, *Goonies*, and stuff like that. At some point, the pizza box was closed, the second bottle of wine was opened, and we were sitting on her couch, sideways, facing each other, knees touching.

Her knees brushed mine, and as the conversation drifted from topic to topic, it seemed like the couch was dipping inward, as if we were sliding toward each other. I'm not sure I'd ever spent this much time just *talking* to a girl, and I was feeling comfortable with it in a way I wasn't sure I was ready to examine too closely.

She hadn't rolled her eyes at me or called me in

a jerk in like…an hour, which was weird, but also encouraging. Maybe I was doing something right.

She talked with her hands, I noticed, flinging them this way and that, gesturing, waving, stabbing, chopping. Once in a while, a gesture would end, and she rested her hand on her knee. Suddenly, there was a shift in the air, in the energy between us, and it began with her hand coming to rest on *my* knee instead of hers.

Maybe she was warming up to me. Could it be?

I felt absurdly excited about that little gesture, the way she let her hand flutter down to settle on my knee. My instinct was to push for more, but I held back. Gradually, I let my hand gradually sort of end up on her knee, a loosely closed fist, at first, just sort of resting there as I listened to her tell a story about getting in trouble in high school. And then, after a few minutes, I let my hand open, spreading my fingers out, sliding them softly along her skin. Her knees were pressed together, tucked under her as she sat sideways on the couch, her skirt tucked modestly around her legs. And then, as I let my hand open and my palm rest on her knee and my fingers on the muscle and skin just above, she shifted a little. She let her knees relax, let the skirt loosen, baring another few inches of the backs of her thighs. She leaned toward me as I related a story of my own, about the time my brothers and I pranked our entire senior class by putting half a dozen cows in the gym, along with a circular freestanding fence to contain them, a bale of hay to feed them and a tank of water.

She was relaxing now, for sure. Her tight body language was softening; her eyes were dancing, shifting, and roaming from mine to my shoulders, my arms, my chest. I used both hands—one empty, one clutching my wineglass—to indicate something in relation to my story, and when I set my empty hand down again, my palm came to rest just a little higher on her thigh. She glanced down at my hand, and then at my eyes, and then subtly shifted her weight so she was angled more closely against me, which had the effect of sliding my palm even further up her thigh. The hem of her dress was a few centimeters from my fingertips, now, with a slight twitch of my hand, I could expose even more of her thighs, and possibly even the lower curve of her ass.

My gaze flicked from her eyes to my hand, and then to the sweep of her dress against the tanned skin of her thigh, and then to the hint of cleavage, and back to her eyes. Was that a smile on her lips? Was she shifting even closer to me?

I couldn't help it anymore—I needed to feel more of her. The curve of her thigh was too inviting, too appealing.

I listened to her talk about her childhood pet, a yellow lab named Polly, and let my hand slide up her thigh, fingers delving under the hem of her dress. Back, then, to her knee. She glanced at me, at my hand, but didn't stop her story, and didn't move away, so I did it again. This time, my hand drifted around to the outside of her leg all the way to her hipbone and back down. I was all but holding my breath as I explored her leg. She met my eyes as I began another trip up her thigh, this time letting my fingers graze gently along the back of her thigh from behind her knee to where her thigh met the couch. And this time, her own hand drifted up my leg, mirroring my gradual exploration.

I was talking, telling her about spending more time serving in-house suspension for fighting than I did in class, but my eyes—and most of my attention—was on her mouth, her lips. On the way she caught her lower lip between her teeth as I cupped the back of her thigh on my downward slide.

I finished my glass of wine, twisting and reaching to set it on the coffee table; when I returned to my prior position, we had to realign on the couch, and this time, instead of being tucked underneath her, she rested her legs on my thigh. In so doing, the skirt of her dress slid backward, toward her body, exposing a mouthwatering expanse of her legs.

This was an agonizingly slow process, but it was thrilling, exhilarating. Nerve-racking, even. I wondered in the back of my head if, even as a kid, I'd ever been this cautious and nervous about touching a girl—I didn't think I had.

Kitty's next story was about her first crush, and getting caught making out behind the bleachers at a football game her freshman year, and I felt a ridiculous bolt of jealousy at the thought of anyone kissing her.

I squashed that with alacrity, and dialed my focus in on Kitty, on the tanned silk of her thighs, turned toward me, resting on my leg, on the way she was closer than ever now, so close I could almost feel her body heat, on how large and brown and expressive her eyes were. I watched her gaze as I skated my palm over her knee and down her thigh, over the top, traveling as far as the edge of her dress before pulling back to her knee, trailing my fingers down the seam where her thighs were pressed together.

Ohhhh shit—the next time I passed my palm over her thigh toward her body, her thighs parted, just a hint. A gap of maybe an inch, just enough to let my fingertips traipse along the delicate flesh of her inner thigh.

As this happened, our conversation became a game of question-and-answer.

"Favorite pet?" This was her question to me, accompanied by her fingertips tracing a vein in my bicep.

"When we were thirteen, we found a squirrel that had been attacked by a cat. She was dead, laying on the ground outside our trailer. And right there with her was a little baby squirrel. How he did it, I'll never know, but Rem managed to catch the little thing in his bare hands, and we raised it in the trailer. Dad hated it, because he kept making nests in weird spots. We loved that little critter, though. We named him Gopher, because his favorite game was to play fetch with acorns. We'd sit outside the trailer and throw an acorn as far we could, and Gopher would run after it in those weird bouncing runs that squirrels do, and he'd bring it back, crawl up your leg, and stand there chittering until we threw it again. Funny as hell."

"What happened to Gopher?" she asked.

"He met a lady squirrel and ran off one day."

"Awww. Were you sad when he left?"

I nodded. "Yeah, he was a fun little fella. Every once in a while we'd find a little pile of acorns on our trailer's porch, which we figured was Gopher letting us know he hadn't forgotten us."

Her eyes followed my hand as I traced the inside of her left thigh down to the hem of her dress, a few scant inches from the promised land of the apex of her thighs. Kitty glanced up at me, brows lowering, teeth clamping on the corner of her lower lip; my fingers rested, pausing on the delicate skin of her inner thigh as I watched and waited for her reaction at the daring of my touch.

It seemed her breath was caught, her lungs filled, chest expanded, breasts high, her eyes searching me. Looking for duplicity, perhaps? This wasn't me, this patient game I was playing. I saw what I wanted, and as soon as I was sure I had a positive reaction, I pounced. Took what I wanted, and gave better than I got in the process. This, though…this was strange, and different.

And I was out of patience.

I was ravenous for this girl. I *needed* her.

And she wasn't demurring from my exploration.

Impatience flared, and I think my explosion of desire showed in a flaring blaze in my eyes—Kitty's eyes widened, and her teeth clamped down hard, turning her plump pink lip white.

I leaned forward, caught her lip between thumb and forefinger, and gently tugged it free of her teeth. "Story time is over, Kitten," I murmured.

"It is?" she breathed, her eyes on mine.

"Watching you bite your lip like that is driving me crazy." I dropped my voice to a whisper. "If anyone is gonna be nibbling on your lips, it's gonna be me, sweetheart."

"Can we still play question-and-answer?" she asked, valiantly trying to sound unaffected.

"Sure." I grinned, leaning close. "You can ask me anything you want, and I'll answer—so long as you ask it while I'm sucking on that luscious lip of yours."

"Sucking on my—*ohhhh* my gosh."

The abrupt shift was due to the fact that I'd matched deed to word, wrapping a hand around the warm, firm nape of her neck and leaning in, capturing that lower lip of hers and sucking it into my mouth. I don't think she was expecting it—she probably thought I'd been teasing, or exaggerating. Expecting a typical first-time kiss.

She clearly had no idea who she was dealing with.

I drew her lip into my mouth between my teeth and then suckled on it, licking it, and she whimpered in surprise. The whimper turned to a moan as I explored her mouth with my tongue, still not kissing, but rather tasting and taking. She responded in the only way she could—giving me her tongue. Her lips. Her whole mouth. She leaned against me, hands twisting into the front of my shirt and then one palm skating over the hard range of my shoulder to dance along my nape. I accepted the offering of her tongue, tangling mine against hers before sliding my lips into place on her mouth, locking us together, claiming a kiss that stole her breath in a gasp—and mine in a snarl.

I backed away, not letting go of the back of her neck. "You bite your lip again, that's what you'll be getting. You bite your lip, I bite your lip."

"Name of your first girlfriend." She hissed this, a hurried mumble, as if afraid she'd forget to ask.

"Never had a girlfriend. Lost my virginity when I was fourteen to a high school senior named Vanessa Cloud."

"Fourteen?" she whispered, sounding shocked.

"Yep." I slid my fingers down her thighs, dancing through the gap between her legs, daring and daring and daring. "Same question for you. First boyfriend?"

"Dylan Porter. Sophomore year." She glanced at me, and our eyes met in a crackle of sparks. "We dated for three months, and then I dumped him because I chickened out about having sex with him."

"Why'd you chicken out?" I asked, dancing my fingers to the very edge of her dress and hesitating there.

"I wasn't ready. My best friend at the time had lost hers before me, and said it had been awful, so I was scared, because I knew he was expecting us to do it soon." She shifted her thighs apart, a silent invitation. "You said you've never had a girlfriend—but have you ever fallen in love?"

"Her name was Jenna Dooley, and—don't laugh, but she was a waitress at a Hooters near where we were training. We'd go in every weekend and she was our waitress every single time we went in. I was head over heels for that girl."

She wasn't laughing. "What happened?"

"I tried to score with her, and she shot me down. Told me I wasn't ready for the big leagues quite yet—I was just barely eighteen, and she was…I don't know. Midtwenties. She let me down easy, though. Told me I was cute, and that I had potential, and to look her up after I'd fought a few fires."

"And did you?"

I laughed. "Oh yeah." I met her gaze. "But you don't wanna hear about that."

"I don't?"

I shook my head. "Nope. It's my turn anyway."

"Your turn?" She was searching me, her eyes darting from mine to where my fingers were still resting, hesitating on the tender skin of her inner thigh, the very tips of my fingers edged under the hem of her dress. "For what?"

I grinned at her, a wolfish, hungry grin that did nothing to hide my desire, or my intentions. "My turn to ask you a question." I slid my fingers forward, under the hem of her dress. "What did you think I meant?"

"I—I don't—I don't know." She sucked in a breath. "What—what's your question?"

She was expecting me to ask something personal, like when she lost her virginity or something like that. Not what I was interested in at all.

I inched my fingers along her thigh, and she bit her lip again as my touch slid closer to her center. "Favorite place to be kissed?"

Her eyes widened. "Um. Like bedroom versus living room?"

I rumbled a laugh. "No, like your throat, or the side of your neck…" I kissed each place as I named it. "Or your lips…" Another kiss, a light one, a teasing touch of my lips on hers, before continuing. "Breasts?" I bent, kissing the apex of the valley of her cleavage; I nudged her dress higher, baring almost all of her thighs, and a hint of white lace between them. "Thighs?" I shifted backward and leaned over, touching my lips in a skipping line of kisses from knee to mid-thigh before pausing to glance up at her.

She wasn't breathing, just gnawing on that lower lip of hers.

"Told you about biting that lip," I muttered, and lifted up to lean over her—she lost her balance in rearing away from me and fell back onto the couch, and now I was levered over her.

I bit the offending lip, nipping hard enough to

elicit a squeak of protest from her, and then soothed it with my tongue, licking and sucking on the lip again.

Her hands caught at my shoulders, clinging to them as if torn between pushing me away and pulling me closer. She'd clamped her thighs closed as she fell, her knees draping to one side. Now, one knee rose up, and her dress fell away. White lace appeared, stark and pure against the tanned skin of her legs, and my eyes were drawn down. French bikini cut, covering her pussy while baring her hips. The white lace was... god—it drove me wild. Made her seem innocent and pure, somehow. An illusion, but one that made me snarl in maddened desire.

"White fucking lace," I growled.

"Something wrong with white lace?" she murmured.

"Everything is *right* about white lace," I answered, letting my eyes devour the sight of her spread out underneath me. "Problem is, it's wreaking fuckin' havoc on my self-control."

She blinked up at me. "Self-control? What self-control?"

I laughed, a bark of amusement that wasn't exactly kind. "Sweetheart, this is me very tightly controlling myself. If I did even half of what I really want to do to you, you'd run screaming for the nearest priest."

"I—I'm not religious."

"You'd still confess by the time I was done with you."

"Confess what?"

I traced a fingertip along the waistband of her underwear, and she sucked in her stomach even as she gasped at my touch. "How much you fucking loved all the dirty, sinful things we did." I hooked a finger into the elastic and tugged. Not down, just away. Teasing. "Things you've probably never even dared to fantasize about."

"I've fantasized about a lot of things," she breathed. "Especially lately."

"Oh yeah?" I removed my finger from the elastic and traced the strap from her hipbone down inside her thigh—she quavered, and her legs fell a little further apart. "Like what?"

"Like what?"

"Yeah, like what. Tell me. Close your eyes and whisper your dirty little secrets to me."

"If I told you, it wouldn't be a secret, would it?" Her voice held a note of snark, a hint of tease; I almost wanted to piss her off a little just because that angry sass of hers was like a drug to me.

"It'd still be a secret—*our* secret." I braced my weight on one hand, my fist buried in the couch cushion beside her head, using my free hand to draw the strap of her dress down over her shoulder, tugging until a hint of matching white lace bra peeked up above the neckline of her dress—and a plump expanse of breast. Not enough, but a start.

She bit her lip again, and then abruptly let it go, almost guiltily. "I don't talk like that."

"Then you have to answer my question."

"Which one?"

"Favorite place to be kissed."

She breathed out sharply. "What if I don't answer either question?"

"I'll torture you till you do."

"Torture me? How?"

I grinned down at her. "Don't tempt me, Kitty."

"I'm not trying to."

"Well, you may not be trying to, but you *are* driving me crazy, and that's dangerous for you, babe. You have no idea what I'm capable of." I lowered my mouth to hers, and I was satisfied to see her lips part, anticipating the kiss.

I avoided her mouth, kissing the corner of her lips, and then when she twisted to catch my mouth, I kissed the other corner. "I'm trying to be good. You seem so sweet and innocent, and I don't want to scare you."

"I'm not innocent, Roman."

I smirked down at her. "Oh, I know. You're just

innocent enough to be awful fucking tempting for a man like me."

"A man like you?" Her eyes met mine. "What's that mean?"

Ignoring her question, I teased her with another kiss, this time letting my lips ghost across hers before ducking away, laughing at her huff of frustration. And then, when she opened her mouth to protest, I actually kissed her. Only, the moment she got over her surprise and started kissing me back, I pulled away. Slid my lips down to her chin, and then down the fragile column of her throat.

"Here?" I asked, breathing hot on the delicate skin. Downward, to the exposed valley of her cleavage. "Or here?"

Her fingers danced, her hands fluttered, trailing over my back and up to my shoulders, to the back of my neck, and then she feathered her fingers over the closely shorn fuzz of hair on the back of my head—and the delicate sweetness of her touch made my head spin, my heart squeeze, and my cock throb all at once.

I slid my lips to the plump curve of one breast, right where it hid under the neckline of her dress and the cup of her bra—and I tugged those down just a bit farther, letting my tongue tickle her skin with the kiss. "Here?"

"Yeah…" she breathed, her voice faint.

I wanted to crow in triumph, but I didn't. I kept my voice even, low, slow. A little bit of Oklahoma drawl crept into my voice. "Right there, huh?" I tugged a bit further, nipping at the skin as I bared it, until I knew she was about to fully pop out of her bra. "Or a bit further on, maybe?"

"God, you—you can't."

"No?" I backed away, letting the neckline of her dress fall back into place.

"I'm not sure if I'm—" She cut herself off, and her fingers dug into the back of my head, pulling me back down. "There. Right where you were. That's my favorite place to be kissed."

I touched my lips to the upper swell. "Here?"

"Lower."

I grazed my mouth downward, to where the neckline of her dress lay flat against her firm, supple flesh. "Here?"

She let out a breath in a soft pant, cupping the back of my head. "Lower."

I tugged her bra strap off her shoulder and hooked two fingers into the cup of her bra, tugging down slowly, gently, until her breast was all but free of the enclosure of the cup. "Here?" I kissed the curve of the inside, near the tip—her nipple and areolae were all that remained hidden inside the bra, and I wanted to see more, taste more. How far could I take this? How far was she willing to go?

I'm nothing if not bold enough to find out, ballsy enough to risk rejection.

"That's...that's pretty close," she breathed.

"Pretty close? But not quite far enough?"

Instead of tugging that same side free, I transferred my weight to my other fist and tugged down both dress and bra straps, and then slid kisses against her other breast, down from the upper swell to the very front, around the inside, kiss after kiss, my tongue leaving wet trails and spots on her flesh.

God, I wanted to see those tits bare. Fuck. So plump, so firm, just begging to be fondled and cradled and nuzzled and kissed. I should slow down, not rush her, not push her too fast—but she was panting, arching her back, staring up at me with wild, lust-hazed eyes. I groaned—I was a fool to think I could restrain myself where this girl was concerned. For such a sweet, innocent little thing, she was a damned devil woman, beguiling me, bewitching me.

With both hands, I yanked her dress down, freeing her tits.

She yelped in surprise, clutching herself with both hands, covering them protectively. "Roman!"

I pinioned her wrists, but didn't try to pull them

away. Let her cover herself for a moment—she'd let them go soon enough. "Damn shame to keep tits that perfect all covered up." I let go of her wrists and pressed both fists in the cushion on either side of her head. Bent over her. Kissed her, full on the mouth, tongue slashing against hers, going from zero to six-ty in a heartbeat.

And god*damn* if the sexy little creature didn't re-spond with breathy, whimpering eagerness. She lift-ed up against me, groaning, taking my tongue and giving me hers with a hunger that spoke of wild-fire-hot need burning under that good-girl exterior. I left it all up to her—all I did was kiss her, but I kissed her with everything I had, using every trick I knew to make her dizzy, make her weak, make her faint with need and ache with barely restrained desire. I nipped her lip and sucked her tongue into my mouth, I teased the kiss and when she pressed hard for more, I gave it to her. When she paused to gasp for breath, I stole her oxygen with a kiss so searing and full of dirty promise we both moaned.

Her hands released, lifting, cupping the back of my head, pulling me closer to demand the kiss never end—and fuck, I didn't want it to either. How long did we kiss? Minutes? Hours? Forever, and not long enough. She gasped a sigh as our lips ghosted against each other, both of us breathless, and I took that opportunity to snag her hands in mine, tangling our fingers together, palm to palm.

And press her hands to the arm of the couch, over her head. Exposing her to my gaze.

She squirmed as I reared back, keeping her hands pinned in place; not hard—if she'd struggled, tried to tear free, I'd have let go. But she didn't. She squirmed in place, putting up a fake fight. For the sake of appearance—for the ruined dregs of her conscience, maybe. I don't know, don't care. I just know that fake squirm was like a drug hitting my veins, making me growl in feral, hungry need. I let my gaze rake with deliberate slowness from her eyes downward, to the uplifted peaks of her breasts.

"Fuck," I snarled.

"Roman, I—"

"Perfect." I pinned both hands in one of mine and gingerly, reverently cupped a breast. "So fuckin' perfect."

"Ohhhhh god. Ohmygod." Her eyes slid closed as I softly caressed her breast, and then the other. "Your hands are so rough. Like sandpaper."

"Hard work all my life, sweetheart. Not much about me is soft." I caressed, stroking a finger around one pebbled nipple. "My hands too rough for you, Kitty?"

Her eyes flew open, and she bit her lip briefly

before answering. "No…" she breathed. "No. I—I like it."

I loosened my grip on her wrists. "Then keep your hands there." I let go, shifting my weight back to have full use of both hands. "Don't move."

I kissed around one breast, around the base upward in a concentric spiral. "This is your favorite place to be kissed?" I asked, stopping just before my lips closed on her nipple. "Right here?" I flicked my tongue against the erect flesh, the sight of her and the taste of her making me throb so hard my balls ached as they never have before in my life.

She gasped, nodding.

"Is that it? Right there?" I suckled her nipple into my mouth, lapped at it, flicked it with my tongue, and she lost her breath in a whimper. "Let me hear you say it."

"Say what?"

"Tell me what you like. Talk to me."

"That—what you're doing. I like that."

I cupped a silk-delicate, heavy, firm globe in one hand, thumbing over the peak. "You fantasize about this?"

She shook her head. "Not this, no."

"Then what?"

I watched her cheeks flame. "Being kissed just like that, but…somewhere else."

I released her, trailing my fingers southward. "You fantasize about *me* kissing you…elsewhere?"

She tilted her head back, gasping as I danced a fingertip over the white lace between her thighs. "No." She caught at my forearm, but more out of desperation than to stop me. "Just…no one. A man, someone. Anyone. Kissing me."

"Where?"

Her blush deepened. "Down…down there."

I trailed my finger over the lace again, tracing the hint of her seam. "Here?"

She nodded. "Yeah…"

"Did you touch yourself while you fantasized about that?" I brought my finger to the edge where the lace touched inner thigh, teasing my touch along the tender flesh and rougher lace.

She nodded, gasping.

"Did you?" I demand.

"Yes!"

I slide a finger under the gusset, tracing the soft, damp, delicate flesh. "Like this?"

"God, Roman—what—what are you doing?"

"Whatever I want." I trace upward. "Whatever *you* want."

"I don't know what I want."

I laughed. "Yes, you do." I halted my touch. "Want me to stop?"

"No," she murmured.

"Do you want more? You like how I'm touching you?"

She nodded, eyes closed.

"Do you?"

"Yes, I like it."

"You like what?"

"The way you touch me," she answered, annoyed.

I met her eyes, and then raked my gaze over her body, her bared, beautiful tits, her lace-covered core, her long, firm legs, one of them bent up and tilted to one side, the other angled past me between my body and the couch. To the gusset where I was teasing her with my touch—I tugged the lace aside, baring her. She squirmed, foot digging into the couch, back writhing—but she didn't stop me, didn't pull away. Just writhed under my gaze, under my touch.

"God*damn*, Kitty," I snarled. "I'm *this* fucking close to absolutely *devouring* you right now."

I let go of the lace, running my palms over her belly to the undersides of her breasts, watching her. "You want that, don't you?"

"Too fast—too soon." She was breathless, struggling for words.

"But you want it." I leaned over her, one knee between her thighs. I touched my lips to her breast, to the pale, fragile, velvety underside, and then between them. "Don't you?" Ran my finger over the lace again, outside, over her seam. I centered my touch where I knew she was most sensitive. "Right...*here.*"

She just whimpered, nodding. Clinging to my shoulders, fingers digging into my muscle, she gasped. "God—how the heck do you know how to touch me so perfectly? You're driving me crazy."

"How crazy?"

"Crazy enough to be letting you do all this." She moaned as I stroked that seam over the lace. "I don't recognize myself, letting you do this—letting this happen. I don't know you." She whimpered, eyes shutting in pleasure as I pressed against her clit over the lace. "I'm not like this. I don't do things like this."

"But you're loving every single fucking second of it, aren't you?"

Her eyes snapped open, blazing. "You're so damned arrogant, you know that?"

"I've heard that before, yes." I held her gaze evenly, confidently. "Am I wrong?"

A rhythmic increase and decrease in pressure over her clit, over the underwear. She shut her eyes and clenched her teeth together over a moan, as if embarrassed by the sound—and her helplessness in making it. Lips to her breasts, nuzzling her nipples, my middle finger against the scratchy lace covering her core; she whimpered, gasped, bit her lip and cried out, and then finally, her hips flexed upward, pressing her against my touch.

"Roman…" Kitty breathed. "God, please…"

I dragged my hands down her body, hooking my fingers to catch in the strap of her underwear. I didn't stop, didn't slow down, just dragged that lacy little scrap of virginal white right off of her. She whimpered at the sudden assault, the abrupt removal of her underwear, but then she was bare, and holy Jesus was she perfect—absolutely as perfect and pretty as the rest of her. That little pussy of hers was tight and pink and the dark golden fuzz was trimmed to a modest but sexy little triangle. Her clit was prominent and begging for me—and I had no capacity to do anything but oblige.

"Please what, Kitten?" I asked. "What is it you want?"

Her eyes on mine were so conflicted, as need and desire warred with…whatever silly, misguided notions were holding her back from just enjoying what I was offering. Which, in all honesty, I truly was offering without expectation of return. I wouldn't demand or expect or even ask for her to do anything to me in return—the sight of her body, the sound of her cries of pleasure, the addicting, erotic, instinctive way she responded to my every touch…that was more than enough for me.

For now, at least.

Yet she gazed up at me with something like re-proach, if not quite outright hatred, as if she loathed me but couldn't help wanting how I touched her, couldn't help loving how I touched her. She didn't want to be enjoying this, but she was. She didn't want to want more of what I could give her, but she did.

And I was asshole enough to not care that she didn't want to want it, selfish enough to crave her pleasure, to take her desire and responsiveness for myself.

"Roman—" She flexed her hips again, and I pressed my fingertip against her clit.

I just laughed. "More, huh?"

"Yes…god, yes."

"Thing is, Kitty, I'm just a big dumb brute, you know? I'm easily confused. I'm not sure what exactly it is you need more of."

Her eyes snapped and blazed. "I've never once acted as if you're stupid just because you're built like Atlas. You're very obviously *not* stupid." She bit her lip as I continued to build the pressure against her clit, erupting in a ragged, helpless moan. "You're just—*ohhh*—just the most arrogant, pushy, demanding, domineering, swaggering alpha male I've ever met in my life."

I rasped my stubbled cheek against the inside

of her left breast, nuzzled the weight of it, and then flicked her nipple with my tongue. Pulling my touch away from her center, I slid my palms over the tops of her thighs down to her knees, and then whispered them back up the insides, caressing the unbelievably soft flesh.

She writhed her hips again, gasping as my touch neared her core once more. "Roman, *please.*"

"Please what, Kitty?"

"I won't say it."

"Then you won't get it."

She let out a wildcat snarl of frustration, eyes blazing. She batted my hand away, her knees came together with an audible clap, and she kicked me backward.

"Get off me."

I immediately rolled away, and stood up. "What's wrong?"

She tugged her bra and dress neckline up into place, breathing raggedly, and then twisted to sit up so the dress covered her core. "You. This. Everything." She stood up and paced away from me, scraping her fingers through her hair in agitation. "You need to leave."

"Kitty, I was just—"

"Manipulating me—seducing me! I thought you were...I don't know. I guess I thought by showing up with pizza and wine and flowers, and sitting and talking with me that you were starting to think about me as more than just a body—more than just a sex object. I see I was wrong."

"Now just hold on a second," I started, taking a step toward her.

She held up her hand, silencing me, stopping me in place. "No, Roman. I want more from a man than to just be treated like all you want from me is my body. I let you in and spent time with you against my better judgment because I hoped you were showing me you were capable of more than that, but like I said, I was clearly wrong."

"Kitty—"

She let out a breath. "Please, just leave."

I blinked for a moment, still struggling to figure out how to salvage this. The conclusion I came to was that it was an unsalvageable situation. In which case…

I leaned against the open doorframe, picking at my fingernails with exaggerated casualness. "So this is probably not the best time to tell you I've named our new bar after you?"

She stared at me. "You what?"

"Yeah." I faked a cocky grin, because I may as well try to sell my own bullshit. "I thought Badd Kitty had a nice ring to it."

"You didn't!" She shook her head, at a loss for

words. "You can't!"

"Can, and have." I shrugged laconically. "Sign's made, already on its way."

"That's—you—you arrogant *asshole!*" Kitty snapped. "Why would you do that? Why would you name your bar after *me?*"

"How do you know I named it after you?" I winked at her—I was probably laying the asshole behavior on a little thick, but I was committed now, and I never back down. "Maybe I just like kittens."

"Bullcrap."

My laugh was one of aroused enjoyment. "It turns me on when you fake swear, you know that? So innocent. Makes me want to see how dirty I can make you talk." He rose and stalked over to where I stood in the middle of the living room, towering over me, one finger trailing up my thigh and against my core over the dress. "Maybe it's just a reference to a pussy—any pussy, not just *yours*. Maybe I just love pussy."

"You and I both know it's not any of that." She glared up at me, shoving me away. "Change it. You're not naming your bar after me."

I just laughed. "Not likely, babe. It's the perfect name."

"Why would you even do that?"

I only shrugged again. "Lots of reasons. It's a great name for a bar, if nothing else. Suggestive, sexy, fun, memorable—hell of a lot more original than Badd's Bar and Grill, that's for damn sure. And for another thing—" Here, I smirked at her. "I knew it'd piss you off, and you're so fuckin' sexy when you're mad. Hell of a turn-on."

Kitty turned away, visibly seething. "You're not just arrogant, Roman Badd—you're...you're an *asshole*. The hubris—it's just flabbergasting! Why would you think I'd be okay with you naming your stupid bar after me? Especially after trying to get me to quit while I was still working for your own *cousins*? We barely know each other! I have to live in this town! How many other Kitty's you think there are around here? The attention the Badd's get is—you can't even understand it! And I'm part of that! Everyone will hear about *your* stupid bar, take one look at that name, think of me, and put two and two together. They'll assume the worst."

I was baffled. "Assume what? And who cares?"

"That I—that I had something to do with it! That I would *want* a bar named after me! That I did something to get you to name it that—I don't know." She hissed, frustration and anger making her nearly incoherent. "I just know that you're a conceited pig and I never want to see you again."

His eyebrows shot up. "Wow, *ohhh-kay*. Arrogant jerk I can live with, but conceited pig? It's just a bar,

Kitty, and it's just a name." I tapped her on the nose, a gesture that I knew would only serve to infuriate her even more—but again, I figured I might as well play it out. "This is about a hell of a lot more than you're letting on, Kitty. Don't think I don't see that. For some reason, my very existence provokes you. I piss you off, and I don't even have to do anything other than exist—just like you turn me on without doing anything other than existing. And you wanna know something else? Part of the reason I decided on the name was because I knew it'd piss you off, and like I've said—you're sexy as hell when you're pissed." I backed away through the open door. "I may be all those things you called me, but there's one thing I've got going for me that you don't: at least I'm honest with myself and others about who I am and what I want."

FIVE

Kitty

I STARED AT HIM IN STUNNED SILENCE FOR A FULL THIRTY seconds before anger blasted my response out of me.

I shook my head. "Let me repeat myself: 'arrogant jerk' doesn't even begin to cover it. Arrogant, manipulative, cocky—" I stabbed him in the chest with my finger at each word, "—selfish, conceited, pig-headed, chauvinistic *asshole*!"

I whirled, paced away, and then stopped, pivoting to address him again. "You showed up here with flowers and wine, acting all sweet. Listening to me, talking to me—acting like—like maybe there was a gentleman in there after all. Like maybe you actually cared about *me*, beyond just wanting me, wanting my *body*. I gave you a *chance*, Roman. I wanted to believe you were being nice. And then you get me all mixed up, you—you turn me on—and yeah, I can't deny that I wanted what happened. I'm to blame for thinking you could ever be anything except a conceited, selfish jerk! Getting me turned on, making me—trying to make me beg, getting me to—gah! You make me so mad I can't even think straight." I walked over to the door, hands shaking, and opened it. "Please leave. And don't come back unless you can figure out how to give a crap about anyone besides yourself, Roman."

He stared at me for a long, long moment, and then walked out the door without a backward glance or even so much as a word, closing the door behind him a little too carefully.

The moment I heard the door to the apartment building slam closed, I sank, shaking all over onto the couch. How long did I sit there, unable to formulate thoughts, unable to let myself even think about what just happened?

Too long.

The door opened and Juneau and Izzy came through together, each carrying leftover containers from different places—remnants of their dinners at work, Izzy at the clothing store and Juneau at the offices of a law firm specializing in Native Alaskan affairs. They each took one look at me, set their containers on the kitchen counter, dropped their purses and kicked off their heels, and sat on each side of me.

"Kit-Kat, what happened?" Izzy asked.

I shook my head. *"Everything."*

"Let me guess—Roman." Juneau patted me on the back. "What did he do?"

"He—we—" I started, but was still crying and had to stop.

Juneau got up and brought me a box of tissues, and Izzy just frowned, eying me and the couch.

"Did you—" She looked me over carefully—I was sitting cross-legged on the couch, habits of modesty forgotten. "Kitty! You're not wearing any panties!" Her eyes bugged out. "YOU SLEPT WITH HIM!" she shrieked.

"Izzy, calm down," Juneau admonished.

"Calm down? How can I calm down? She slept with him, and now she's crying. Either it was that *good* or that *bad*. Which one was it, Kitty?"

"Okay, for one, I didn't sleep with him." I sucked in a breath, steadying myself. "Well, not exactly."

Izzy pointed at me. "Your panties are *missing*. You had sex."

"Izzy," Juneau snapped. "She doesn't need an interrogation right now."

I frowned, glancing at the floor around the foot

of the couch. "Where are they?"

"What, your panties?" Izzy bent forward to look, and then flipped upside down to lift the flap of the couch so she could peer underneath, using her phone as a flashlight. "Not here."

I blinked, trying to remember. "We were on the couch when he took them off me. It's hard to remember—I thought he just tossed them aside." Renewed anger sizzled through me. "If he *took* them—?"

Izzy clapped a hand over her mouth. "Kitty! You saucy little minx! You had sex on the couch! In broad daylight! With a man you met once!" She hug-tackled me. "I'm so proud of you!"

I shoved her away playfully. "Don't be. It was...I shouldn't have." I sighed. "And we didn't have sex."

"Then explain," Izzy demanded.

"It *does* somewhat leave one with the impression that you guys had sex," Juneau added.

I tried to figure out where to start. "We—I hadn't seen him in like, almost three weeks. Not a word. Like he'd just given up, you know?" I sighed. "He showed up a few hours ago with flowers, two bottles of wine, and pizza."

"Well, that'll open *my* legs lickety-split," Izzy said, laughing. "So, you can't be held responsible."

"A light breeze opens your legs, Izzy," Juneau said, making all three of us laugh, since the zinger was a rarity for her, as she was almost unfailingly kind.

"Just so it's clear from the outset," I continued, "we *did* drink both bottles of wine, but it was over, like, three hours of talking and eating, so—so I can't blame what happened on that. I was maybe a little buzzed, but that's it. You both know I can hold my wine."

"Got it," Izzy said. "Not drunk. Continue."

I close my eyes. "I—he—we—I don't know how it happened, honestly. He was being sweet, listening to me, telling all these funny stories. And—he was actually *listening*."

Juneau nodded seriously. "There's very little that's sexier than a man who can listen well."

"Truth," Izzy said.

"It was lots of little things. I mean, aside from the fact that he is, objectively, just gorgeous. He'd touch my leg, I'd touch his, and—the way he was looking at me, the way my whole body just *tingled* every time he touched me? I just—I *wanted* him."

"Not sure what there is to cry about so far," Izzy said. "That's called attraction, Kitty, and it's absolutely normal."

"Let me finish, first." I drew a breath, gathering my thoughts. "He just—he knew how to work me up. One little thing led to another, until I was just...all mixed up. So turned on I didn't know whether I was coming or going or what."

"Coming, I hope?" Izzy quipped.

"If you were *going*, I can see why you'd be cry-ing," Juneau said, snickering.

I glared at them both. "Stop! This is serious."

"Sorry," they both said.

"Continue," Izzy said, rolling her hand. "One thing led to another…"

"And I was…I don't know. Out of control, I guess. Had me basically begging." I admitted this quietly, my voice dropping. "And yes, at some point, I let him take off my underwear, and I thought he put them on the floor but now I don't know. And he had my dress half off, and—he wasn't even shirtless."

Izzy was staring at me incredulously. "He got you to *beg*?" She whistled. "He must be *good*. You're, like, the queen of composure."

"Except where he's concerned, apparently," I said, bitterly. "Because I had none. Zero composure. Totally just—enthralled. Hypnotized. I don't know. He got me to say things, and I—the whole thing…I just can't even believe it was *me*." I met their eyes in turn. I groaned, words failing me. "And he kept saying this stuff—it was all just…so *wicked*. So filthy. I've nev-er heard anyone actually say things like he was saying to me. I couldn't believe it."

Izzy fanned herself. "Hooooooo *girl*—you're

making me horny."

Juneau eyed me, laughter on her features. "So, you know I'm on your side, but I'm still not seeing what there is to be upset about. Sounds like a hot hookup."

I shook my head. "You don't understand what he's like. He's infuriatingly arrogant. He's gorgeous and sexy and ripped and if he does sex as well as he did whatever you want to call what just happened, then he's also probably *amazing* in bed. In incredible shape, smart, quick with a comeback—and the worst part is, he *knows* all this. He knows *exactly* the effect he has on me. He laughs at me. Teases me. He pisses me off like no one I've ever met in my life, and he thinks that's *hot*. He makes me angry on purpose because he thinks I'm sexy when I'm pissed."

Izzy's eyes were wide. "I've never heard you talk about anyone like this, Kitty."

"And that's a *bad* thing." I shook my head again, sighing. "You don't get it. He turns fatheaded arrogance and conceited swagger into an art form. He's probably had more lovers than he can count."

"So?" Izzy countered. "None of that makes him a bad person, nor does any of that mean you shouldn't take this opportunity for all the crazy amazing orgasms he can give you."

I blushed, ducking my head. "I called him a

conceited pig. I sort of yelled at him and kicked him out."

Juneau's eyes widened. "Wow. You never yell. Or call names, for that matter."

"He just brings out the worst in me," I moan.

Izzy patted me on the shoulder. "He really does. I mean, Kitty, honey—you had *that* man, here, *alone*. He gave you an orgasm, and you didn't even give him a handy in return? Did you kiss him? Did you offer to return the favor?"

"I stopped him before he could get me all the way there," I said.

Izzy stared at me blankly. "You...you *what*?"

"Well...he made me mad. He was just being so... so manipulative. So arrogant. Like he knew he could get me to do whatever he wanted, and I only let him in because I thought by showing up like he did that he could be more than just a guy interested in sex, but then he turns into that anyway, and on top of it all he was trying to make me *beg* for every little thing *he* wanted to do. So no, he didn't give me an orgasm, and no, I didn't touch him. He never even took his shirt off." I groaned. "And he took my underwear, apparently."

Izzy just gaped at me. "You kicked him out before he could finish making you come? Are you crazy? How is that even possible? Why the hell would you do something like that? At least let him finish making you come first!"

"Are you missing the part where he's an arrogant jerk?" I demanded. I hesitated. "And did I mentioned he named their new bar after me?"

Neither knew what to say to that, immediately.

As usual, Izzy was the first to muster a response. "He what?"

"Exactly."

"What'd he name it?" Izzy asked.

"Badd Kitty."

Izzy's face went through several expressions. "Um. That's actually really good. I'd go to a bar named Badd Kitty."

I stomped a foot. "Good name or not, he didn't ask me, and he refuses to change it. He already bought the sign, apparently."

"It's kind of flattering, actually." Izzy made an *I'm sorry* face and shrugged. "I can see why you're pissed about it, though."

"It's just another example of his arrogance." I tried to slow my breathing. "He just...he does whatever he wants, takes whatever he wants without any regard for anyone. It's beyond galling."

"And a little hot," Izzy said.

I stared at her. "There's seriously something wrong with you."

She shrugged. "Maybe. But I'll take an arrogant guy over one with no balls and no confidence any day." She waved a hand dismissively. "And anyway, who cares? You don't have to marry the man, just fuck him." Izzy sighed and took my hands in hers. "You probably don't want to hear this, but I think you aren't being honest with him *or* yourself about your feelings for him, or what you want, or, basically, anything."

"This isn't exactly the kind of support I was expecting," I said, standing up and pacing away.

"Probably not," Juneau said, from the couch. "But it *was* an opportunity to really get over Tom, which you desperately need to do."

"I *am* over Tom!"

"You are not," Izzy argued. "Have you slept with anyone since him?"

I ducked my head. "One guy. And it was terrible, and I felt guilty."

"Felt *guilty*?" Izzy frowned, utterly puzzled. "About *what*?"

"I don't know. It just didn't feel right. I mean, aside from the fact that he didn't really offer much by way of foreplay, and I didn't even get close to coming before he was done, and he didn't offer to help me out afterward. It just…we went on a few dates, and you kept telling me the best way to get over someone is to get under someone else, so I tried it, and it sucked, and I hated it, and I felt guilty because I didn't even really like the guy all that much, I was just using him to try and get over Tom."

Izzy smacked her forehead. "Kitty—you dumbass, that's not how it works. In order for getting under someone to work at getting you *over* someone, you have to *want* the person you're hooking up with. Rebound sex one-oh-one, honey—it's gotta be good, or it won't work."

"How are you supposed to know beforehand whether it'll be good?" I asked.

She shrugged. "You just know. It's a feeling. I mean, do you get the sense that if you had sex with Roman that it would be bad?"

I felt my entire body tense and heat at the suggestion. "No. It wouldn't be bad."

"What do you think it would be like?"

I could barely manage a whisper. "It would be incredible."

"How incredible?"

I didn't answer for a long time. "Probably so incredible I'd never want to have sex with anyone else after him."

"Which is *exactly* what you're afraid of!" Izzy shouted. "You're scared he'll ruin you for all other men."

Juneau had something to say, I could tell. She

had that look.

"Spit it out, June," I sighed.

"Just...I think maybe you're also scared that it's not just going to be good or amazing sex, you're scared that it'll end up being *more* than just amazing sex, and that he'll make your relationship with Tom look...lame. Or...something." She winced at me. "Sorry."

"I hate you both." I sighed. "Plus, you really have no clue how arrogant and crude and jerky he can be."

"You only hate us because we're right and you know it." Izzy flipped open the lid of the pizza box that was still on the coffee table, removing a slice. "Oooh! Pepperoni and bacon. Awesome." She eyed me as she ate. "Good news is, it's not too late to fix things."

"What if I don't want to fix things?" I moaned.

Izzy rolled her eyes. "You're trying to tell me you don't want to have sex with Roman Badd?"

I didn't answer.

Izzy pointed at me with the pizza. "Exactly. You do. So, now, you just have to eat a little crow, admit maybe you like him not just in spite of the fact that he's an arrogant jerk, but even, maybe, a little bit *because* he's an arrogant jerk."

I hate it when Izzy is right.

SIX

Roman

OF ALL THE TIMES FOR MY STUPID BROTHERS TO BE gone, this was the shittiest. I needed them. They'd talk sense into me. Beat it into me, if necessary.

I'd managed to kill two full days without thinking about Kitty, or what she'd said, or how she'd acted.

The custom neon sign I'd ordered had arrived, so I hung it in the window. According to articles and wikis on Google, the next phase was to stock liquor, purchase pint glasses, shot glasses, and rocks glasses...and a new ice machine...and bar towels, and a special dishwasher for glasses to go under the bar, and...a huge list of things, all of which cost a shitload of money. We'd been approved for a loan we were assured would cover the total cost of buying, renovating, and reopening a bar, but it was…

Well, it was a lot harder than I'd anticipated. Not that I'd ever admit that to Rem or Ram, who had laughed me out of the trailer when I first proposed the idea. I'd assured them it wouldn't be all that hard, and that we could do it.

Turns out, there's a lot that goes into running a bar, and the amount of helpful information available on Google was…sadly, limited. I mean, I pulled up plenty of articles just by googling "how to open a bar," but how did one go about trademarking the name and logo? And how do you even get a logo? We'd hired a real estate agent and an attorney to handle the actual purchase, which thankfully included the transfer of the liquor license, so at least that was done…but all the minor details were killing me. And I wasn't a details kind of guy.

Thankfully, the amount of work to do was so tremendous I was able to bury myself in it instead of dwelling on Kitty.

Or on her words: "Please leave. And don't come back until you can actually be different."

Okay, then. Fine. Whatthefuckever.

She can go fuck herself. I don't need her. I don't even want her all that much. It was just the thrill of the chase. The novelty of a chick playing hard to get, and playing it well.

A little too well, maybe.

Or…god forbid—what if she wasn't playing?

She hadn't sounded like it.

I tried my damnedest not to think about it, but it was impossible.

I mean, shit. That *girl*.

That body. Those eyes.

I'd washed my hands a million times, but I still smelled her on my fingers. I'd taken a dozen showers and brushed my teeth a dozen times, but I still tasted her—still felt her kiss on my lips. I blasted Pantera as loud as I could stand it while I was working, but I still heard her sweet, innocent, breathy little voice…

I'd watched more porn than I cared to admit over the last forty-eight hours, but I still saw *her*. I saw *her* tits, big and round and tanned golden and shaking as she quaked from my touch. I still saw *her* pussy. Her mouth, open with a gasp, just begging for my cock.

I watched my favorite porn star taking it hard, but my cock didn't respond to that—only to the memory of Kitty's tits in my hand, the taste and feel of her nipples in my mouth.

God, god, god.

Her.

I wanted her. I fucking *wanted* that girl, and the taste I'd gotten wasn't anywhere near enough.

I never want to see you again.

I'd heard that before, of course. But only *after* I've fucked the girl into next week. I only heard that particular phrase after I'd assured the girl, saying I was serious about not wanting to call her the next day, or ever. It was usually a retaliatory thing—*yeah, well, I don't ever want to see you again, either...*because I'd already made it clear I'd gotten what I wanted and I was done.

Fuck.

I knew I couldn't keep avoiding thoughts of her when instead of writing out a list of things I still needed to purchase for Badd Kitty, I was doodling her name, like a damned lovesick teenager. And yeah, there may have also been a few doodles of tits on the paper, which, considering I'm not in any way a sketch artist, did in fact resemble Kitty's particular pair of breasts. Namely, big, round, tear-dropped, with quarter-sized areolae and nice plump little nipples.

I wasn't getting anything done.

Fuck.

I leaned back in the folding chair that was currently the only place to sit in the makeshift office of the bar; the metal chair creaked in protest under my weight. I tapped Ramsey's number, letting it ring and ring—and go to voicemail. I didn't leave a message. Remington's phone went right to voicemail, and I didn't leave a message there either.

"Do *NOT* go to her house, asshole," I said to myself, out loud. "Don't do it."

I was the owner of a bar, but we didn't have any actual liquor yet, so I couldn't even get drunk here. There were plenty of other bar options available in the area, but somehow I ended up on foot, walking down the quiet sidewalks toward Badd's, sometime around ten at night.

The front door was propped open, live music pumping out—the twins, I assumed. I stood outside, peering in. Bast was behind the bar with Zane and Lucian, and Kitty was scurrying around with a tray full of drinks, and the twins were on stage with both of their wives or whatever up there with them, singing in four-part harmony. I saw another waitress I didn't recognize and Bax, with a bus tub between his hand and hip, was tossing empties into it as he passed between tables.

If I went in there, I'd make a scene.

And for once, I wasn't in the mood.

Conceited pig.

Why the hell did that sting so bad? It's not like I haven't been called worse. But for some reason, coming from Kitty, it just fucking *stung*.

I walked past the entrance, turned right at the next block, and found an open liquor store. Like the lonely sop that I was, I bought a fifth of Maker's, stuffed it into a paper bag, and took it with me toward the docks.

I sat down and drank.

Alone.

Stewing.

Remembering.

Thinking.

Why did I care what she thought? I shouldn't. I didn't.

She was just some girl.

Nobody.

Not even that hot. Now, Lana, a local girl from Oklahoma I'd hooked up with just before heading up here, now *she'd* been hot. Stinger waist, HUGE tits, platinum blonde, perfect teeth, tiny hands. Nice twangy drawl in her speech, and a way of using her tongue that had me weeping for joy.

Of course, she'd been the one to hightail it the second we were done, and she'd done it while I was in the bathroom cleaning up. I'd even brought her a warm washcloth, thinking it'd be courteous. Assuming we'd at least do some shots down at the bar and go back up for round two. But no. She was gone when I got out of the bathroom.

Ugh. Even thoughts of Lana's tits and the thing she'd done with her tongue wasn't enough to distract me.

I took another pull and capped it, realizing I'd gone through almost half the bottle already. I should find Kitty and tell her I wouldn't bother seeing her again. No point. Why chase someone who don't wanna be caught, right?

Fuckit.

Even that tight round ass of hers wasn't worth the effort if she was gonna be that flat-out *mean*. Conceited pig, my ass. I knew what I had to offer, dammit. I knew what I looked like, and I knew how I could make a girl feel. Doesn't make me a conceited pig, goddammit. Confident, sure. Even a little arrogant. I know that about myself. Jumpin' outta airplanes into fires, you gotta be a little arrogant. That edge is what keeps you alive.

I looked around, realizing I'd started walking again at some point, still carrying the half-empty fifth of whiskey. Or...more than half empty. I guess I'd started drinking again.

There were a few tourists around, heading back to their hotels and cruise ships for the night, and the dock area was fairly quiet. Where the hell was I?

Wait, I recognized that building.

Goddammit. I was at Badd's again. I was pretty toasted, which meant going there was a bad idea. A *Badd* idea, if you will. Haha. I'm so punny.

I set the mostly empty fifth down on the sidewalk outside the bar, took a few deep breaths, and tried to convince myself one more time *not* to go in there.

She's not worth the drama.

Fuck it, of course she was. Who was I kidding?

I swaggered in, ready for trouble. Looking for Kitty.

What I found was a mostly empty bar. The stage was empty except for a mic stand and an amp, and the only patrons were a trio of middle-aged ladies giggling together in a back booth, and a guy and girl making out in the hallway near the bathrooms. There was a massive stack of glasses on the bar waiting to be washed, and Bast was back there washing them and wiping down liquor bottles, while Zane counted cash at the register. Bax was pushing a broom around, and Lucian was carrying cases of beer out from a stock-room somewhere.

"She went home already, asshole," Bast said, not looking up at me.

"Who?" I said, taking a seat at the bar.

Bast turned to face me, a bottle of Tanqueray in his hand, a bar towel in the other. "Kitty. That's who you're looking for, I assume."

"So what if I am?"

Bast just shook his head. "If you came looking for trouble, Roman, you came to the wrong place.

Especially since you're alone and drunk."

"Ain't drunk."

Bast snorted. "Okay, buddy. Keep telling your-self that. But don't think I'll serve you. We have a strict policy against serving people who are clearly intoxicated."

"I'm your cousin, and you're closed."

"And you're hammered."

I shrugged, and nodded. "Maybe a little."

"What do you want, Roman?" Bast set the bottle on the bar and braced his forearms on the edge, lean-ing toward me. "For real. What do you want?"

I shook my head. "Fuck if I know."

"How about some water?"

I blew a raspberry at him. "Fuck water. Can't drown the sorrows of rejection at the bottom of a glass of water. Beer me, bitch!"

"If you're thinking you can score an easy hookup with Kitty Quinn, you're barking up the wrong tree. She's not a hookup kind of girl." Bast reached into a cooler behind him, twisted off the top of a bottle of Coors, and handed it to me. "Plus, she deserves better than you, frankly."

I took a swig and beer, and glared at him. "Fuck you, Bast. The fuck you know about me?"

"I know enough to know it's true, dickhead." He twisted the top off a second and drank from it. "You think you're the best thing to happen to women, and the world in general. You think you can just swoop in and scoop up whoever the fuck you want, do whatever the fuck you want, and there won't be consequences. I've got a newsflash for you, bub—that ain't how it works. You can go into any bar in the world, and I have no doubt you could have your pick of women." He tapped himself on the chest. "Look who you're talking to, fucker. Think I wasn't the same way? Only, I didn't even have to leave this place to have my pick. I could point, curl my finger, and get anyone I wanted."

"So? What's your point?"

He shrugged. "This is a gross generalization, but the kind of chicks who'll let you pick 'em up at the bar and fuck 'em without even knowing each other's name are not worth your time beyond a quick bang, man."

"Who says I want anything but a quick bang?"

"Obviously that's all you're interested in. But my point is, Kitty ain't that girl. She's not a quick bang. She's the real deal, man." He took a long swig, and pointed at me with the bottle. "And from her perspective, you're the male version of that same kind of person. The quick fuck. The easy pickings. If she wanted to sleep with you, she would. If all she wanted was something quick, she could have it. All she'd have to do is look at you sideways and you'd be all over that shit. But I guarantee you, if she wants something that means more than a few minutes of fun, she won't be looking your way. So just don't think you'll get anywhere with her if that's what you're looking for, because Kitty Quinn is worth a hell of a lot more than a quick fuck. And she knows *you're* not."

I shot to my feet. "Fuck you. You don't know the last fucking thing about me, or what I want, or what kinda person I am." I swayed, and sat down on the stool faster than I'd anticipated. "You're lucky I'm drunk or I'd knock your fuckin' block off for that shit."

"Welcome to try anytime, fuckface."

I felt a presence beside me. I twisted and glared up at Bax, who was standing behind me with my bottle of Maker's in his hand.

"The fuck *you* want?" I grumbled.

He shook the bottle. "You gonna kill this?"

I stared at him, trying to figure his angle. "What's it to you?"

He shrugged. "Shame to waste good whiskey is all." He took a swig and re-capped it. "Hey, you ever have Blanton's?"

I shrugged. "Nah. Never got around to buying a bottle."

He waved a hand in a *come-on* gesture. "I've got a bottle back at my gym that I've been working on for a while. You can help me kill it."

I stared at him still, suspicious of his intentions. "What's your angle, man?" I swayed in my seat, staring at him. "Why be nice to me?"

He laughed, jerking a thumb at Bast. "Pay no attention to my brother. He suffers from a terminal condition called 'grumpy asshole.' His wife is on her period and not putting out, so he's particularly cranky. Plus, he's a little territorial. And, also, just a dick." He grinned at me. "And unlike him, I know that if you're a bottle into a bender meant to make you forget something, you can't quit until you're all the way gone. And I got no beef with you, so we may as well drink ourselves stupid."

"Don't you have a wife to nag you about that shit too?"

"Not married yet, and she's on a girls' trip with some of the others up to Anchorage for a spa day, so I'm a free man for now." He grinned. "Plus, my lady is the shit, and wouldn't get on my case even if she was here."

I drained the Coors, dug a five-dollar bill out of my pocket and tossed it on the bar in Bast's direction. "There. Keep the change, dick."

"Thanks, cockhead." The sarcasm in his voice was pure venom.

I laughed, unsteadily following Bax outside and

down the sidewalk. "I can't decide whether I like him or want to break his face."

Bax laughed with me. "Welcome to being related to Bast, my friend. I'm his brother and I've felt that way my whole life. Still do, some days." He waved a hand. "He's a great dude. You just have to get past the crunchy, cranky asshole exterior in order to get to the nice guy nugget inside."

"I don't think he was kidding about what he said, though."

Bax shook his head. "Nah, he wasn't. He doesn't pull punches, and he doesn't sugarcoat shit. Plus, he kind of does have reason to be a little salty toward you." He eyed me warily as we turned a corner. "Considering how you guys showed up and all."

"What? Our little plan to horn in on the action you boys have going on up here?"

Bax laughed. "Yeah, that. Plus the way you tried to poach Kitty out from underneath us at our own bar. Ballsy move, dude."

I shrugged, swaying a little and bouncing off a wall. "Hey, I make no apologies, man. It's a free market economy."

"But we're your *cousins*, Roman. We're family—and none of us even knew we *had* family till you guys showed up. I can understand opening a bar because you see opportunity, but opening a bar in direct competition to your own family, with the stated intent of stealing our business? That's kind of shitty."

"Family, sure. But we're strangers. We don't know shit about each other." I followed Bax around another corner, and then waited while he dug keys out of a pocket and unlocked a door; we entered into an office space, and through an open door I could see the darkened silhouettes of exercise equipment and a boxing ring.

"So, shitty, sure," I said. "But not *that* shitty. It's just business."

"Yeah, we may be strangers, but you guys show up here, rock our world and flip our understanding of our own family on its head, and then don't make any effort to get to know us." He flipped on a light, sank into a well-used leather desk chair at a battered desk, pulled open a drawer and withdrew a bottle of Blanton's, as well as two rocks glasses that clearly came from his family bar. "*And*…when you do finally show up again, you're drunk and spoiling for a fight. That's just shitty behavior all around no matter which way you slice it, my friend."

The office was small and smelled of sweaty equipment. It was lit by flickering fluorescent tubes hanging from the ceiling, and had posters on the wall outlining powerlifting guidelines and standards, as well as more than a few Sports Illustrated Swimsuit Edition centerfolds, heavy metal concert posters, and lots of framed photos of famous boxers and MMA fighters. The centerpiece was a black-and-white photo of Bax himself, covered in sweat, one eye swollen and bleeding, lips cut to shreds, cheek gashed, fists wrapped in reddened tape that had once been white; he was standing over a fallen opponent, arms outspread, victorious, having just taken the winning shot. I eyed Bax with renewed respect, seeing that photo. There was a couch directly under that photo; an ancient, deep leather sofa, and I sank into it with a sigh, accepting the full glass of whiskey he handed me.

"Shitty is shitty, man, and family is family, even if we don't know each other all that well—yet." He poured a generous glass for himself, and lifted his in a toast. "Keyword being *yet*."

I toasted, drank, and eyed him. "Why are you being nice?" I drank again.

He kicked his feet up on the desk. "I'm being nice because I'm a decent guy. And because I think you are too...or you could be. You just don't know how to be a good dude. You've never tried, and no one's ever tried to make you. Besides, I feel like you and I are... I don't know...kindred spirits or some shit."

I laughed. "Now there's something no one's ever accused me of before."

"I mean, anyone who can take down a fifth of

Maker's and keep going is all right in my book."

I toasted him again. "Here's to fifths of whiskey and a hell of a headache in the morning."

We chatted about drinking escapades for a while, downing finger after finger of Blanton's until I wasn't sure I'd be able to get up from this couch. Eventually, Bax took his feet off the desk and leaned toward me.

"Gotta level with you, man—my brother was right about Kitty." He held up a hand to forestall my outburst. "Not about you—that's just his way of expressing himself. He'll come around, as long as you put some effort into being cool. But Kitty? Man, she's one of a kind. Don't fuck with her. And I mean that in the sense of don't mess with her head. She's a sweet girl, and one of the truly good people I've ever met that I'm not related to by blood or the bond of significant other-hood that is essentially akin to marriage. And she sure as hell deserves someone that's not... shitty to everyone around him."

I drained my glass of whiskey and set it aside—the room was swimming. "She's got me fucked up, man." I eyed him—or where I thought he was, at least, since there were three of him. "It started out like Bast was saying—something quick to kill the night with. But she's different, and I knew that right off the bat—but that was part of the fun, you know?

A challenge. And also just…different. She's a different kind of beautiful. She's sweet, but she's got attitude, man. Serious spunk and personality in that fine little package."

Bax nodded. "She's got layers. When Bast first hired her, I thought she was honestly…a little plain, and kind of boring. Too nice, too sweet, not enough fire. And my brothers and I? I gotta be honest, when push comes to shove, we're more like you and your brothers than we are different, so a nice, sweet, innocent girl like Kitty? I didn't figure she'd last a week, you know?" He laughed. "She's got fire, all right. And the more time I spent working around her, the more I realized she's not plain, not by a long shot. She's seriously beautiful, in a bone-deep sort of way. She doesn't need to accent it or play it up, and she doesn't try—especially not at work. She does that on purpose, I think, so customers just see as her as part of the scenery at the bar. She doesn't want to call attention to herself."

I eyed him with amusement. "Pretty detailed observations for a guy shacked up with another woman."

He laughed. "This is all stuff I've talked to Eva about, dude. She's not jealous. Eva knows I'm gone for her, and that I'd sooner cut off my own balls than ever betray her, or what we have together." He said this casually, without drama, and it kind of stunned me.

"Really? Your girl is that amazing?"

Bax laughed all the harder. "Bro, you have *no* fucking clue. You'll understand when you meet her."

I nodded. "I saw her when we all first met, although I can't say we really met. She's fine as fuck, man." I wiped my face with my hand. "But then, all of you bastards have managed to score the finest women I've ever seen. It's ridiculous."

Bax cackled. "We really did."

"I mean, your youngest brother, what's his name—Xander?"

"Xavier," Bax corrected.

"Right, Xavier. Dude, the kid landed one of the hottest women on the planet!"

"Right? Shocked us all to hell. Like, oh by the way, I'm dating Harlow Grace. No big deal." He laughed so hard I thought he'd have a coronary. "Kicker of it is, when he first started hanging out with her, he had no idea who she was. He didn't find out until things were already hot and heavy between them."

I stared at him from the couch. "How did he not know? She's literally famous in, like, the ass-end of nowhere."

Bax just waved a hand. "Eh, that's Xavier. You met him, you mocked him—he's different. Smartest human being I've ever known and ever will know, but socially...not the most adept. He doesn't need to be, though. That's not his thing. He's on his way to being the next...shit, I don't know—Einstein? Musk? I don't know."

"I didn't know that about him when I first met him," I protested.

"True, but even not knowing what makes him different doesn't mean it's okay to mock him. Doesn't excuse it."

I sighed. "Fine, whatever. I'm sorry."

Bax quirked an eyebrow. "See? An hour with me and you're already improving."

"Whatever, dickbag."

He just laughed, but quickly became serious. "What's your deal with Kitty?"

I shrugged. "I dunno. I can't stop thinking about her." I hesitated, wondering how much to say to a relative stranger, even if the stranger was a relative. "I...I went over to her place. We spent some time together. An impromptu date, you could say. And...things happened. Didn't bang, but she...well, it's obvious she feels something for me on some level, but it's also clear she just...she doesn't *like* me."

"And that chaps your ass, does it?"

"I've never given a shit about whether anyone likes me. As long as I've got Rem and Ram, and I can hook up with honeys whenever I want, I'm good. But Kitty made it painfully clear I'm not cutting it…I don't know." I groaned, laying my head against the back of the couch. "She let me touch her—let things go pretty damn far pretty damn fast, and then she freaks out and tells me I'm a conceited pig."

"Ouch."

"Right? I mean, normally name calling just rolls off my back, but for some reason, I can't let go of that one." I sighed. "But then, I *did* name our bar after her."

"Whoa, whoa, whoa—*what*?"

I peered at him through one cracked open eyelid. "Yep. Badd Kitty. Got the neon sign up already. Rem and Ram are gonna give me hell for it since I didn't tell them I was doing it, but shit, it's good name, right? Buuuuut, Kitty didn't appreciate the gesture, you might say."

"I wouldn't guess so," Bax said, laughing in disbelief. "That's ballsy as fuck, man."

"She was pissed." I laughed, chuckling and groaning at the same time. "And dude, she is *soooo* hot when she's mad."

"Wow. Okay. So, that was kind of dumb, if you were trying to get her to like you."

"I wasn't, though!" I protested. "I just wanted to bang her! I don't even know when that changed,

either." I laughed at myself. "Shit. I'm just now realizing that things *did* change the second I laid eyes on
her. And let me tell you, *that's* never happened to me
before."

Bax snorted, swiveling his desk chair around,
opening a mini fridge and withdrawing a bottle of
water, which he tossed to me. I caught it—with my
forehead, and fell over laughing.

"Dude, you're so wasted," Bax said, cackling.

"No kidding. I'm trashed, man." I cracked the
bottle open and drained half of it. "Seriously, when
did I stop just wanting to just bang her?"

"What is it you want now?"

I groaned, taking another long drink of ice-cold
water, which was exactly what I needed right then. "I
don't even know, to be honest."

"Bullshit." Bax tossed me another bottle of water. "Drink up, bro."

"Thanks. What are you calling bullshit on?"

"You, pretending you don't know what you want
with Kitty."

"I *don't* know." I eyed him as I slugged back more
water. "And aren't you, like, supposed to be telling me
to stay away from her and shit?"

"I'm not her brother, and really, I'm not even her
boss. We're friends and coworkers. I mean, the eight
of us co-own the bar together, but technically, Bast

is the general manager and the big boss. He's been running that place since he was a teenager. He makes it look easy."

I laughed. "Dude, it's *so* not easy. I thought it'd be easy, and I'm finding out how naive I was to think that."

Bax cackled so hard he almost fell backward out of his chair. "You three knuckleheads really thought you could just waltz up here and open a bar? Do you even have any experience?"

"No, we don't have any experience. Not beyond drinking in bars, at least. And yeah, we did kind of think it wouldn't be that hard."

"And how's that going for you?"

"Well, we have the place fixed up, but it turns out that was the easy part. Actually turning it into an operating bar is…proving a little trickier than expected."

"I really, *really* wish I was in a position to say I told you so, but I'm not, so instead I'll just say it serves you right."

I finished the second bottle of water and stretched out on the couch. "What did you mean about calling bullshit on me regarding what I want from Kitty?"

Bax bobbled his head side to side. "Well, just that guys like us, we always know what we want. Sometimes, though, we get pretty good at pretending we don't, because we don't always like what the thing we actually want says about us."

I raised my head off the couch and peered at him. "Huh? The fuck's that mean?"

"Eva and me—the whole thing just started out as…a really intense attraction. She was this new type of chick I knew nothing about, you know? Like, super classy—East Coast old money kind of classy, as in her family is basically the American version of aristocracy. Smart. Talented. Essentially *good*." He gestured at the photograph of himself hanging above me. "That? That's me. I mean, obviously it's *me*, but that photo represents who I was—who I thought I was and all I thought I could be. And Eva—she…she was this pure, shining angel, you know? Like, how the *fuck* could I deserve her? I couldn't. I didn't. So I tried to convince myself that I didn't want her, not in the way I knew deep down that I really did want her."

I slow clapped. "Cool story, bro."

"Don't be a dick," Bax snapped. "You're only acting that way because my story resonates with you, and if you're as much like me as I think you are, nothing pisses you off faster than realizing you have to open your eyes to your own essential faults, admit your own deep down desires and needs, and understand that you may just have to work at improving as a human in order to get anywhere past where you are."

"All right, Confucius. Whatever you say." I threw my arm over my head.

Damn the man—he was speaking my language, and speaking truths I didn't want to hear. It was hard enough to process when I was as wasted as I was, but it was worse knowing that I'd remember every word of this in the morning.

I was silent for a while as I tried to come up with a wittier, more burning comeback to Bax, something to shut him down. Instead, all that percolated in my whiskey-soaked brain were questions.

"Is it worth it?" I asked.

"Is what worth what?"

"The pain in the ass I'm assuming it is to become a better human, or whatever pussy-ass phrasing was you used. Is it worth it? Because that seems like a lot of work just for a chick."

He sighed. "Yeah, it is. But it's not just for the chick, Roman. It's not even really about the woman." He paused. "Okay, well, that's not exactly the truth. Yes, it is about her, and yes, the right girl is worth it. But it's more about that it's *her*. She's not just some chick, but she's *the* chick. But if you want the real nitty-gritty Confucius truth, it's that I needed to know I really *deserved* Eva. *I* needed to know I was worth it.

"Evolving as a person is hard. It means facing some shit that may not be pretty, but when you can look back after a few years and go, dude, look at all the bullshit I've overcome to get to where I am." He gestured with two long, burly arms at the office and the gym beyond it. "I own this. Flat out, free and clear, no debts—I *own* this place. Everything that comes in is pure profit, money in the bank. I have the love of an amazing woman, a huge family that has my back, a business that I love, which makes coming in to work every day not work, but something I enjoy and look forward to. It's meaningful. I get to hang out with my brothers and my sisters-in-law at a cool-ass bar, slinging drinks and watching people have fun. Just a few short years ago, all I had was a football career that would have seen me wealthy but lonely, an empty apartment in Calgary, a line of women who didn't give a shit about me beyond the size of my cock and the numbers in my bank account, and brothers I hadn't seen in months.

"It took work and facing some shitty truths to get to where I am, but it's absolutely been fucking worth it. And, I gotta say, Eva was a big part of me getting to this point."

I stared at him. "Must be nice."

He nodded unapologetically. "It sure is."

"Is this the part where you sell me a self-help course?"

He snorted. "No. This is the part where I tell you

to pass the fuck out. I'll lock the door on my way out. There's water in the fridge behind my desk, a bathroom just outside to the left, and a trashcan under my desk if you need to hurl."

"Takes more than this to make me hurl."

"Just saying."

I eyed him as he stood up. "You're all right, Bax."

He grinned at me, a lopsided smirk. "Don't get mushy on me now, Roman."

"Shut the fuck up and leave me alone, you big ugly piece of shit."

He flipped off the lights. "That's more like it." He paused halfway outside. "Feel free to hit the weights when you get up."

"Thanks."

He was still hesitating. "If I give you one more piece of unsolicited advice, will you remember it in the morning?"

I laughed. "I don't black out. I once drank two full fifths of Jack by myself and remembered every last god awful, embarrassing detail of the night."

"Impressive." He fiddled with the doorknob. "Try being honest with yourself, Roman. If you're honest with yourself about what you really want out of life, and with Kitty, you'll find it easier to be honest with her. And a woman like Kitty—I promise you there's very little she values more than honesty."

I groaned a laugh. "Duly noted. Now, if you don't mind, you've thrown way too much heavy shit on me for one night."

"Better than getting your ass kicked by your cousins in a bar fight, though, right?"

I raspberried him. "I'll still kick your ass, pussy boy."

"Okay, dude, whatever you say," he scoffed. "I'm an undefeated bare-knuckle boxing champion, my friend. So if you ever want to strap on some pads and go a few rounds, let me know."

"Undefeated?"

"Believe it, son."

I shot him the finger. "Go away. I'm sleeping."

He slapped the doorframe with a big paw, closed the door, locked it from the outside with his key, and ambled away, whistling. He seemed every bit as sober as when we'd first arrived, but I know we'd drunk at least a quarter of that bottle. He should be feeling *something*. The bastard could drink, I'll give him that.

Undefeated bare-knuckle boxing champion.

Plus a Navy SEAL brother.

And Bast looked like he could tear some shit apart if he had to.

Rem and Ram and I could do some major damage, but I was realizing I needed to think twice the next time I showed up drunk and looking for trouble.

Those boys could bring it, a fact I would do well to remember before my arrogant ass started writing checks I couldn't cash.

Honesty. Huh. I was good at honesty of a certain kind, but not in the way Bax meant. I was good at pointing out other people's shit, but not so good at pointing out my own.

What *did* I want with Kitty?

Well, for one, to get her naked and make her scream. That part hadn't changed.

But I wanted to see more than frustration in her eyes. I wanted to see more than anger, more than confusion, more than mere lust.

What I hadn't told Kitty when she'd asked if I'd ever been in love was that I was pretty hung up on Jenna, the Hooters waitress. When I went back a year or so later to look her up I actually found her. She had quit Hooters, gotten a cosmetologist's license, and was dating a fancy-ass pretty boy lawyer. I'd pined after that chick for a solid year, putting in work and thinking I'd show up, sweep her off her feet, and prove who I really was. She'd smiled at me, patted me on the cheek, and told me I was three months too late, but I got an A for effort.

That had hurt and I had sworn off having feelings for women ever since.

So, what did I want with Kitty?

Nope. Too drunk and too maudlin to go there. I wanted things I'd never had, couldn't have, and would never have.

See? Sappy, pussy, feelings bullshit. No thanks.

I'll deal with this bullshit later.

SEVEN

Kitty

IZZY HAD BEEN RIGHT—MY RELATIONSHIP WITH TOM HAD been kind of boring. I'd loved him, and he'd loved me. We spent eight years together, lived together for five. Things had gotten…complacent, I guess.

But I'd started to want more—more than just living together. I'd hinted at marriage, and more than hinted. I pointed out locations that would have been good wedding venues. Told him my ring size, and what kind of diamond cut and setting I liked. He'd ignored it all.

Finally, I'd flat out asked him if he intended to propose to me. He'd admitted he knew that's what I wanted, but he just wasn't sure it was what he wanted, even though he did love me and care for me. After some go-rounds and arguments and lots of crying on my part, and even some on his, we'd agreed the best thing was to break up, since we couldn't see eye-to-eye on something so important as marriage and children.

That had been over a year ago.

What had been wrong with me that Tom hadn't wanted to marry me?

Deep down, I was scared to admit it that I knew I wouldn't get what I wanted from Tom. I'd wanted more. I wanted him to chase me a little. Show me real hunger, not just... "Hey babe, wanna have sex?" Not just grope for me in the dark. Not just kiss me a little, paw at my tits, push in, come two minutes later, and go to sleep.

Not that that's all we ever had. He would get a little crazy sometimes, but not often, and the sex that I found fulfilling was usually instigated by me.

Ugh. Why was I thinking about Tom?

Because it was easier than thinking about Roman?

Roman challenged everything I thought I knew about myself, everything I thought I wanted for myself and from a man, and from a relationship.

He was forcing me to admit to myself that I *liked* the way he dominated me and made me admit things I found scary. I *liked* the way he looked at me—like I was prey and he was the lion. I even liked the arrogance—a little, in a weird way that I didn't un-derstand. I just…I didn't know what to do with him. How to handle what he made me feel, what he made me want.

I knew I'd reacted poorly to his naming the bar after me, but I also think I was justified in being pissed. It was an odd thing for him to do, and it still makes me feel uncomfortable. But at the same time, it *is* the tiniest little bit flattering. But still weird.

Overall, I just wish…

I wish I'd gotten the chance to explore more of how he makes me feel, on a purely physical level. Yes, yes, yes, I know—there's an emotional component I'm being too immature to think about. But I just don't want to like him. I don't want to want him the way I do.

I'm dreaming about him. Wet dreams, weird dreams, romantic dreams. I see his swagger, the cun-ning, mischievous, wicked glint in his sky blue eyes, the power in his body, the mastery in the way he touched me that night.

God, that night…

Darn it. I have to stop thinking about him. It's been a week—if a man like him doesn't renew the chase after a week, he's given up. Which, admittedly, doesn't seem like him.

Gah.

Stop already! I needed to do something to keep busy. Maybe go for a run and wait for the girls to get home from work. I bet they'd like to drink wine and watch rom-coms tonight.

My buzzer went off at that moment, startling me out of my rumination—I headed over to the intercom, my heart palpitating at the thought that it might be him.

"Hello? Who is it?" I asked.

"Delivery for Kitty Quinn."

Darn it. Wait—am I disappointed or relieved? A little of both maybe.

"That's me," I said. "Bring it up." I hit the button and heard the front door open, and thump closed.

A minute later there was a knock on my door. The young man on the other side wasn't from any of the usual delivery places, and he wasn't holding a plain old box, or even a dozen roses. He was holding a garment bag and an envelope.

"You're Kitty Quinn?" he asked, and then offered me the bag and the envelope.

I nodded. "Yeah. Who—who's this from?"

He grinned at me. "He said you'd ask that, and he said my answer should be, 'who else would it be from?'"

I sucked in a breath. "Roman?"

The delivery man—boy, really—was barely

twenty, blond, with a scraggly goatee and tattoos on his hands. "I dunno what his name was. Huge dude, like…like Dolph Lundgren meets Arnold Schwarzenegger."

"You didn't ask his name?" I asked, incredulous.

"He handed me those items, told me your name and address, and paid me cash. My job is to deliver things, not ask questions."

I rolled my eyes, accepting the bag and the envelope. "I've never had a delivery like this," I said, hesitantly. "Do I tip you?"

His eager, earnest grin only widened. "Nah, he took care of that, too." He waved at me as he turned away. "Have a good night, ma'am."

"You too."

I closed the door, relocked it, and brought the bag and envelope into my room. I wish I could say I opened the envelope first, because that's the polite thing to do, but that'd be a lie. I unzipped the garment bag and slowly withdrew the dress inside.

I actually inhaled audibly. It was jade green, short, with a plunging neckline and back, and would cling to me like cellophane. I knew just by looking at it that it would fit me perfectly, which only made me all the more curious. The question of how he knew my exact dress size was easy to answer—Izzy. All he'd have had to do was show up, tell her he wanted to surprise me, and she'd tell him anything he wanted to know.

I held the dress up to my body and yep; for sure it was my size. I'd look pretty sexy in this.

I set the dress aside, poking in the bag to make sure I wasn't missing anything. Thank god I did, because there were matching shoes—strappy, sexy sandals with a wedge heel. And a little black box tucked in at the very bottom, containing tiny but beautiful diamond earrings.

Seriously?

What *was* this?

Time to open the envelope.

Inside was a piece of ivory linen cardstock, blank on one side, with heavy, angular, neat, masculine handwriting on the other.

Kitty,

I've handled this whole thing all wrong, and I'm sorry. Let me make it up to you, please. If you're up for a little surprise, a car will be outside waiting for you in thirty minutes. I figured you might need some time to get ready. The car will be a white Lexus, and the driver's name is Tony. He'll know you by name, and he'll bring you to me.

I know this is where I tell you something reassuring about there not being any expectations connected to this, but that wouldn't be true. Kitten, there are DEFINITELY expectations. So go into this eyes open, okay? Give me a chance.

—Roman

Nerves fluttered in my belly—not just a few butterflies, but a whole kaleidoscope. There were definitely expectations. I wouldn't have believed him if he'd tried to say there weren't—that would have been disingenuous of him at best. Trust Roman to be forthright about this, at least.

There was no question in my mind whether I would go—that was a no-brainer. A gorgeous man sends you a dress, heels, jewelry, and a driver, you go along with it. Plus, I was dying of curiosity.

Thirty minutes wasn't enough time to get ready though. Not by a long shot.

Oh boy.

I put the card in the envelope, set it on my bed, and stripped out of my clothes. I put on my sexiest lingerie—a set Tom had actually gotten me, if you want the truth. Regardless of where the set came from, it was still high-end lingerie that did amazing things for my cleavage and backside. Hair and makeup was next. I rarely did more with my hair than a bun or ponytail, but if there was ever a time to use my curling iron this was it. I put my hair in tight ringlets, which dropped down into looser spirals due to the length and weight of my hair. I left a few wisps loose around my face. Simple makeup—some foundation, eye shadow, color on my lips, mascara.

I was still working on my makeup when the door opened and Izzy and Juneau came in together—they almost always did, as they worked on the same street and got out at the same time. They found me in the bathroom, panicking because I couldn't get my mascara to go on right, and I was trying for a smoky eye that wasn't too obvious, but it wasn't working.

Izzy and Juneau stood at the bathroom door, staring at me.

"Um, Kitty? What's going on?" Juneau asked.

"Duh, girl—she's got a date." Izzy's voice gave her away.

"It was you, wasn't it?" I asked.

"What was me?" Izzy asked, endeavoring to sound innocent.

"You told him my dress size."

She shrugged. "And shoe size, and the fact that you prefer simple round diamonds to anything big or ostentatious." She peered at my reflection in the mirror. "Um, what's going on with your makeup?"

I sighed. "It's not working."

Izzy winced. "Yeah, that's not working *at all*. You look like a raccoon trying out nineties-style makeup."

"I don't do makeup that often, so sue me."

"Take all that off. I'll do it for you." Izzy twisted to look into my bedroom. "So what did he send you?"

I waved a hand at my room. "Take a look. He's not subtle, that's for sure."

I used makeup wipes to erase my failed attempt while Izzy and Juneau checked out the dress—and the note, judging by the paper rustling sounds.

"That dress is *amazing*," Izzy said, excited. "It'll look incredible on you."

"I'll look like a skank going to prom is what I'll look like."

"Honey. That dress will make his cock rock hard and keep it that way without you having to move a muscle. You'll be the sexiest thing in Alaska in that dress, no joke."

Juneau sighed. "It's a beautiful dress. Not subtle, and definitely picked out by a man, but you will look pretty stunning in it."

"He just appreciates her form, is all," Izzy said. "And you're welcome for telling him that you look best in green."

"Did you warn him about being careful with me?" I asked, pointedly. "Did you tell him if he hurt me, you'd find him and hurt him?"

"Nope!" she sang. "I told him that you were scared of getting into a relationship, in desperate need of amazing sex, and that you're the most genuinely kind person I've ever met. Except with him, apparently, since he really does bring out the worst in you. But that's only because he scares you. Which is good. If it doesn't scare you a little, it's not real enough."

"Isadora Styles, you did NOT say that to him," I said, turning to face her, incredulous.

She nodded, winking at me and clucking her tongue. "I sure did, girlfriend." She patted my hand. "I also told him that if he messed you up or hurt your feelings again, I'd cut his balls off and make shepherd's pie out of them and feed them to him through a straw, because I'd also break every single one of his stupidly perfect teeth."

"Izzy."

She shut me up by bringing lip stain up to my mouth. "You really think I wouldn't have your back?"

"Did you really tell him I was in *desperate need* of amazing sex?" I said, smacking my lips together after she applied the color.

"Well, you *are*." She met my gaze in the mirror. "Is there a word stronger than desperate?"

"I'm *not* desperate."

She sighed. "I didn't say you were desperate, I said you were in desperate need of amazing sex. Big difference. You're not in a dry spell; you're choosing not to have sex. You could have basically any man you wanted without effort. You're just scared. Gun-shy."

"It's not about sex, Izzy, it's about—"

"The idea of a relationship," she cut in. "I know. But after eight years with Tom, you don't need a relationship. You need a man who will show you what it's like to be truly lusted after." Her eyes were unapologetic as she cut through me with her words. "Tom never lusted after you. He loved you—as in he cared for you. Which is great. But he never lusted after you. Not once. I never saw that, and I was with you guys all the time."

"And with this guy it's the opposite," I said. "He may lust after me but he doesn't give a crap about me as a person."

"You don't know that," Izzy said, tossing my eye shadow back onto the counter. "There. Finished."

Juneau appeared, leaning into the bathroom as Izzy finished my makeup. "The driver is here."

I eyed myself in the mirror. "You are so much better at that than I am," I said, marveling.

She'd done my makeup as I'd envisioned but failed to achieve—minimal, just enough to make my eyes look wider, brighter, a little sultry, with some pop to my lips and color on my cheeks.

She leaned against me. "I put makeup on every day, hon. You put it on, like, once a month."

"I don't see the point of doing it for work, and

that's pretty much all I've been doing lately."

"Yeah, well, that's a different conversation, sweet-ie," Izzy said, grabbing the dress from off of my bed. "Get your sexy ass into this dress so you can go get yourself a man." She held it up, found the zipper on the left side and opened it, handed it to me, and then stopped, laughing. "Kit-Kat, honey, did you even look at the dress?" she asked.

I frowned at her. "Yes, why?"

She gestured at me. "Because this is a plunging neckline and you're wearing a bra."

I bit my lip. "I can't wear a bra with that dress?"

She shook her head. "Nope. Really, you shouldn't wear anything under it."

My breath lodged in my lungs. "I don't know if I can do that." I eyed the dress, and then myself in the mirror. "Plus, I feel sexy in this set. If I wear the dress naked underneath, I'll be self-conscious, on top of being worried my boobs will fly out."

Izzy laughed. "Well you'd wear boob tape, obviously."

"Boob tape?"

Juneau laughed. "Yeah, it's a thing."

"I don't have boob tape."

Izzy vanished into her room and reappeared with a roll of clear tape. "This isn't the kind of tape that's supposed to work in place of a bra—it's not support.

It's just meant to keep your tits attached to the dress so they don't go *Free Willy* on you."

"So I'll be saggy, but they won't pop out unexpectedly." I sighed. "Great."

Juneau rolled her eyes at me. "Kitty, don't ridiculous. For how big your boobs are, they're super perky. Like, it's against nature and I'm a little jealous."

I rolled my eyes back at her. "Oh shush, June—yours aren't saggy either." Reluctantly, I slipped the bra off and hung it on the doorknob.

"No, but they're not as perky as yours." She stood behind me and tapped the undersides of my breasts. "Look at these things. Perky as an eighteen-year-old's."

I rolled my eyes again, shrugging away from her touch. "You're being ridiculous. They're not *that* perky."

"Yes they are, so shut up," Izzy said, holding out the dress for me.

I stepped in, tugged it up, and shrugged into the teeny little straps, and Izzy, bold as you please, reached in, grabbed my tits, and adjusted them inside the deep plunging neckline. She peeled sections of double-sided tape off the roll and affixed them to my breasts just to the inside of my areolae, then zipped the dress, and pressed the fabric against my breasts so the tape stuck to the dress and my skin, keeping the edges of the dress in place. I stood in front of the mirror adjusting my cleavage and the lay of the dress against my curves.

"Oh...dear...*god*," I breathed. "I look like a trollop."

Izzy cackled. "Trollop? Who says trollop? What are you, a ninety-year-old grandma? Jesus criminy, Kit-Kat." She tugged the neckline down and plumped my breasts up, making sure the tape was still sticking in place. "You look...honestly, you look hotter than I've ever seen you look, babe."

Juneau grinned. "You really do. He won't be able to keep his eyes off you."

"Or his hands," Izzy added.

I twisted, glancing at my backside—the dress scooped down to almost the small of my back, clinging to my hips and thighs, the hem ending at mid-thigh. The cut of it made my already generous hips and butt look even wider, more bell-shaped, and my cleavage was, conservatively, eye-popping. The low neckline meant I was showing off serious side-boob.

"I look like a skank." I tried to tug the neckline up, but Izzy batted my hands away.

"Leave it. You look just skanky enough. Classy and sexy without being trashy." She lifted a shoulder and made a face. "I have to admit, the man can pick a dress."

"You picked it, didn't you?" I asked.

She lifted both hands palms out. "No, I didn't, I swear by the girlfriend code. I told him your dress and shoe size and that was it."

"My hips and butt look enormous," I complained, smoothing my hands over them, as if could make them slimmer by doing so.

"Your hips and butt look *incredible*," Izzy countered. "Stop being self-conscious."

"I can't help it," I whined. "It's just been so long since I dressed up like this."

"You look beautiful, Kitty," Juneau said. "For real. I'm straight as an arrow and you're making *me* horny."

I laughed in shock. "Juneau!"

She laughed with me. "What? You really do look that good."

Izzy caught at my hands, her eyes telling me I wouldn't like her next statement. She held out a hand to me. "Panties."

"I'm not going without underwear, Iz."

"Yes you are." She wiggled her eyebrows at me. "It'll feel weird at first, but you'll thank me later."

I glared at her, and then at my backside again, in the mirror. "It's not necessary. You can barely see the panty lines."

Izzy just lifted an eyebrow. "Barely see them still means you can see them. Off." Her expression softened. "Just trust me, Kit-Kat, please?"

"Gahh, fine!" I shimmied the dress up around my hips, wiggled out of the underwear, kicked them off, and tossed them from the bathroom onto my bedroom floor. "Happy now?" I demanded, giving myself one more look-over in the mirror.

And damn her, but Izzy was right—the effect *was* improved without the underwear. The dress clung to my butt and hips, highlighting their curves, and without the underwear lines, it was all round curve.

"Yes, much better."

"I could have just put on a thong," I muttered.

"True, but it's better this way. You'll see." She winked at me. "You look hot."

I rolled my eyes as I left the bathroom, snagging my purse from the counter. "Okay. I should go." I transferred my phone, wallet, and keyring to my white Coach clutch. "I'll text you when I get to wherever he takes me. If you don't hear from me in a few hours, assume he's kidnapped me."

Izzy laughed, shoving me out of my bedroom, making me trip as I slipped my feet into the strappy sandals. "If I don't hear from you in a few hours, I'll assume he's kidnapped you and plans to fuck you six ways to Sunday."

"Isadora!" I protested, laughing. "You're so bad!"

"You should try being bad sometime. Like

tonight. You could use a little irresponsibility and recklessness in your life." She winked at me, kissing me on both cheeks. "For real, have fun. Loosen up. Give in to your basest desires. I have a good sense about this guy, Kit-Kat. Give him a chance."

Juneau had vanished, and reappeared with a string of studded Magnum condoms; she unzipped my clutch and stuffed them in. "Just in case."

I stared at her. "Really, June? Studded Magnums?"

She stared back, wide-eyed with innocence. "There was a reason I slept with Chris as many times as I did. I would have kept sleeping with him had he not tried to trick me into a threesome with his booty call or whatever she was." She leaned close to us, whispering conspiratorially. "He was hung like a horse."

I laughed. "Oh, June. You never cease to surprise me."

She leaned in and kissed my cheeks too. "I'm picky about my guys, but when I find one I like, I don't mind being a little naughty."

"I have so many questions, now," I laughed, heading for the door.

"Later," she promised. "As long as you have some juicy details for us, too."

"I'll give him a chance," I said. "This *is* a pretty romantic gesture."

Izzy popped me on the butt as I exited our

apartment. "Have fun!" she called after me. "Do everything I would do! Channel your inner Izzy!"

"I don't know about that," I called back. "There's not much you wouldn't do!"

"Exactly!"

A sleek white Lexus SUV was waiting at the curb, with a middle-aged man in a trim black suit leaning against the front passenger seat, staring at his phone. As soon as he saw me, he tucked his phone into an inner pocket of his suit coat and stepped forward.

"Miss Quinn." He smiled at me, reassuring and kind and welcoming. "My name is Tony. May I say you look absolutely stunning this evening?"

"Hi, Tony. Thank you."

I angled for the front door, but he intercepted me, opening the back passenger door. I tucked my knees together and scooted up into the seat, smiling at Tony as he shut the door after me. He slid into the driver's seat, started the car, and pulled away from the curb.

"Do you know where we're going, Tony?" I asked.

He grinned at me in the rearview mirror. "Of course. We're going to the Yacht Club."

"Really? The Yacht Club?"

He nodded, and withdrew a piece of paper from an inner pocket. "Mr. Badd told me to give you this."

I took the paper from him—it was another piece

of linen cardstock with his handwriting on it.

Kitty,

I want you to be comfortable, and I figured you'd want to know ahead of time what we're doing so you can check in with Izzy and Juneau. I've chartered a private boat for the evening. Her name is The Bonnie Lee, and we'll be having dinner and taking a tour to the north. I've chartered her until tomorrow at noon, but we can return at any time, and Tony is on call to bring you home, if that's what you end up wanting to do. You know damn well how I want this evening to end, but I've given you escape options in case you have other ideas. I have to admit I desperately hope you don't use those options, but they are available.

> *See you soon.*

> *—Roman*

P.S. I can't wait to see you in that green dress.

Instead of trying to communicate all that to my roommates via text, I just snapped a photo of the card and sent that to them in our group thread.

Juneau texted back first: **OMG. That's so thoughtful!**

Izzy: **Seriously. This dude is pulling out all the**

stops. This is an all out attempt to woo you.

Me: *Woo? Now who's the ninety-year-old grandma?*

Me: *I'll text you again from the boat, when I figure out whether I'm staying.*

Izzy: *if you don't stay, I'll kill you.*

Juneau: *Unless you have a legitimate bad feeling about him. Obviously trust your gut and be safe. But don't use not feeling safe as an excuse to chicken out.*

I sent them a GIF of Michelle Tanner from *Full House* rolling her eyes, and then put my phone on vibrate before tucking it into my purse.

I tucked the card into my clutch and watched the scenery pass out the window, trying to calm my nerves. I was not exactly successful, however. The butterflies were in full flight in my belly, leaving my hands trembling a little, especially as we neared the Yacht Club.

I had to admit that this was easily the most romantic thing anyone had ever done for me. Tom had taken me on plenty of dates over the eight years we'd dated, but never anything like this.

As we pulled into the parking lot I thought also about Izzy's advice—give him a chance. Be a little reckless. Irresponsible, even. Well, I wasn't sure about reckless and irresponsible, but I would give him a chance.

EIGHT

Roman

I STOOD NEAR THE PROW ON THE DECK OF *THE BONNIE LEE*, one hand on the railing, watching the sun sink toward the horizon. I'd be lying if I said I wasn't nervous, which irritated me. Girls didn't make me nervous. I hadn't been nervous when I lost my virginity, or when I fought my first wildfire as a hotshot, or when I parachuted the first time. Nada. No nerves, just excitement and anticipation, the rush and the thrill.

Right now?

Nervous as fuck.

My hands were shaky and clammy, and it felt like a whole damn zoo had escaped and was running wild in my stomach.

I tried not to glance back at the dock again—something I'd been doing obsessively for the last forty-five minutes, waiting for Tony to get here with Kitty. I tugged at the sleeves of my dress shirt, and then adjusted the tie at my neck—I hadn't buttoned the very top button, but I did have a tie on. My suit didn't quite fit—it was snug in the shoulders, chest, and arms, and the pants were tight around my thighs and ass, as I'd put on a bit of muscle since the last time I'd worn this thing. I hated it, but I wanted to look my best. This wasn't a jeans and button-down sort of date, which was my usual attire for anything that resembled a date, something that, honestly, I didn't do as a rule. If I really liked a girl and wanted to extend things with her beyond a night or two, I'd take her to a mid-level restaurant, buy some food and wine, sweet talk her a little, and that was about it. More out of courtesy than anything else.

This was different.

Kitty was different.

I'd never done anything like this before. Never wanted to. Never even considered it. Why would I go to this kind of trouble for a hookup? I wasn't sure what she was, but I knew one thing for sure and that was that Kitty was *not* a hookup. So what was this thing I'd arranged? I hadn't answered that question yet, even in my own mind. I couldn't. I just knew if I wanted there to be even a possibility of anything with Kitty, I had to step up my game. A smile, a little charm, some sweet talk and smooth moves...it wasn't enough for her.

She deserved more, and she knew it. She was a girl who knew her worth.

Of course, she'd let me get pretty far last week, but then she'd flipped out and shut down. She'd used naming the bar after her as an excuse, but I knew it was about more than that. She was embarrassed, ashamed, and pissed off at herself for letting me get her worked up, and pissed off at me for using her own desires to manipulate her.

I felt shitty about that, honestly. I knew she'd been hesitant, but I knew that she was attracted to me on a purely physical level, and I'd worked her horniness against her, until she was so mixed up and raging with libido that she couldn't think straight. It had been a dick move.

Granted, most chicks I'd ever spent time with hadn't cared. They'd been all too eager to have my hands and mouth on them. In all honesty, Kitty was the first girl who'd ever shown any reticence, let alone had actually stopped me once I got started.

I sighed bitterly, remembering Bax's words to me: *I needed to know I deserved her.*

Did I deserve a woman like Kitty?

Fuck no.

I heard an engine and tires crunching across the parking lot. Turning, I spied Tony's Lexus pulling around. He parked with the rear passenger door close to the dock, exited, walked around and opened Kitty's door. My breath caught, relief slicing through me—it wasn't until that moment I realized I'd been half expecting her to stand me up. But no, she was here.

One of the green, sparkly sandals I'd bought her lowered to the parking lot, and then, carefully, keeping her knees together and moving slowly and somewhat stiffly, she slid out of the SUV. My breath was already hitched in my chest, and I gasped audibly at the sight of her.

Holy mother of all fucks. I had seriously underestimated the beauty of Kitty Quinn. She was sexy in work jeans and a bar T-shirt. Breathtaking in barely there pajamas. Achingly perfect in a little sundress. An object of perfection and purity with that dress tugged down and pushed up, baring her pale, creamy, silky skin.

In that green dress, each curve was highlighted and hugged and shown off. Her hair was down, just the way I liked it, and curled into loose spirals, framing her lovely face…Jesus. There weren't words to describe her.

I was still over a hundred feet away from her and

barely able to make out specific details, but I was having trouble breathing at the sight of her.

My fist tightened on the railing of the bow until my knuckles hurt.

She paused, ran one palm down a hip, lifted her chin, let out the breath, and took a step forward. I could hear her heels on the wood planks of the dock as she walked toward *The Bonnie Lee*. It was late in the evening, nearing sundown, and the club was mostly deserted. A boat owner was cleaning his vessel on the other side of the marina, and another was putzing with his fishing gear a few slips down, but otherwise *The Bonnie Lee* was the only boat lit up, engines idling, and I was the only person visible.

Her eyes latched onto me as she made her way toward the slip, and I noticed her hands obsessively running down her waist and over her hip; she transferred her purse from hand to hand now and then too, and her empty hand was always smoothing over her hip.

Self-conscious? Nervous?

How could a woman as stunning as Kitty be self-conscious? She seemed to be confident and centered—except when I went out of my way to piss her off.

I shoved my hand in my trouser pocket, still gripping the railing to keep from giving in to my own nervous habit: running my hand through my hair. I'd gelled and spiked it, obsessing over each strand until Remington had threatened to shave it off if I didn't quit. I tried to pose, to stand tall, shoulders back, chin high. Put a little smirk on my face, like I'm as cocky as ever instead of shit-my-pants nervous.

After what seemed like an eternity, Kitty was standing at the side of the yacht, smiling nervously at me. I crossed the deck and extended my hand to her. She hesitated a moment, and then placed her hand in mine, pressing her palm against mine as she stepped across onto the boat. Once in, she was still holding my hand, staring up at me, blinking slowly and breathing even slower.

"You're a fucking goddess, Kitty," I murmured. "The sexiest woman I've ever seen in my life."

"Thank you." She ran her hand over her hip again. "The dress is...very tight."

I rumbled a laugh. "Had to get you in something that showed off your perfect figure."

She blushed. "Haven't you already seen my figure?"

"Nowhere near enough of it." She blushed harder, her teeth threatening to go straight through her lip, and I growled. "Remember what I said about you biting your lip?"

She nodded. "Yeah?"

"You're biting your lip again."

"I'm not allowed to bite my lip?"

"You're allowed to do anything you want, Kitty. Problem is, when you bite your lip, it makes me crazy."

"I'm sorry?"

I shrugged. "Don't be sorry, just be aware, if you bite your fuckin' lip again, I'm gonna do what I did last time. Which will cause me to short-cut past all the stuff I had planned for us this evening in favor of getting right to...*dessert*."

She trembled. "Dessert? What's dessert?"

"You are." I pinched her lower lip between thumb and forefinger. "This plump little lip first, followed by everything else."

She closed her eyes and inhaled deeply, as if to steady herself. "Roman, slow down."

I laughed, backing away half a step. "See? Exactly. That's what you do to me when you bite that damn lip." I snagged her wrist as she went to run her hand down her hip yet again—the millionth time since she'd got on board. "And this hand is another problem."

She blinked at it curiously. "It is? Why?"

"Because you keep running it over your hip, and it's doing things to my self-control." I ran my thumb over the tender skin on the inside of her wrist. "So... stop doing that."

"I'm not conscious of doing anything." She smiled weakly. "Honestly, it's a nervous habit. I'm self-conscious in this dress because it's more...revealing...than anything I've ever worn. Plus, I'm just nervous."

I tangled my fingers in hers to prevent her from making the gesture again. "Couple things. One, you shouldn't be self-conscious, because like I said, you are, very truthfully, the most beautiful woman I've ever seen with my own two eyes. That's no lie, and it's not a line. It's the truth. You're fucking gorgeous. And two, I'm nervous too."

She stared up at me in surprise. "You are?"

I laughed, nodding. "I don't get nervous. Not ever. Not about anything."

"Not even when you're about to jump out of an airplane into a fire?"

"Especially not then. I get jittery from excitement, but not nervous." I ran my thumb over the web her hand between thumb and forefinger. "*You* make me nervous."

She laughed. "I do? Why?"

I went for broke. "Because I don't have the slightest clue what the fuck I'm doing with you, Kitty."

"You sure seem to know *exactly* what you're doing."

"It's all bullshit and bravado, babe. Especially

right now."

A throat cleared discreetly behind us, and we both turned. A tall, slender man with close-cropped gray hair and weathered, tanned features stood before us, wearing pressed black trousers and a white short-sleeve button-down.

"I'm Captain Martin," he said, in a gravelly, powerful voice. "We've got perfect conditions for a romantic evening sail so, if you two are ready, we'll set off."

"Take us out, Captain," I said.

"Very well, Mr. Badd. "If you'll both take seats in the saloon, we'll be underway. Once we've cast off, Ms. Cowell will begin the food and beverage service."

Captain Martin vanished back into the cockpit, and I led Kitty by the hand toward the saloon—the living room area near the rear of the vessel. Sliding glass doors enclosed three sides of the saloon, and all three sets of doors were opened, making the saloon open-air. There was a white sectional couch facing a massive television, and a small table covered in a white tablecloth, set with two places, wineglasses, and several white candles of varying heights, lit and flickering gently, with a single red rose in a slender vase near one place setting.

Kitty paused, taking in the scene, and then glanced at me. "Roman...wow."

I smiled at her. "The couch, for now?"

Her eyes went to the couch, and then to me. "Um. Considering what happened the last time I sat on a couch with you, I'm a little leery," she said with a laugh, but I could tell she was also serious.

"I'll be on my best behavior, I swear."

She eyed me warily. "You made it abundantly clear how this evening is going to go, Roman."

I sighed, sitting on the couch; Kitty followed suit, sitting near me but not touching, setting her purse on the couch beside her. "Kitty, listen—you know I'm attracted to you, and that I want you. I'm not gonna feed you any bullshit about that, okay? But I'm also not sitting here *expecting* things to go a certain way."

The engines rumbled to life, revving as the captain moved us out of the slip and toward the open water, slowly angling away from the marina. After a few moments, the engines revved up a notch and there was a more distinct sense of movement, and a bit of bob and sway from the water. Before Kitty had a chance to reply, a young woman dressed in the black and white of a server entered the saloon; she smiled at us brightly as she approached us, taking a seat on the edge of the couch next to us.

"Hi, I'm Eliza, I'll be taking care of you this evening. We are a full-service vessel, equipped and prepared to accommodate almost any desire or request, so you only have to ask. Chef Matthias has prepared a menu for your dinner experience this evening based around the freshest possible catches. I'll go over those in further detail as we get closer to dinner time. For now, I can bring you something to drink, maybe something to nibble on as we get started? I know you'd like to spend as much time alone as possible, so I'll be as unobtrusive as possible while still making sure your needs are met." She pulled an iPad out of her apron, opened it, rotated it to face me, and handed it to me. "This is a comprehensive drinks list, arranged by wine, beer, and liquor. Do you know what you'd like?"

I glanced at Kitty, not taking the iPad. "You have a preference?"

She shook her head, shrugging. "Nothing too sweet, other than that I'm fine with whatever."

I handed the list back to Eliza. "Some red wine then. Surprise us?" I watched Kitty's reaction, and she seemed fine with my choice. "And a cheese plate."

Wine wasn't my thing, but it seemed like a better choice than slugging back whiskey like I usually did. Eliza returned a few minutes later with a bottle of imported Italian wine and a plate of assorted cheeses, along with spicy mustard, crackers, jams, berries, and cuts of meat. After she poured the wine she left, promising to stop by in a while to see if we wanted anything else.

Alone with wine and cheese, I decided I needed to clear the air a bit before we talked about anything else. "Listen, Kitty, about what happened on your couch...I—shit, this is hard, because I've never said anything like this before. Um." I resisted the urge to tug at my tie. "I'm not proud to say this, but I left your place with the clear impression that you'd felt like I'd somehow...I don't wanna use the word manipulated, but that's all I can think of. You were pretty upset."

She smeared Brie onto a cracker, ate it, washed it down with a sip of wine, and then sat back to meet my eyes. "That almost sounds like an apology, Roman Badd."

"If you felt, or still do feel like I pressured you or tricked you, or in some way manipulated you into doing anything, or letting me do anything, I will apologize for that. But if you were fighting your own feelings for me or attraction to me and I got you to give in to that, well...I sure as hell won't apologize for that."

She hesitated a long moment. "I can't with any honesty say you tricked me or manipulated me."

"But you're not happy with what happened."

She shrugged, cutting a piece of cheese, wrapping it in a slice of meat, and handing it to me. "I don't know. I've always been a pretty in-control person. I drank some in high school and college as most people do, and I had my experiences with getting drunk, and I've tried smoking pot a few times. But on the whole, I don't really enjoy getting too drunk or losing control. I never have." She turned her warm brown eyes on mine. "And that night, you—you made me feel out of control in a way I'd never experienced before. It's like you had some kind of remote control to operate my—my entire psyche and body. The things you said, the way you said them, the way you touched me, it was all...so overwhelming, and it just...it short-circuited my ability to think straight, to react like I normally would. There's just something about you in general that does that to me. You make me feel out of control. I don't yell at people, I don't get angry very often. But with you, I just feel like I'm a different version of myself which I don't recognize." She shrugged. "I guess it makes me scared or worried or uncomfortable, which only upsets me more and makes me react to you in ways I normally wouldn't with other people."

"I get it. I'm outside your comfort zone. Everything I am, the way I am, what I do, how I do it—you're unfamiliar with it and uncomfortable with me and around me."

She hesitated, glancing at me. "I don't like being made to beg. I don't beg. I don't find it funny or sexy or cute—it's demeaning, and if that's the kind of thing you're into, you should find someone else, because I won't be that girl, now or ever."

I sighed, nodding. "You're right. I'm sorry. It won't happen again."

"Promise?" she asked, watching me carefully.

"Swear on my soul."

She held my gaze for a long time—too long. So long I was the first to look away.

I dipped a piece of cheese in mustard and held it out to her, and instead of taking it from me, she ate it from my fingers, which I think surprised us both.

"I'm not sure why I did that," she said, laughing.

I smiled at her, not bothering to dampen the heat of it. "I don't mind at all," I murmured.

She busied herself cutting another piece of cheese. "You said you'd behave, Roman."

"I am."

She topped the cheese with a slice of strawberry and handed it to me; I ate it from her fingers as she'd done to me, grinning predatorily, making sure my lips slid along her finger.

She yanked her hand away as if burned. "When you look at me and smile at me like that, I get nervous."

"Why?" I asked.

She shook her head faintly. "I don't know. Because after what happened on my couch I know exactly how easily you can turn a look and smile into—into some sort of hypnosis that has me doing things I'd never normally do."

"Like let a man you barely know get you mostly naked?"

She blushed. "Exactly."

"You can't blame that entirely on me," I said.

She spread more Brie on a cracker and, again, fed it to me. "Sure I can."

"Why are you feeding me?" I asked. "Not that I'm complaining, mind you."

She huffed a laugh, shaking her head with a rueful grin. "I don't know. My hands seem to have ideas my brain hasn't caught up to."

"Well, feel free to go along with whatever ideas your hands may have." I grinned at her lasciviously, so she couldn't miss my meaning.

Her blush deepened. "Roman!"

"Just saying." I dipped cheese into jam and fed it to her, and this time, she let her lips linger on my fingers—just for an instant. "So, how do you figure you can blame what happened between us squarely on me?"

"Not guilty by reason of insanity?" She suggested.

I laughed. "Okay, well, for one thing, what happened wasn't a crime—unless you're claiming it wasn't consensual."

"No!" she protested, vehement. "No. It was con-sensual. I'm not saying that in any way at all." She hesitated a long, long time, and I waited through the silence. "I knew what was happening every step of the way, and I let it happen. And...and I enjoyed it. Up until you pissed me off and I stopped us, at least."

"But?"

She sighed. "But I didn't *want* to enjoy it."

"Why?"

She remembered her wine just then and took a hearty gulp. "Um? I guess because it was—and is—easier to pretend I dislike you. To pretend I—I don't know. Like I have some kind of moral high ground to stand on, or something. To pretend like you *did* ma-nipulate me into letting you do the things you did."

I frowned. "Moral high ground? What, like I'm some—some dirty sleazebag or something?"

"No. Maybe." She shrugged. "I don't know. I just didn't want to like you. I still don't want to like you."

"But do you?"

Another shrug. "Maybe." A trace of a smile gave her away, though. "A little. As long as you behave."

"But what happened...it's not a matter of blame, because it wasn't wrong. It wasn't an accident, or a mistake. I was making you feel good, Kitty. That's all. No expectations, no promises, just a woman enjoying the pleasurable sensations created in her body by the touch of a man." I met her gaze steadily. "It doesn't even have to mean anything, if you don't want it to."

"What would it mean?"

"Hell if I know. I'd be guessing if I had to construe what it meant."

"What would you guess at, then?"

"Hmmm. Maybe that you were promising me more. Like, by letting me touch you, you were promising me more, later, when you may not want more, or maybe you changed your mind about it." I thought for a moment. "Or maybe you'd think I'd make assumptions about you, about your character." I frowned. "We've both been saying '*what happened*', like it was an incident. It's not *what happened*, it's what *we did*. You may not have touched me, but you participated. You were part of it. It was something we did *together*, not just something I did *to* you."

She nodded. "Yeah, you're right."

"So… I guess I'm saying regardless of how you feel about it, you have to own it."

She nodded again. "I know."

"Are you ashamed of it?"

She shrugged, scraping at the last of the brie instead of looking at me. "I don't know."

I touched her chin. "Kitty." She turned her eyes up to mine. "Are you ashamed of what we did together?"

"Not ashamed, just…embarrassed."

I pondered this. "Why embarrassed? I don't get that at all."

She twisted away from the coffee table and the now-barren cheese board, wine goblet in hand, and sat angled toward me. "Because like I said, I lost control. And it took you making me angry for me to regain it."

At that moment, Eliza entered with a small black folder containing the evening's menu, and we moved from the couch to the dinner table. She went over each dish in detail; Kitty ordered salmon and I ordered halibut. Eliza poured us each another glass of wine, brought out salads, and left us alone again. As we ate our salads, we continued our conversation.

"So, why is losing control such a big deal to you, Kitty?" I rolled a cherry tomato to the edge of my plate, watching her reactions. "Seems to me that the whole point of sex is to let go a little bit, right?"

She frowned, considering. "We've obviously had different experiences regarding sex, then, because I've never thought of it like that."

"Then explain your experience, or how you think of it, how you feel about it."

She saw me rolling my tomatoes away from the rest of my salad and reached out to stab them. "I can't believe you don't like tomatoes. I love them." She thought a moment or two before answering. "I guess for me, sex has always been about…sharing, I guess? Sharing an experience. Sharing emotions. Finding a part of the other person in a way that's just not possible except through sex."

I nodded, rolling my fork in a circle. "I'm following. Go on."

"I don't want to talk about past experiences in any detail when I'm here with you in this setting, but—"

I interrupted. "This is all about conversation, Kitty. You're not going to upset me, or weird me out. I want to hear what you have you to say so I can understand you better."

Oh, shit. Did I really just say that? Since when do I want to understand a woman better? It was true, though—I did want to understand Kitty. I wanted it in a way, and to a degree, that I'd never even thought I was capable of.

Kitty seemed just as surprised by my admission as I was. "Wow, okay. You really want to hear about my ex?"

I shrugged. "I mean, only talk about what you're comfortable sharing. But yeah, I want to know what informs the way you feel about this. Because I feel like we're coming at it from two totally different places."

"Well, Tom wasn't my first boyfriend, but he was my first serious boyfriend, and my only serious relationship." She hesitated. "I guess it goes beyond just Tom, though, if you want to get into the psychology of how I think about sex and why. My parents aren't, like, conservative Christians or anything, but they are very spiritual people, and they are conservative about certain things. They raised me to respect my body, to be modest, and to treat the physical aspect of any relationship as...well...sacred, I guess. They didn't really preach no sex before marriage, exactly, but that was very much their line of thinking. They taught me that sex is very special and very important, and that I shouldn't enter into a sexual relationship unless I was very sure it was in the context of a meaningful, monogamous relationship. Casual sex was something that was...not *wrong*, exactly, just...I don't know. I guess 'wrong' is the only word I can really think of that applies. Not morally wrong, just a misuse of sex. They believed, and taught me to believe, that sex is a tool to increase intimacy, not something to just...chase after as an end in itself."

"I can say with perfect accuracy that I grew up with the exact opposite mindset. But go on." I extended an arm along the back of the couch, and she shifted, very subtly, closer to me, not quite within the curl of my arm but almost.

She laughed. "That doesn't surprise me at all." A sip of wine, a gathering of thoughts, and then she continued. "So, I had a couple boyfriends in high school and in college. I gave my virginity to the guy I dated all through my senior year. We both knew it wasn't true, ever-lasting love, but we really liked each other and we both knew we were going to different colleges after high school, so I guess it felt safe, because he was coming from a similar background. I don't think either of us wanted to go to college still virgins, nor did we want to fall in love with someone and still be a virgin."

I frowned. "No? I thought that was, like, the big thing with people who grew up like you."

"Well, that was what my parents taught me, yeah. But by senior year I had my own ideas and beliefs, you know? Like, I wasn't ashamed of still being a virgin at eighteen when all my friends, literally *all* of them, had lost theirs already. I wasn't proud of it, either. It was just a thing. I wanted to experience sex, though. And I felt like, I wanted to fall in love, but I didn't want to fall in love still a virgin because I wanted to be able to experience the whole thing—falling in love, the whirlwind of feelings, staying up all night having marathon sex sessions, that whole romance novel thing, right? And if I was still a virgin, there'd have to be this awkward stage of learning. I knew that much from talking to my friends. None of them had been like, wow, my first time was *amazing*. That's not how it works, and I knew it." She paused, sipped, and continued. "I met Tom toward the end of college. I'd had a few boyfriends, slept with a few of them, and was confident in what I thought I wanted in a guy and in a relationship. And when I met Tom, I was sure I'd found it. He was sweet, funny, good-looking, charming, had a good future. Knew what he wanted and where he was going, and that aligned with my life goals, too. We just worked together. We waited until we'd been dating a month to sleep together, and it was...good."

I winced, and she frowned at me.

"It's weird to be talking about this with you on a romantic date like this," she said.

"It's important stuff, though, right?"

She nodded. "I guess so. But this isn't how I thought this date would go, I have to admit."

I laughed. "You probably thought as soon as you got here I'd lock you in the cabin and fuck you up against the wall right off the bat, right?"

She blushed. "More or less."

"What would you have done if that had been my intention?"

"I—I don't know."

I leaned forward, eyes on hers. "Would you have gone along with it?" I held her gaze. "Be honest."

"I—I'd have tried to slow things down a little."

I felt my chest swell, and my zipper tighten. "But you wouldn't have shut me down?"

"You've been very open about intending to have sex with me, and—and I guess the more I thought about things and talked to my girlfriends about it, the more I realized I want things that I haven't been letting myself admit."

"Like what?" I asked.

She whispered back. "You?"

"Can you be any more specific?" I murmured, tracing my finger down the outside of her bicep.

She shivered at my touch. "I want a lot of things, Roman. More of what we did. More of the way you make me feel." She lifted her eyes to mine, biting her lower lip. "And to...to make you feel things."

"Oh, you make me feel things, all right."

She blushed hard. "I mean, I want to touch you." She bit her lip again, and I had to restrain myself from taking that lip from her and licking it and tasting it. "I want you. I just want *more*."

"How much more?"

"A *lot* more." She whispered this across the rim of her wineglass.

I sat back, grinning, as Eliza entered with the main courses, made sure we had what we needed, and left again. I let the heat of the previous moment dissipate, returning the conversation to her past.

"So. You and your ex." I watched her try to shift tracks, probably assuming I'd pursue the other train of conversation. "You hesitated when you said it was good. Why?"

She didn't answer for a beat. "Um. I don't want to give you the wrong impression of my relationship with Tom. It wasn't—"

"Just tell it like it is, Kitty. Don't dress it up or play it down."

"I—we—" she fumbled, and started over. "Things with you have changed my feelings on it, a little, I guess."

"How so?"

She shrugged. "Things with Tom and me were good. I liked being with him. We lived together for five years and were together for eight. That's a long time to be with someone, you know? So...it was good. I was content with what we had."

I eyed her as she held a silence. "But?"

She huffed a laugh and dropped her head forward. "God, you're relentless, you know that? How do you always know when I'm leaving something out?"

"I don't know. I can just read you."

She sighed, took a bite of her salmon, and then continued. "*But*...I guess too much contentedness can be a bad thing. I sometimes found myself wanting...I

don't know how to put it, other than just that I wanted *more*. I wanted him to want me in a way I didn't
feel like he did. We had sex regularly, don't get me
wrong. But he just seemed totally happy with it being
pretty much the same thing every time, and sometimes I wanted a little variety. A little more heat, or
spice or whatever."

"So is that what killed the relationship?" I asked.

She shook her head, loose curls bouncing. "No,
not at all. I don't think I ever really even thought about
that aspect of my breakup with Tom until recently."
She glanced at me. "Until you." She shook her head
again, and I couldn't help admiring how the shake
of her head sent her tits gently swaying and jiggling.
"No, me and Tom breaking up was about the fact that
we dated for three years, moved in together, and lived
together for five years, and he never proposed, never
wanted to talk about marriage or kids or anything."

"And you wanted that?" I asked.

"I mean, I thought that's where it was going,
yes." She scooped up a forkful of basmati rice. "And
he wasn't sure what he wanted, but he said he was
pretty sure it wasn't that." A pause. "He said, and I'm
quoting as closely as I can remember, here—'we have
a good thing going, so why change it?'"

"We had a saying in my smokejumper unit:
Complacency kills." I finished my food in a few bites,

and then continued. "Which seems true for a lot of things. I've never been in a real relationship, but I think that if I ever were in one, I wouldn't want it to be just this okay, content, blah thing." I held her gaze. "I don't know if you realize this about me, but I like things to be exciting."

"Yeah, I think I've *maybe* gathered that about you, Roman."

"So, let me ask you this." I covered my plate with my napkin and sat back in the chair, eying her. "How does all this tie into you being hesitant to give over control, or to let go, loosen up, or whatever?"

"Because with Tom, sex was…about togetherness. It was sweet. Loving. We held each other afterward, and whispered sweet nothings that would probably make you barf." She laughed self-consciously. "Sex wasn't about being crazy, or going wild, or…or losing control. Nothing I've ever done has been about intentionally losing control. I guess it was an unspoken thing in everything my parents taught me, a subtext—that we should always be in control."

I thought for a while. "That does explain a lot, actually."

She finished her food, pushed her plate away, and stretched a little. "So, tell me about your experience, where you're coming from." She held my gaze. "And be as honest as you made me be. Real talk."

"Real talk, huh?" I figured why not let her have it. She asked for it, right? "So my dad was—is, I guess— an alcoholic. We all knew this from an early age. He never hit us, nothing like that. Isn't one of those sob stories. He was just a heavy drinker. Our mom took off when we were seven, and our dad just…well, he did the best he could. You heard a lot of this when I told it to my cousins. But he was one old drunk and we were three uncontrollable hellions. We did basically whatever the fuck we wanted. He worked, and he drank until he passed out. Which left us to our own devices. We also lived in a rural area, which is putting it nicely. Fuckin' boonies, is what it was. Not much to do out there but drink, smoke, fight, and fuck. So that's what we did. We learned it real early from the folks around us—our friends, most of whom grew up similar to us. Not a lot of supervision, no one to care much beyond keeping us fed and alive."

"That sounds like a very…rough…upbringing."

"Yeah, you could say that," I laughed. "We three were the biggest, meanest kids around, so everyone was always trying to take us down a peg, and we were always too stubborn to quit, so we were always in a fight. I think I grew up sportin' a black eye and a broken nose more often than not. I think most folks assumed it was from Dad, but he does love us, and somethin' fierce, too. Just in his own way.

"Anyway." I paused to consider. "When I was fourteen years old, I hooked up with a senior named Vanessa Cloud—I think we talked about this. Of course, I'd messed around plenty before that, but that was the first time I had actual sex. Since then, it's been a steady stream of girls. The pursuit of sex and hot chicks came second only to graduating high school. We just wanted to get the fuck outta there and fight fires in Cali, which had been our dream from way back. We saw one of those Smokey the Bear commercials, and decided we were gonna fight wildfires. And then, once we were gone, it was just our way of life—fight fires, hit the bars, hook up."

I paused, choosing my words carefully. "In my experience, sex is about feeling good, connecting for a while with someone you like. It's about a physical feeling, a sensation. It's about the moment. The experience. The high, the rush, the thrill. It's about the opposite of control, for me. In my line of work, I have to be in control, at the top of my game, hyperaware of my surroundings and my crew and everything, the fire, the woods, the air, the dirt, my body, my gear—everything, every single moment. Sex is a chance to let go of all that. Just *feel*. Just *be*."

She shivered, her eyes warm and intense on mine. "That sounds...I like the way you make that sound."

"It's a visceral thing, Kitty. It's the purest

experience of life. It's fleeting, it goes by so fast, but in that moment, you're just—you're fully alive, fully immersed in the moment and the sensation, and that's all there is. No worries, no stress, no bills, no pain, or exes or anything—just that moment, that feeling." I hold her gaze. "It's about surrendering control, Kitty. Willingly giving it up, letting it go, and just living in your body, in that moment, with that person."

"What about the emotional aspect of it?" Her voice was quiet, almost inaudible.

I shrugged. "Never been important to me."

"Not at all?" She sounded almost…sad.

"Nope." I paused, my breath catching in my chest, honesty emerging out of me. "Not until now."

NINE

Kitty

MY HEART CONSTRICTED, SQUEEZING INSIDE MY CHEST. I wanted to believe he meant until me. That I made him feel emotions, or want to feel them. That I made him want to explore the emotional component of sex with me.

"Until now?" I asked, breathing the words.

He opened his mouth to reply, but Eliza entered at that moment, carrying a tray full of desserts.

"Would either of you care for dessert?" she asked, angling the tray toward us.

I shook my head; normally I'd be all about the tasty-looking items on that tray, but in that moment, all I wanted was to be left alone with Roman.

He watched my reaction, and then smiled at Eliza. "No, thanks. I think we're okay. Maybe bring another bottle of wine, and then just let us have some privacy for the evening?"

"Absolutely." She vanished with the tray, returning moments later with another bottle, uncorked, which she set on the table for us. She indicated an intercom panel on a nearby wall. "I'll be up in the cockpit with Captain Martin. If you need anything, just press the green button and speak, and we'll both hear you."

"Thank you very much, Eliza." Roman's smile was charming, but I could tell he was impatient for her to leave.

Eliza headed for the door, and then paused. "Just as a by the way, the cockpit and cabin where Captain Martin and I will spend the evening is acoustically sealed from the rest of the ship, and has a limited view, meaning he can see in one hundred and eighty degrees from the helm, but cannot see rearward past mid-ship." Her smile was polite, discreet. "So, you will have absolute privacy in the saloon, in the main bedroom quarters, and outside toward the stern. We will carry on with our planned tour northward along the Inside Passage unless you inform us otherwise, planning a return to Ketchikan around sunrise."

"Sounds perfect," Roman said, visibly impatient

now, which Eliza noticed. "Thank you."

She smiled again, backing out of the saloon. "I'll leave you alone now. Thank you for the opportunity to serve you."

And then, finally, she was gone. As soon as she was out of sight, Roman left the table, snagging the bottle of wine and our two glasses, heading out to the stern. There was a couch built into the side of the boat just outside the saloon, with a table secured to the floor. He set the bottle and glasses down, poured us each a glass, and handed one to me. Instead of sitting down, however, he moved to the very rear of the boat, leaning a hip against the side, bracing a hand on the railing. The boat left a white wake in the green-gray water. Trees rose in a thick blanket to our right, open water to our left. Roman had timed this whole thing absolutely perfectly—the sun was just now setting, an orange ball plunging itself into the sea, bathing everything in a golden orange-red light, staining the sea, the boat, the sky, everything. The only sound was the faint rumble of the engines and the gentle sweep of the prow of the boat against the waves, an occasional seagull cawing overhead, wheeling and tilting.

For a while, we just stood side by side at the back of the boat, watching the sunset, sipping delicious wine, and enjoying the moment. We didn't speak, and the silence was comfortable.

I finally turned my gaze away from the red crescent of the sun as it prepared to vanish entirely beneath the horizon—Roman was staring down at me, his blue eyes sparking with intensity.

"So, what did you mean, 'until now'?" I asked, the question burning a hole in my heart.

He didn't answer for a moment. "Just that until I met you, I never cared about the whole idea of emotionally connecting with someone through sex. I never wanted to emotionally connect with anyone. That's just not what sex has ever been about for me. And, honestly, I wouldn't know how to…" He shrugged, at a loss for words. "How to even *do* that, I guess."

I couldn't help a laugh. "How to do what? Emotionally connect with someone through sex?"

His grin was wry and rueful. "You laugh like that's ridiculous."

"Because it is!" I shake my head. "Do you really just go through life without feeling anything? You're just numb to everything except the desire to have sex and…what else? Fight fires and punch people?"

He laughed. "Yes, Kitty, that's exactly it. Those are the only things I feel in my life—have sex, fight fires, and punch people."

"Well, you did say your entire life was about fighting, sex, smoking, and drinking."

He laughed again. "What I actually said was, growing up where I did, the only things to do were drink, smoke, fight, and fuck." He lifted an eyebrow at me. "I didn't say that's all my life consists of *now.*"

I quirked an eyebrow back at him until he started laughing.

"Okay, fine, it pretty much is. Except I don't smoke, and while I do drink, not as much as you're probably assuming." I think about the other day, and the amount of whiskey I put away. "At least, not typically. I also don't get into too many fights anymore."

"You don't? You swagger around like your greatest joy in life is to knock people's teeth in."

His grin was predatory. "Yeah, well, that's the vibe I like to give off. I act like I'm the toughest, meanest guy in any room—and usually, I am—which means most people won't mess with me." He gestured at himself. "When you look like me, guys get intimidated, and when guys are intimidated, they wanna show how tough they are by trying to start shit with me to prove they're not intimidated. Which is dumb, because that's just a good way to get your teeth knocked in. So I swagger around like I know I've got the biggest, brassiest balls around in part as a way to prevent assholes from starting something with me." He winked at me. "Plus, I generally do have the biggest, brassiest balls around."

I rolled my eyes at him. "And so humble." I sighed. "So you don't drink that much, don't fight that much, don't smoke at all…which leaves the last one as your primary activity."

"Not gonna sugarcoat it, and not gonna lie about it." He stared down at me, his gaze unapologetic and unwavering. "Until I moved up here, yes, fighting fires and having sex was the way I spent the majority of my time."

"Having sex without any emotional connectivity," I clarified.

"Pretty much." He shrugged. "It's not like it was just this…blank, emotionless transaction, though, Kitty. I don't know what you're picturing or imagining, but I *do* feel things. I *have* emotions. I'm not a robot."

"So what do you feel, then?" I asked.

The sun was gone, leaving a reddish smear on the western sky. I shifted, leaning my butt against the stern and eyeing him sideways.

He thought about his answer for a moment. "About what?"

I gestured with a hand, a circular, all-inclusive movement. "I don't know—everything. In life, during sex, with your brothers, with your cousins…" I hesitated, meeting his eyes as I laid out the last one. "With me."

"In life? I worry about my dad. I feel doubt about the bar Rem and Ram and I are trying to open, and whether it was a good idea, whether we really have the skills to make it happen right. I feel love for my brothers. We're super tight, super protective of each other. But this bar is making things tough. I think I maybe railroaded them into doing it with me, and I'm not sure they're feeling the project the way I am. Or this town, or the cousins. I don't know. We haven't talked much about it, so I'm not sure where they're at, but I just feel like things are in limbo.

"In terms of my cousins? That's a tough one— there's a lot there. It's weird suddenly having a family. I grew up thinking it was just Rem, Ram, Dad, and me. And with Dad drinking the way he did, I figured it was only a matter of time before he died, leaving the boys and I alone. He had a heart attack earlier in the year, which was what brought us back to Oklahoma from California." He hesitated. "That and what happened in the last fire we fought."

"Can I ask about that? Or do you not want to talk about it?"

He shrugged. "It's heavy."

I gazed up at him, taking his hand in mine. "For me, this date is about getting to know each other, so if you don't mind talking about it, I'd like to know."

Roman hesitated, and then let out a slow, tight

breath. "Okay, since you put it like that." He took a moment to gather his thoughts, and then started the story. "We were sent to jump into a fire in the Klamath area. Super remote, a wicked intense fire that was spreading fast through some challenging terrain. It started out like a fairly routine fire—although, there's never such a thing as a routine wildfire. Each one is different, with its own challenges and dangers. This one should have been over quick, though. We got there early, dropped into a nice position and went on the attack. We were getting ahead of it, establishing a boundary." He shrugged. "You probably don't care about the details, though. Upshot is, she jumped our boundary and started running on us. Got away from us, and we got split up. Rem and I were paired up, working our way along the base of a ridge, trying to connect with Ram, Kevin, and Jameson who were around the other side of the ridge. Peterson and Mackie were north of us, up on the ridge heading down—the idea was for the three teams to converge, heading the worst of the fire off before it spread any further."

He paused, staring at the wake.

"A tree fell. That shit happens all the time, and part of the job is staying alert, watching the forest, watching the fire. But sometimes, shit just happens. A tree snapped suddenly, without any real warning." He paused again. "Um. So the tree knocked Ram aside, and left Jameson on the other side of it, alone. Kevin was beneath it. He, um. He took the worst of it right on his shoulder, and then it landed on him. Basically crushed him immediately. Ram went nuts, trying to lift the fucking thing off Kev. Jameson called us over to help, but by the time we got there, Kev was dead. And we still had the fire to get under control. We chopped the tree into a manageable piece, got it off him, got his body clear of the fire, and had to go back to work."

"Roman, god, I'm so sorry."

He turned away from me, jaw grinding. "Kevin was our best friend. We'd known him since we joined the Forest Service, went through training with him, transferred to the Redding Smokejumper crew with him. He was like our fourth brother. When that tree went down, and I wasn't there, couldn't get there in time to save him? I fucking—it messed with me. I know I couldn't have saved him. He was dead the moment the tree hit him. I know that. But if I'd gotten there sooner, if I'd…yada yada yada, bullshit, whatever. I know better. But my head still keeps spinning these stories about what I should have done differently. Same with Rem and Ram, too—Ram especially. He was there, he watched it happen, watched Kevin die and couldn't do shit to stop it. It really fucked him up, and when one of us is fucked up, we all are. And then Dad had a heart attack, and we just...we needed time away."

"So will you go back to it?" I asked.

He shook his head and shrugged. "I honestly don't know. He wasn't the first jumper to die in the line of duty, and not even the first I'd worked with. But his death just hit me hard, and I'm not sure if I can or if I even want to go back to fighting fires. I miss it, don't get me wrong. I miss the challenge, the rush, the intensity. I loved the work, but I'm just not sure at the moment."

"So you're still dealing with that? The loss of your friend?"

He nodded. "Yeah, I mean, of course. You don't just get over something like that—losing a best friend. Not quickly, maybe not ever. I mean, I'm okay, I'm not stuck in grief or anything. I miss him, I'm sad, I'm grieving his loss, but I also know I have to move on with life. He'd kick my ass if I wallowed around wasting my time mourning him or whatever. But yeah, it's a loss I'll be dealing with for a while." He laughed, scrubbing his jaw. "So there's the story. Anything else you want to know?"

I gazed up at him, resting a hand on his shoulder. "Thank you for sharing that with me, Roman."

He turned to face me. "You have to know I don't

talk about shit like that with most people, right?"

"So I should be honored?"

He nodded, no humor in his eyes. "Yeah, you should. With most women, we don't talk about personal shit."

"You don't do much talking at all, I'm guessing."

"You'd guess right."

I pushed that aside, and focused on him. "Just so you know, this, what we're doing? Talking? Getting to know each other? This is part of emotional connectivity—you being vulnerable with me, letting me see more of you besides the big, macho, dirty-talking sex cowboy."

"Sex cowboy?" he asked, laughing.

I slapped his chest. "Shut up. You know what I mean."

He laughed harder. "No, I really don't." He stood in front of me, towering over me, one hand on the railing beside me, the other clutching his now-empty wineglass. "What's a sex cowboy, Kitty?"

"You, I guess." I let my hand rest on his chest, feeling the hard, heavy muscle. "The way you are about it."

"How am I about it?"

I shrugged, finding it hard to breathe with the intensity and heat of his presence, his body. "Rough, domineering, approaching it like a game. Like something to win."

"You like that, though." He took my empty glass from me and held them both in one hand, leaving my hands free; I rested them on his chest, let them slide around a bit, beginning an exploration of his muscular torso.

"I don't know that I do," I argued.

"It's new to you. It's unfamiliar, so you're unsure. You're out of your element." He let his gaze wander downward for the first time in a while, soaking up the expanse of my cleavage before returning his eyes to mine. "You don't want to like it, but you do."

"How do you know?"

"Because of the way you responded to me." He grinned at me. "You responded to my touch like you'd never felt anything like it before. You wanted more. You couldn't get enough, until you stopped. Your mind, your heart—those weren't exactly along for the ride, but your body was."

"That's part of what's hard for me," I said, pushing the edges of his suit coat aside to explore more of his shoulders and chest with my hands. "Having my heart and head at odds with my body is weird, and I don't like it."

"Can't you just go along with what your body wants?"

"Spoken like a man," I laughed, shaking my

head. "No, Roman, I can't. I'm not wired that way. I'm a woman, which means—for me at least, although I know everyone is different—it means that I need some kind of emotional connection for sex to be meaningful. Sex and emotions are hardwired together, to me. For me to really get into it, my head, heart, and body have to be aligned."

"You seemed plenty into it," he shot back, smirking.

"It was an overwhelming experience," I admitted. "And you make it hard for me to think straight when you turn on your whole charm-and-seduce routine."

"It's not a routine," he protested.

"Yes it is. It's how you get women to sleep with you."

He frowned. "Hmmm. I mean, I see what you're saying, but I don't like calling it a routine, like it's a formulated process."

"It's not?"

He shook his head. "No. It's not like I do the same thing every time—that'd be disingenuous and any woman I was trying it on would see right through it."

"Then how do you do it?"

"It's about observation, noticing responses, reading body language and reactions." He leaned close to me, towering, huge, hard, and I sucked in a breath.

"See? Like this. When I get this close to you, you react. You breathe in and hold your breath. Your nostrils flare. Your eyes widen. To me, that means you like me being close, you're reacting physically just to my proximity. It means if do something like *this*—" He trailed a fingertip down the outside of my arm, around to my front where the plunging neckline left my skin bare, dragging his finger up the center of my body in a fiery, tingling line. "You'll react even more strongly. You're shivering, clenching your jaw, breathing deeply—you *like* the way my touch feels. But you're nervous, because you don't know what I'll do next."

"You're very observant," I said.

"Yes, I am." He shuffled closer yet, so our bodies were almost touching. "See, you can call it my charm-and-seduce routine all you want, but I just call it doing what comes naturally to me—turning you on. Making you *feel*—sensations, rather than emotions."

"What if I want to feel emotions as well as sensations?"

"I wouldn't even know how to go about that. What am I supposed to make you feel?"

"I don't know—something besides raw lust?"

"What's wrong with lust?"

I shook my head. "Nothing in itself. There's just…there has to be more to sex than lust."

"Like what?" he asked.

I sighed, trying to formulate my thoughts into words; in thinking it through, I found myself sliding his suit coat off his shoulders. He took it from me, folded it, and tossed it onto the nearby couch. I wanted still more of him, of feeling his body and his massive physique, so I held his tie in place and tugged the knot free, stuffed it into his hip pocket, and then unbuttoned his shirt, untucking it. I bit my lip at the swell of his muscles against the white undershirt, wanting still more. The cuffs, then—I freed his wrists from the prison of the buttoned cuffs, and pulled the shirt off of him. Python-thick biceps stretched the sleeves of the T-shirt, and his chest strained against the cotton, hanging free around his trim waist. I met his ice-blue eyes as I tugged the hem free from the waist of his suit trousers; he only reached up, one gentle thumb prying my lip out of my teeth. I wanted to see his body—his bare skin, the muscles, the curve and line and hardness of him. He lifted his arms over his head, and I peeled the undershirt off him, tossing it onto the couch with his button-down and suit coat. He was naked from the waist up, now…

And utterly magnificent. Glorious. A living god made flesh—every inch of him was sculpted to perfection, enormous muscles rounded and hard and taut, bulging with power. His abdomen was a rippling field of shredded muscle, his chest a broad swelling colossus of strength, his arms cables of rigid steel wrapped in tanned flesh.

"God, you're gorgeous," I breathed, the words torn from my lips.

His answer was to set the glasses on the table and return to stand in front of me, blue eyes burning. "You didn't answer my question," he murmured. "What else is there to sex besides lust?"

"Besides the obvious?" I asked.

He frowned down at me, seemingly perplexed. "What's the obvious?"

I laughed, shaking my head. "Love!"

He tensed. "Love."

I nodded, biting my lip—intentionally, this time, hoping to elicit a reaction from him. "Yes, Roman, love."

He tried to back away, but I hooked my fingers into his belt loops and held him in place.

Roman blinked down at me, a palpable wall going up behind his eyes—one which I was starting to understand the source of. "If that's what you're hoping to get from me, I'm afraid you'll end up disappointed."

I wasn't bothered by his response. I just smiled at him, tracing a finger over the bulge of pectoral muscles. "I'm not so sure."

"How about besides the obvious, then?" he said,

in an obvious gamble to change the subject.

"A lot of things," I answered, running my palms over the mountain ranges of his shoulders, down to the valley between his pecs, over the ridges and runnels of his abs. "Respect. Affection. Intimacy. Selflessness—meaning, the desire to give of yourself to the other person without needing anything in return. Vulnerability. Trust. Safety. Protection. And yes, protection for you, too, Roman. Men are protectors, and I get that—but men need protection, too."

"From what?" he asked, his voice pitched low, rife with hesitancy and suspicion.

"You men act tough and hard and impenetrable, and with you, I sometimes think you really are that way. But then I get glimpses of the man under all that armor, and I see a man who has mommy issues, and relationship issues, and intimacy issues—a man who's never let anyone in except his brothers. Your emotions are deep down, but they're there, and they're fragile, and tender, and delicate. Assuming you could be truly vulnerable with me, you'd need me to protect those emotions, Roman." I gazed up at him, letting him see my emotions in my eyes—my desire, my nerves, my doubt, my hope. "And I could do that, if you let me."

"Fragile, tender, and delicate, huh?"

"And that's a good thing," I said. "You can't be tough and hard and strong all the time."

"Yes, I can." He tapped his chest with a fist. "That's how I've always lived."

"Which is why you don't understand how to do emotions with sex."

"And you've never had sex without the emotions."

"So we both have something to learn."

"And you think you could teach it to me, do you?" He sounded skeptical, which would have been insulting had I not seen past it.

"I'm willing to try. And I'm willing to learn, too." I stared steadily up at him. "Are you?"

"Is that the bargain you're driving, Kitty?"

I shook my head. "No, not at all. There's no bargain." I decided on brutal honesty. "You want the truth?"

He nodded. "Absolutely."

"I want you. I want *this* with you." I palmed his chest on the emphasized word, knowing he'd understand my meaning. "You make me feel things I've never felt, in ways I've never thought possible. And I want more of it. And yes, Roman, I plan to take this as far as it can go with you—tonight. *Now.*" I held his gaze, caressing his chest and arms as I spoke. "But you have to understand something, Roman—I can't do this without emotions. It's not how I work, as a person. So I'm going to sleep with you, and I'm going to try to learn from you how to let go, how to just feel, just be, like you were saying. But I'm also going to feel things for you, emotionally. I'll probably get invested in you, in the idea of us. I'll end up wanting that—wanting more from you than just sex. I already do, to be totally honest. Which scares the bejesus out of me, because I know darn well you're not that kind of man."

"Kitty—"

"You're an asshole, Roman Badd. The things you say, the things you do, most of them are just selfish and self-centered. I was half-convinced, until today, that you had few, if any, redeeming qualities aside from your looks and sex appeal. And yes, as you've pointed out, and as I've already admitted, I want you, and I don't want to want you. I don't want to feel the things I'm feeling for you. But then you do something like this," I gesture at the boat, the saloon, the wine, "and you surprise me. You do something like this that makes me think there's a really great guy in there, trapped somewhere deep inside, especially in the way you've opened up with me a little this evening. I'm not naive enough to think I can bring that guy out of you by myself. You'd have to want to do that for your-self. But I can't help wanting you, wanting the things you can give me, sexually. So I'm giving in to that and letting myself hope a little, but not too much. I'll probably end up getting hurt, and I'm going into this knowing that full well. But I have good friends who will be there for me when it's all over, and I know I'm strong enough to be willing to at least try, despite what I suspect the results will be."

I continued to hold his gaze.

"Can you say the same?" I asked the question with my eyes on his, my heart on my sleeve, everything laid out for him.

He seemed rocked to the core. "Not how I expected this to go."

"Thought you'd make a romantic gesture, sweep me off my feet, seduce me, and go along your merry way, huh?"

He shook his head. "No, actually. Typically, yes—that's exactly what I'd expect. But I've never made a gesture like this for anyone. I've never cared enough to put the effort in. But I do care, Kitty." He ground his jaw, thinking, formulating. "You saying you weren't sure I had any redeeming qualities kind of hurts, if I'm being honest. I know I'm an asshole, but I did kind of think I had something to offer besides big muscles and being good at sex."

"You haven't offered me anything besides that, Roman," I said. "Until now."

"I wouldn't have set this whole date up if I wasn't trying to offer you more." He held my gaze, but his eyes were conflicted, deeply thoughtful. "If all I wanted was sex, I'd have gotten it. If I wanted to fuck you,

I could have gotten that from you already, and you know it. You'd have given it to me willingly—you'd have resented me afterward, probably, but we'd have fucked."

I frowned up at him. "And then you say something like that and I wonder about you all over again."

"I can read your physical responses like a book, Kitty. I know you want me, physically. You want my hands on you; you want my mouth on you. You want me inside you, all over you, everywhere." He breathed this, inches from my face, his breath hot, his words hotter. "It would have been so easy, too."

His hands brushed over my cheeks, tilting my face up—I was helpless to want anything except the kiss his touch promised. I parted my lips, but instead of kissing them, he ran his thumb over my lower lip; with a subtle tilt, his thumb pressed against my mouth, and I tasted the salt of his skin, felt the rough callus. Instinctively, I closed my lips around his thumb and he drew it out slowly, tasting him on my lips and over my tongue, an erotic glide of flesh on flesh. A tease—a taste of him, of us.

He rumbled a laugh. "See? See how easy it would have been?"

"But?" I questioned, my lips moving against the pad of his thumb, my eyes tilted up to his.

"But I wanted to…to deserve more from you."

He clenched and released his jaw several times before continuing. "I couldn't deny that I wanted something more with you than just to fuck and be done."

I sucked in a breath. "So you do want more?"

He nodded, the movement slow and heavy. "Yes, I do. I just—I don't mind admitting I have not the slightest fucking clue what that looks like, or how to do it."

"Just be honest. Be open. Be vulnerable."

"What does that mean, though?" he asked. "You keep telling me to be vulnerable, but what does that look like?"

I caressed his shoulders, down his chest, ran my hands down to his waist, around his sides, up his back, and then clung to him, my fingers dimpling the powerful muscles of his back, just beneath his shoulder blades. "It means letting me see parts of you that aren't strong and in control and tough. It means not having to be the big, swaggering, balls of brass macho man all the time."

"I'll never be some sissy, touchy-feely sap, Kitty. Just not who I am."

"I'm not asking you to be, Roman." I gritted my teeth and admitted a truth I'd been hiding from until then. "Honestly, I *like* the way you are. You frustrate me, and your bluster and bravado can be infuriating, and your arrogance can be off-putting, but at the same time, it's part of your charm and what makes you so attractive. All I'm saying is, it's okay if there's more than that—if only with me."

"I'll try."

"That's all I'm asking."

His blue eyes searched mine, intent, focused, and open for once. "You're asking me to try?"

I nodded. "I am."

"What is it we're trying?"

"Sex with emotions. Sex where you don't run away afterward. Where there's more than just sex."

"To be clear: you want sex regardless, but you'd rather it be more."

I shook my head. "No, that's not what I'm saying."

"Then I'm confused, 'cause that's what it sounded like."

I rested my chin on his chest and gazed up at him. "What I'm saying is, yes I want sex with you regardless of the emotional component. But I don't just *want* it to be more than just sex—I *need* it to be more. I'm just willing to accept the consequences of sleeping with you even if you can't give me more."

His smirk was the arrogant half-smile that sent frissons of infuriated arousal through me. "Then you must *really* want to fuck me."

"Must you be so crude?" I asked, eyes narrowing

up at him.

"Sorry, princess, let me rephrase—you must really want to ride my cock."

"How is that any better?"

"It's not." He wrapped his hands around the small of my waist. "But you like it when I'm crude. You just won't admit it."

"Arrogant jerk."

"I notice you're not telling me I'm wrong."

"About what?"

He leaned down and captured my lower lip between his teeth, nipped it, released it. "That you want to ride my cock, and that you like it when I'm crude."

I shivered. "I really wish I could tell you you're wrong."

"But you can't." His eyes blazed. "Got anything else you need to say, Kitty?"

"I don't think so, why?"

"Because I'm done talkin'." His Oklahoma accent tended to come and go according to some whim or vagary of his personality, and when he said this to me, his eyes were on fire with lust, and his accent was a thick, syrupy drawl.

"Oh."

His fingers danced around to the small of my back, found the skin where the dress left it bare, and traced their way up, up, to my shoulders. And then back down. His smirk was there on his lips, arrogant, knowing, infuriating, intoxicating. He found the tab of the zipper under my left armpit, and drew it down. My dress sagged apart, hanging from the tape and the straps, clinging to my hips. He ran a fingertip up the expanse of flesh bared by the open zipper, from thigh to underarm.

His eyes flicked to mine. "Why, Kitty Quinn... you're not wearing bra *or* underwear, are you?"

I shook my head, the only response I could formulate.

"Holy shitballs." He sucked in a breath. "How fucking perfect can you be?"

The raw need and appreciation in his eyes was worth every moment of self-consciousness I'd endured throughout the evening.

He shook his head. "You've been sitting there across from me all night, naked under that dress?" Roman's jaw clenched, grinding. "It's been torturous enough without knowing that."

"Torturous?" I breathed.

"Yeah—keeping my eyes on yours instead of that incredible goddamn rack of yours."

"You've done an admirable job of keeping your eyes on mine, I must say. I'm impressed." I said this with a smile, a warm, genuine one. Because I really did appreciate it—it made me feel like he was truly listening and interested, and not just viewing me as a set of curves to be ogled.

He ran a finger down the center of my chest, from my throat to the V of my dress's neckline. "How do you manage to not fly out of it every time you move? That's what I've been wondering."

"Good question," was my only answer, along with a provocative curl of my lips.

He answered my smirk with one of his, and slid his finger back up to where the strap curved over my shoulder. He pushed the strap over and down, and then did the same on the other side, and the dress sagged even more, now held up solely by the tape and the generous swell of my hips. Taking his time, he pulled the fabric away from my body, in doing so peeling the tape away from me—my skin stretched away, snapped back into place as the tape gave way, sticking to the dress instead.

"Tape?" he said, laughing.

"Boob tape," I said, laughing with him. "It's a thing, I guess. I don't dress up much, so I didn't know about it until tonight either."

"Boob tape." He peeled the other side away, gently, carefully. "Who knew?"

"Lots of people, apparently, just not me."

And then neither of us was laughing—he tangled his fingers in the fabric of the dress just below my hips and tugged down, once, firmly. The material slinked over my hips and fell to the deck in a pile of green, leaving me utterly naked. The wind caressed me, as did Roman's eyes.

I wanted to cover up, to cringe, to hide—but I didn't. I stood straight, shoulders back, chin up.

"*Fuck*," Roman breathed. "You are *so* beautiful, Kitty."

My chest constricted. His gaze made me feel beautiful—and not just beautiful, but desired. Wanted.

With a growl, he reached for me, and I knew, from the first rough scrape of his hand over my flesh, that tonight would be a night like no other.

TEN

Roman

WANT, NEED, DESIRE, LUST—WORDS FAILED ME. Kitty Quinn standing naked on the deck of that boat was the single most erotic, arousing, intoxicating vision I'd ever seen in my entire life. My cock went rock hard in an instant, throbbing painfully against the zipper of my pants. I wanted everything, and I wanted it immediately. I wanted to bend her over the railing and lift her up onto it and put her on her hands on knees on the deck and on the couch in the saloon…

I wanted to kiss her stupid.

Kiss her breathless. Kiss her until we were both dizzy.

I wanted to just touch her—just put my hands on that perfect body and revel in the privilege of being allowed to touch her at all.

Where did I start? An impossible decision. Especially because for once in my life I didn't want to rush, didn't want to hurry right to the good stuff. Usually foreplay was just a means to an end, getting my partner primed for maximum pleasure, so I could take mine from her. With Kitty, it would be different; I knew this instinctively. I knew it in my gut, in my blood, in my bones. In my very synapses. I couldn't rush this. Didn't dare. I knew I might never get another chance to glory in such perfection—I didn't deserve Kitty Quinn. I just didn't. I was a brute, a fuckboy, a roughneck redneck with a filthy mouth and a sordid past. She was a quintessential good girl—the kind of goodness that was intrinsic in the fabric of who she was.

Her essential nature was just *good*. Mine was... not.

She was used to love and gentility and respect and care—more often than not I fucked rough and hard and discarded them after with hardly a thought or a care; I knew how to pleasure a woman, so they never left unsatisfied, but it was not my habit or my nature to give two shits about my partners, because their only purpose in my life was to provide me with a few minutes of pleasure, relief, release, absence of control for a handful of moments. Kitty deserved more than that.

I wanted to give it to her. For the first time in my life, I truly, deeply *cared* about the other person.

So, when I tugged that sexy jade-green dress off of her, leaving her utterly bare to the wind and the crimson light of a dying sunset, I was nearly paralyzed by indecision. Nature and instinct told me to take her and fuck her until she was begging me to stop. The truth was that my desires ran deeper than nature, deeper than instinct, something intense and breath-taking, something which drove me to take great care with the priceless treasure standing before me.

I wrapped a hand around her back, her silky flesh warm under my palm. "You're so fuckin' perfect I don't even know where to start," I admitted, my native drawl emerging beyond my ability to suppress it. I'd spent long enough in California that my Oklahoma accent only tended to show up at certain times.

Her liquid mocha eyes gazed up at me, blazing with arousal yet still warm and soft with tenderness. "Tell me more."

I grinned wolfishly. "I've been fantasizing about getting you naked like this for so long that now that I have you like I want you, I don't know what to do first." I slid my hand down over the taut roundness of her ass, cupping it greedily. "Do I just touch you until I've gotten my fill of your curves, or do I kiss you until neither of us can breathe, or do I bend you over this railing and fuck you until you're weak in the knees?"

Her breath left in a squeak. "Um. Yes?"

I laughed, pulling her away from the railing to stand freely in the middle of the deck, her feet braced wide against the gentle roll of the deck, the movement of the boat making her breasts sway side to side, jouncing every once in a beautiful while when the prow went over a wave and smacked back down. I backed up a step so I could just look at her. I needed to take a moment to soak up the vision, to memorize everything about her.

Her hair was loose around her slim shoulders, dangling in loose spirals, and in the sunset it looked more brown than blonde, setting off the fiery chocolate brown of her wide eyes. Her face was heart-shaped, symmetrical, with high cheekbones and delicate features. Lovely, beautiful, breathtaking—pick an adjective and it would apply in spades. I could just stare at her face all day and not get enough, and every angle revealed a new facet of her beauty. Her makeup was done with absolute artistry, minimal and subtle, just enough to highlight the wide dark almond shape of her eyes and her plump kissable lips and flawless complexion. I let my gaze wander downward, next.

Pale, creamy skin, dotted here and there by sprays of freckles—never just one freckle, but five or six in a group. Like the clump of freckles on her chest, just above the slope of her left breast. Or on her belly, just beneath her right breast. Or on her left shoulder, right on the round where shoulder became bicep. Or on her right hipbone, just where it indented toward her center. God, I wanted to kiss each freckle, lap at them with my tongue, nip at them with my teeth.

And I would.

But first, I needed to look at her some more.

She was growing impatient, I knew, but that would only emphasize the anticipation of awaiting me touching her.

Her breasts were absolute perfection—classically teardrop shaped, heavy, round and squishy and real, with wide, dark areolae and thick pink nipples. I only barely resisted the urge to bury my face in them and moan in raw pleasure.

Fuck it.

Why resist?

I licked my lips, staring at those luscious tits, needing to feel them, kiss them, luxuriate in their wondrous glory. Kitty's eyes widened as I closed the space between us with one step, and sank to my knees in front of her. Moving slowly, I lifted my hands to cup her breasts from underneath—I met her eyes briefly, reading her self-consciousness and mounting need. Then, finally, I did what I wanted to do the first time I saw her, and even more so when I bared them at her apartment—I sank my face between the soft, creamy, silky, pillowy globes, rubbing my face and stubble against the flesh. My lips stuttered across the tender inner flesh, and my hands lifted them, framed them where I wanted them. I ran my thumbs over those plump pink nipples, flicking them to life, twiddling them in slow circles until I heard her breath catch. Gazing up at her from between her tits, I smiled, rubbing my face against them once more before backing away and standing up to resume my slow, appreciative approval of her body.

Her grin was confused and bemused. "What was that about?"

I shrugged. "I've wanted to bury my face between your tits from the first moment I met you. So I did."

She frowned. "You've seen them already, though. You—you had your mouth on them."

"Not the same thing," I growled.

"So you're saying you just had an urge to motorboat me?"

A laugh burst out of me. "Motorboat? That was *not* motorboating."

"No?"

I shook my head. "No. That was just me appreciating with my face how soft and ample your tits are." I moved closer to her again, cupped her breasts and lifted them up, buried my face between them and motorboated her properly. She cackled as if it tickled, and I backed away. "*That's* motorboating. And while it's fun, it's not really all that sexy. It's funny more than anything."

"Oh, I see." She frowned at me. "Why do you keep backing away and just staring at me? It's weird."

"Because I just like looking at you. I want to memorize what you look like right now." I smiled at her, a slow, hot grin. "Why? Are you getting antsy for something else?"

She bit her lip, nodding. "Yeah," she breathed.

I tugged her lip out from between her teeth with my thumb and forefinger, pulling it away from her mouth, let it go, and then bent over her and sucked that lower lip into my mouth until she whimpered. "I told you about biting that lip."

"I can't help it," she whispered. "It's a nervous habit."

"It drives me wild." I backed away again, letting my eyes roam southward down her body, to her thighs and the dark V between them. "You drive me wild. Everything about you."

"You don't seem that wild yet," she said, her eyes

sparking, daring.

"I'm trying to take it slow. I don't want to rush this."

"Why?"

"Because I'm going to take my time with you," I told her. "I don't dare rush."

"But why don't you dare?" she pressed.

I hesitated. "How truthful should I be?"

"All the way truthful."

"I don't dare rush this with you because I'm worried I may never get a second chance with you. You wanted vulnerability, well there it is, Kitten. Getting to have this with you, it feels like a once in a lifetime opportunity and I will *not* fuck it up by rushing it."

"Oh." Her eyes met mine, and I knew I'd said the right thing. "Roman, god...I don't know what to say to that."

"The truth, raw and unvarnished."

She stepped up to me, running her hands up my chest, over my shoulders, down my biceps. "The raw, unvarnished truth, then, Roman, is that you'll get a second chance. And a third, and a hundredth. If you can offer me yourself, if you can show me you care, if you can show me that I'm more to you than just a body and a night of sex, that you care about *me*...then you'll have me."

"I can't promise I won't be an arrogant jerk most

of the time."

"And I can't promise I won't want to smack the arrogance out of you most of the time." She blinked up at me, and she bit that lip again, on purpose.

"Keep biting that lip like that and see what happens," I growled.

A hot grin curved her mouth, even as her teeth kept hold of her lip.

"I plan to," she whispered.

"You may get more than you bargained for."

"What do you mean?"

I clutched her against me, palming her ass with both hands, caressing it possessively. "I mean, I've been holding back with you, Kitty. I've been holding back a *lot*."

"Why?"

"Because I don't want to scare you."

Her eyes were wide. "Scare me?"

"I'm not a gentle man, Kitty."

She pushed me backward a few inches, slipping her hands between our bodies, catching hold of the silver buckle of my slim black leather belt. "I don't mind being a little afraid, Roman."

"What are you saying?"

"I'm saying stop holding back. Stop being nice."

"You sure you know what you're asking for?"

"You." She gazed up at me, her eyes honest and

fiery. "Just…you."

That delicate whisper, the quaver of need in her voice, it snapped the last of my restraint. I snarled, springing into action. I caught her wrists, pinioned them in one hand and held them up over her head, lifting her breasts. Her breath hitched with a gasp, setting those beautiful tits to jiggling, and I spent one last moment just appreciating them.

And then I was done appreciating.

Need ruled me.

I glared hungrily down at her, keeping her wrists in my fist. "I hope you're ready for this, Kitty."

"Ready for wha—?" she started, but didn't get any further.

I released her wrists, caught her waist and lifted her up onto the ledge at the very stern of the boat— all that separated her from a tumble into the white wake was my hold on her. She quit breathing entirely, peering over her shoulder, not quite panicking but almost.

"Roman?"

"Better hold on, princess."

Her hands caught at me, frantic, clutching at my shoulders. "What—what are you doing?" Her voice was tiny, a breathy whisper.

I just grinned at her as I sank to my knees, my hands on her thighs. "Can't you guess?"

She scrabbled at my shoulders, and then caught at my head with desperate fingers. "I'll fall!"

"Can you swim?"

"Yes, but—"

"Just hang on, Kitty." I gazed up at her, brushing my thumbs over her center. "Trust me. I'll never let anything happen to you."

Her heels dug into my back as she wrapped her legs around me, clinging to me fiercely, and her fingers dug into my scalp, trying to knot into my short, gel-spiked hair. I kissed the inside of her left thigh, and then her right, nipping the tender velvety flesh closer and closer to her seam, letting my thumbs play over her entrance, one rubbing up and down the damp slit and the other circling her hardened clit. She sucked in a sharp breath, and then let her thighs splay apart as her heels dug into my back all the harder.

"Roman—" she gasped.

I let my thumb prize apart her slit, delving in. "Yes, Kitty?"

"Please—please don't tease me."

"Where's the fun in that?" I drew my thumb out, only to replace it with my middle finger, curling it up and in, seeking that magical spot high inside her tight, hot, wet pussy. "I love teasing you."

"Why?"

"Because you're so sweet and good that hearing

your innocent little mouth say dirty, filthy things to me is a turn-on."

"I'm not all that sweet or good," she murmured. "Especially not right now."

"No?" I pressed my thumb to her clit, gently circling it until she whimpered. "Then what are you?"

She nodded, her hands wrapped around the back of my neck—she pulled me against her. "Please, Roman."

I flicked her clit with my tongue. "Is that what you want?"

She whimpered, nodding again. "Yes. Please, that, please."

"Tell me what you want me to do, Kitty." I teased her clit with my thumb again, enough pressure for her to feel it, not enough to put her near the edge.

She groaned, and her eyes flicked open, raging with erotic fire. "I want you to lick my pussy until I scream your name, Roman. Make me come." She flexed her hips, needy and desperate. "Make me come not just once or twice. Make me come until I can't take any more."

"Ohhhh fuck, Kitten," I snarled.

"What?"

"You talking like that? Gonna make me explode before I even have my fucking pants off."

Before she could respond to that, I buried my

face between her thighs and gave her exactly what she asked for—my mouth on her clit, my middle finger caressing and massaging inside her, and then two fingers, and then three, stretching her. Her clit was sugar on my tongue, sweet and tart and delicious, a hard little nub begging for my attention. I gave it to her, aggressively, starved for the taste of her. I licked it, swiped it side to side, circled, flicked it up and down, suckled it into my mouth and sucked until she screamed, and then licked it again with the flat of my tongue, faster and faster until her hips were writhing and she was clinging desperately to my neck with both hands, balanced on the ledge of the stern, nothing but white wake and gray-green ocean beneath her, the risk making it all the more thrilling. Wind tossed her hair behind her, caught her whimpers as they ratcheted up to screams. I wrapped my one free arm around her back, clutching her close, making sure I had a firm hold on her, so she'd know without a doubt that I had her safe and secure.

No teasing, no drawing it out—this was about raw, primal hunger. I made her come in record time, drawing the screams from her with my greedy mouth and eager fingers, and when she came apart, she screamed my name to the wind, wrapping around me with arms and legs until I had no choice but bring her off the ledge. I wasn't done, though. Not by a long shot. She'd asked me to make her come until she couldn't take any more, and I planned to deliver exactly that. So I lifted her off the ledge, cradled her in my arms and carried her across the rear deck to the couch, and set her down. She was still quaking and gasping from her first orgasm, and I knew her clit needed a moment to recover. The rest of her didn't need that break, though; I nipped at her breasts, kissing the heavy underside of one and around the inside and up to her nipple, which I sucked between my teeth and flicked with my tongue. Sensitive, she gasped, jerking against me, and I kept going, transferring my mouth to her other breast, teasing closer to the nipple until she was trembling in anticipation. I suckled on the thick, rigid protrusion of her nipple until she arched her back, pressing her breast harder against my mouth, and then I let my fingers dance up her thighs. She had them pressed together, and at my touch, she flung them wide open, scooting her butt to the edge of the cushion, her hand on my face, cupping my cheeks as I worshipped her breasts, one and then the other. I stroked her slit upward, letting my finger drag across her clit, testing her reaction—she groaned raggedly, and I knew she was almost ready for number two.

Instead of going for it, though, I decided I wanted to explore her channel more—stimulate her from the inside. I started with one finger, but I didn't go for the G-spot. Instead, I slid it in as deep as it would go, feeling her pussy clamp around it from the last of the aftershocks, or the precursors of the next one, I wasn't sure which. I explored her with one finger, swiping along the sides, feeling the smooth, wet, slick walls under my touch. And then I added a finger, and then after a few moments, a third, the digits cramped into a delta. Curling them, I drew them out, slid them in. She moaned, hips flexing. In and then out, faster, now. More. Her groan was guttural, raw, dragged out of her chest as I ground my fingers in and out of her faster and faster, making sure to start hitting that spot. Groan after groan tore from Kitty's lips, each more ragged than the last—until I used the fingers of my other hand to massage her clit in synch with the movement of my other hand. Her knees drew up, heels pressing against my shoulders, seeking a better angle, opening more for me. Slowly and then with increasing desperation, she sank into the orgasm, hips starting to buck, her whole body writhing, head thrown back, beautiful tits shaking as she quaked and thrashed under me. Faster, faster, until she was screaming my name in a chant—

She came with one last wordless scream, spine arched, whole body racked and trembling.

My intent was to keep going, take her right

through to number three, but she had other plans.

As soon as the tremors of her orgasm released her, she kicked me away, and not gently, either.

"Had enough already?" I said, with a laughing growl.

She went to her feet, standing over me, staring down at me—I was on my knees, sitting on my shins, gazing up at her. She shook her head, biting her lip.

"No, Roman, I haven't. I haven't had anywhere near enough."

"Then why'd you stop me?"

She reached down and took my hands, lifting me to my feet. "Because I want more than to just let you make me come."

"Like what?"

Kitty lifted my hands, slid my middle finger into her mouth, and slowly dragged it out, her tongue curling around it, tasting herself on my finger. She repeated this with each finger that had been inside her, each erotic slide of my finger between her lips making my cock throb harder, making my heart slam more furiously in my chest.

"Like...everything," she said, and reached for my belt, lust blazing in her eyes.

ELEVEN

Kitty

I WAS STILL SHAKING FROM THE ORGASMS HE'D GIVEN ME— the second of which was utterly unlike anything I'd ever felt. The way he'd touched me, massaging me deep inside, only going for my clitoris when I was already crazed with need? The orgasm had originated deep inside, making my core clench harder than ever before, making my entire body seize with paralytic, scream-inducing ecstasy.

And now, after two intense orgasms and hours of buildup, I wanted more than just my own pleasure.

I needed Roman.

I'd come here with the intention of giving him a chance, of exploring what could be between us. Sex, at the very least. More, possibly.

But in this moment, the only thought on my mind was to touch him, to taste him, to give in to my own desire for him.

Time to give him a taste of his own medicine. Make him wait—and me too, in the process. I just stood there, letting my gaze rake over his body; he was shirtless, his broad chest and mountainous shoulders and thick arms bare, rippling abs tensing as he breathed. Black suit pants, black leather belt, black dress shoes. The pants were tight around his thighs, hugging his trim waist, and the zipper was bulging, straining to contain him. I wanted badly to just free him, take him in my hands, caress him and show him how much I needed him. Instead, I glanced down at his feet.

"Why are you still wearing shoes?" I asked.

He smirked. "Been a little busy."

I thought about trying to play tough girl, ordering him to take them off...but that wouldn't be me. It would come across as funny rather than hot, probably. So, instead, I dropped to my knees and cupped his calf, pulling his foot toward me. He balanced effortlessly on one foot, and I propped his shoe on my thigh. I untied the laces, loosened them and tugged the shoe off, setting it aside. I trailed my fingers up under the cuff of his trousers, tickling his hairy, muscular calf. Hooked a finger inside his black dress sock and tugged it down, and then off. Slowly, I repeated the process on his other foot.

He glanced down at me in bemusement. "I had no idea having my shoes and socks taken off could be so hot."

"So I taught you something new?" I asked, standing up.

"You're teaching me a lot of new things, Kitty."

I trailed my fingers up his thighs, feeling the hard knots of muscle bunch under my touch. "Like what?"

"Like the fact that I've never known true need until I met you."

"Same," I replied, biting my lip as I palmed his thighs, and then ran my hands upward, caressing the bunched muscle of his powerful quads.

"You don't understand, though," he muttered.

"What don't I understand?"

"How bad I need you to quit fucking around and touch me."

I just smirked at him, bringing my hands closer together, nearer to the center of his pants, closer to the zipper and the massive presence behind it. "What's that phrase? Oh, yeah: turnabout is fair play."

"Fuck," he snarled. "I'm tryin' to let you have your moment, Kitty, but you're makin' it hard."

I frowned at him. "Let me have my moment?"

He gestured at my hands as I traced the outline of his package with my index fingers. "This. You playin' this out."

"Is it really so hard for you to let me have my moment?"

He curled his hands into fists and tucked them behind his head, causing his biceps to swell to eye-popping proportions—which only made my desire blaze hotter. "Yes, Kitty, it is exactly that hard."

"How hard?" I asked, turning the question into an innuendo with little more than a smirk and a teasing look.

"You're about to find out, princess." His murmur was a promise, a threat.

"I am?" I asked, innocent. "When?"

"Keep playin', Kitty," he growled. "You'll find out."

I ran a finger along his length, my fingertip stuttering over the cold teeth of the zipper. "You wanted to make sure you didn't rush it, you said. You made me stand there, naked, self-conscious, while you just stared at me. You wanted to appreciate the moment, you said."

"Yeah, and?"

"And now it's my turn." I slid the end of the belt out of the loop, tugged the prong free, and let the belt hang open. "Surely you can manage to just stand there a few minutes and let me appreciate you."

"I want you to appreciate me with your mouth, is what I fuckin' want." He said this through gritted teeth, hands knotted together behind his head, massive arms swollen as he tensed them to keep from grabbing me and doing who knows what to me.

"That's so crude, Roman," I protested.

Was I protesting out of habit? Did I really mind his crudeness all that much? Not really. It was hot, in the moment. And I knew that's what he wanted—he'd said so before, how he wanted my mouth on him.

The question was whether I was prepared to give him that. It wasn't something I did very much with my ex, and when I did, it always resulted in things going faster than I'd intended, leaving us with an awkward space before he was ready again, which typically meant the heat of the moment was lost, as was my desire.

With Roman, however, I had a feeling it would be different, as everything was.

"Crude, but true." He let out a snarling breath. "You're fuckin' killing me, Kitty. You're taking for goddamned ever."

I ran my hands around his hips, cupping the hard round cannonballs of his buttocks. "Toughen up, Roman. You've tortured me enough—surely you can take your own medicine for a few minutes."

He laughed, gruff, rough, mocking. "Don't be so sure, Kitty. You did tell me not to hold back, and now you're preaching a different sermon."

"That was then, this is now."

"So you just want me to stand here and do nothing?"

"No, I want you to stand there and let me enjoy the process of getting you naked and touching you for the first time. Don't be impatient."

"Have you met me?" he asked, half laughing, half growling. "Patience ain't my strong suit."

I laughed, bringing my hands back around front. "I know—believe me, I know." I traced his outline again. "Just look at this as...an opportunity to strengthen that muscle a little bit."

He let out a long slow breath. "Tryin', but I'll warn you, babe—you've got maybe sixty seconds before my control is gone. So make use of the time you've got left."

My eyes widened as I realized he wasn't kidding. His eyes were raking over my body eagerly, hungrily. He still had his hands fisted behind his head, biceps flexing, and his breathing was ragged.

"It's really that hard for you to just stand still and let me take my time exploring you?" I asked.

"You've got no fucking clue, Kitty. Takin' everything I've got."

"Oh." I bit my lip, knowing it drove him crazy.

Sultry eyes, gazing at him from beneath my eyelashes, breathing slowly, not touching him now at all. Just standing, meeting his stare, letting my eyes make promises of what I'd let him do, once his restraint was gone.

"Don't fuckin' look at me like that, goddammit," he rumbled. "Those eyes of yours are fucking…"

"What?"

"Killing me, that's what," he muttered, closing his eyes briefly with a ragged sigh.

Lip caught in my teeth, just to make him crazy, I kept looking at him like that, my sultry, aroused need not at all faked or played up. I was lost to this, lost in my need. I'd probably cringe in mortification later, thinking of all this, but right now, I didn't care. I just wanted him. Having felt the thick burden behind his zipper, I had a pretty good idea what I'd be unleashing, and I knew it'd be breathtaking.

No way I was ready, but I wanted it.

Lust blazed in me, pulsed through my veins. This man—this arrogant, infuriating, surprisingly sweet, crude, beast of a man…I've never wanted anyone or anything with the wild intensity of my need for Roman Badd in that moment.

My own ability to wait, to tease him, to draw this out was used up.

I ripped the belt out of his pants, tossed it aside. Popped the button and dragged down the zipper—he swelled into the opening, tight black briefs straining to contain his manhood. His pants dropped to his ankles, and he toed them aside, standing now in just his underwear. My eyes wandered his physique, from the planes of his shoulders to the hard swell of his chest, his furrowed abdomen, trim wedge of a waist, thick thighs…and that absolutely enormous bulge behind the stretchy cotton of his briefs.

I needed contact with him before I bared him. I needed reassurance, a hit of the drug of his touch, his kiss.

I pressed up against him, letting my breasts flatten between us, his manhood a thick ridge against my bare core, separated only by a thin layer of fabric. My hands clutched at his back and shoulders, roaming, caressing, my eyes seeking his, my expression open—he knew exactly what I needed, somehow. He brought his hands to my face, cupping my cheeks.

He kissed me, for the first time that night. His mouth was firm and warm, his lips damp and strong, sliding against mine in a slow, arousing dance. His tongue angled between my teeth, seeking my tongue; his breath was mine, and mine was his. My chest ached, swelling, tightening as Roman kissed me, and my fingers dug into the backs of his shoulders, clawing at him. My lungs screamed, but I kissed him anyway, taking his breath instead of oxygen. Sucking his tongue into my mouth, I snared the back of his head with my hands, then broke to catch my breath.

His lips brushed mine, his breath hot on my mouth.

"Kitty…" His growl was as ragged as I felt.

I let go of his neck, kept my forehead against his, watching my hands as they delved between our bodies, hooked into the waist of his underwear and tugged them down past his hips in a quick and unceremonious jerking movement. He stepped, kicked them away, and was naked with me. Eyes open wide and staring, lip caught between my teeth, I could do nothing but gasp, stunned breathless as expected at the scope of his magnificent manhood.

Curved inward ever so slightly, circumcised, the broad fat pink head leaking a droplet of clear liquid, the girth was all taut dusky flesh and straining veins. I'd need both hands to encompass all of his length, and I doubted my fingers would meet around his thickness. Heavy balls hanging tight against him, the shaft bobbing with his breath, the tip touching his navel.

My forehead resting on his, I wrapped one hand around the thick head and slid my grip downward— and no, I couldn't bring my fingers together.

"That tiny little hand—Kitty, *fuck...*" His growl was tense, taut, snapping with need.

I stroked him with the one hand, taking an eternity to pass my hand from head to base. Then my other hand, just the one, sliding my fingers around him from root to tip. He groaned, his hands descending to a vise grip into my hips. His eyes were closed, jaw tensed, flexing. And then, when I wrapped both hands around him, his eyes flew open to watch as I caressed his length.

"Goddammit, Kitty," he barked.

"What?" I asked, genuinely perplexed. "I'm not trying to tease you."

"No, I'm just—" he cut off with another long, guttural groan as I twisted my hands around the head. "Fuck. That's it—I can't handle this another fucking second."

He yanked away from me, eyes raging with lust and furious need. Roughly, quickly, he pinioned my jaw in one hand, jerked me to his mouth for a hot kiss that lasted too short of a time, and then he had my shoulders in his hands, his grip powerful and rough, making me feel delicate and weak. His grip pressured me downward, his eyes on mine. I knew what he wanted, and I wasn't sure I was ready. Was I ready? He was too much. God, so much, so huge, so thick. When was the last time I'd done it, taken a man in my mouth? I couldn't remember. A night of half-drunk, sloppy horniness with Tom, a year ago? Two? Who knows, who cares?

I hesitated another moment, my eyes on his. He let go, thumbs brushing over my cheekbones, and then I sank to my knees, my hands roaming his hard abs, sliding around to his butt, clawing into the muscle, clutching him, and then palming up his huge chest and back down.

I stared up at him, wide-eyed, nervous—his touch was all power, all control, demanding. His eyes were snapping with fire, blue flames burning with need that would brook no refusal.

"I need your fuckin' mouth, Kitten," he rasped, his voice taut. He fisted his cock, angled it toward me. "Let me watch you wrap that sweet, innocent little mouth around my cock."

Oh god—I was going to.

I had to.

I *wanted* to. His command sliced through me, set fire to my needs, erased my inhibitions. I felt free, in a way I'd never felt before—it was just him, all that he was.

I was hesitating, and he didn't like it.

"Take my cock, Kitty."

"Roman—"

"*Now.*" He traced my lips with the tip. "I'm done

playin', done messing around. I need you, and I need you right the fuck now."

I stared up at him, my hands lifting to wrap around the outside of his. He let go, let me take him in my hands, his fingers sliding into my hair, tangling, knotting.

I licked my lips, tasting him, blinking up at him.

"Open for me, baby." A command, but a soft one.

I parted my lips, keeping my eyes on his. I felt him at my mouth, felt the veiny flesh sliding along my lips. I gasped at the intrusion of him into my mouth, the gasp suddenly muffled as he filled my mouth. I whimpered, a sound of amazement, or protest, I wasn't sure which. Both. My eyes flew wide, his flesh was all I could taste, my lips stretched around him, jaw cracking to take all of him. I had both hands around him, one at the very base and the other just above, and all I could take of him was a few inches—just the very head and a little bit past the rim.

I don't know what I expected, honestly. For him to start driving, hard and fast. Or for him to expect me to know what to do, what he wanted. All I knew to do was flick my tongue against him, tasting him, circling, lapping at the tangy, smoky salt of the essence leaking from him, hands pulsing on his shaft. He groaned, eyes watching as he filled my mouth, stretching me open.

"So fucking hot, seeing your mouth wrapped around me," he groaned. "So—*fucking*—hot."

And then he pulled away from me, oxygen flowing into my mouth, tension released from my jaw, lips tingling, his flavor burning on my tongue. What now? Would he push back in? Would his essence fill my mouth? Would he come?

I should have known better.

He wrapped his hands around my butt and lifted me, settling me on his waist, his shaft nudging against my core. He walked with me into the saloon, set me on the couch, bent over me, leaning against me. He covered me with his bulk, his broad body blocking out the light, the stars, the saloon, everything. He braced one hand on the couch cushion beside my head, and the other cupped my cheek, tilting my face to his.

Yes, yes, please yes—kiss me.

God, kiss me.

I was already breathless, and now I had to suck in a breath at the slash of his lips against mine, the first of a questing series of kisses, some just lips, some with a swipe of his tongue. Each kiss left me needing the next one more and more, until I was wild with desperation for him to kiss me, kiss me, kiss me. He gave me his mouth, and his hand slid down to caress my breast, kneading it as he dove his tongue into my mouth, demanding that we take the kiss deeper. And deeper it went, no longer did we break for breath or to realign our mouths, we only kissed, lips locked, tongues tangling. My spine arched to press my breasts into his hand, and I felt his shaft angling against my thigh, heavy and hot and hard and thick, and I reached between us to grasp it, needing to feel him in my hand again, loving the stroke of my palm and fingers around his throbbing manhood.

Finally, the kiss broke as we gasped for breath, his heart hammering against my ribs.

"You're so huge," I whispered, stroking him. "*This*—" I squeezed. "I love this."

He laughed. "It loves you. The way you touch me is—god, it's more than perfect. Keep touching me." His teeth seized my lip, tugged playfully. "Tell me you love my cock, Kitty."

"I can't say that."

"Why not?"

"I just don't use language like that. I don't like being crude."

He pinched my nipple until I squeaked. "Say it." We both watched my hand caressing his massive erection; when I hesitated again, he pinched my nipple even harder, enough to make it hurt in a way that sent a pang of something hot slicing to my core.

"*Say* it, Kitty."

"Need me to stroke your ego as well as *this*?" I asked.

"No, I just want to hear your pretty, sweet little mouth say dirty things to me." He threaded his fingers between our bodies, past my hand as it moved on him, to my core, circling my clitoris until I was gasping, and then he stopped. "Say it, Kitty."

"I love your cock, Roman," I whispered. Saying it sent a surge of thrill through me, a frisson of excitement. Simple, possibly stupid, but it coursed through me, and I shivered. Stared into his eyes, stroking him faster. "Roman, I *love* your big, hard cock."

He narrowed his eyes, jaw grinding. "What else, Kitty?"

I twisted my head; glancing up to see my purse where I'd left it at the beginning of the evening. I reached up with my free hand and dragged it over to me. He watched me, curious, as I used one hand to keep caressing his cock, and with the other worked open the button flap of my clutch purse. I found the strip of condoms Juneau had put in there, tossed the purse aside onto the floor. Set one crinkly square in my teeth, tore it free, and tossed the rest onto the nearby glass coffee table.

I ripped the wrapper open with teeth and fingers, withdrew the latex ring, and spit the wrapper out; Roman plucked it off my chest and set it on the coffee table.

"You came prepared," he remarked, looking a little shocked.

I kept caressing him. "Roman, I want you." I writhed my hips against him, daring rifling through me, making me say things I've never said, would never have even dreamed of saying. "I want your cock inside me. Right *now*."

"*Fuck*, Kitty," he moaned, the two words drawn out into a tortured sound.

I smirked up at him. "Yes, please."

He laughed, but sobered quickly. "Put it on me, then."

He watched, and so did I, as I fit the ring to his tip and rolled it down his length, hand over hand, each brush of my hands down his cock making him shudder and twitch.

He lined himself up against my slit, gazing down at me. "Are you ready, Kitty?"

I grasped him by the base, whimpering as I slid him between the taut lips of my core. "No," I whispered.

"Too bad."

He groaned between gritted teeth as he pushed in, slowly—agonizingly slowly.

Tears started in my eyes at the burning, tingling

ache of him stretching me. "Oh—oh god, *Roman*—"

He bent, suckling my nipple until I whimpered. "Can you take it, Kitty?"

I had barely more than the tip of him inside me, and it was almost too much. I shook my head. "I—I need a second."

"How about this?" He reached between us, his finger finding my sensitive center. "Does that help?"

I whimpered at his touch, arousal sizzling through me in renewed intensity. He held absolutely still, except for his finger swiping at me, circling. I felt myself responding, needing more, needing him.

"Suck on my tits, Roman," I breathed.

"I love it when you tell me what you want." He bent to obey me, his lips moving against my breasts. "Keep talking dirty to me, Kitty."

I caught my breath with a sharp gasp as he sawed his teeth against my nipple, and then flicked it with his tongue, soothing where he'd bitten. With his one hand, he palmed and caressed my other breast, and now the stimulation of his hands and his mouth on both nipples and his finger against my clit, I began to ache, a heavy throb starting low in my belly.

I felt myself growing slick around him, and somehow he didn't feel so painfully too big. I flexed my hips to take more of him, but he retained control, pulling away from me.

"I'll give it to you when you're ready," he murmured. "You just focus on feeling good."

I gave my hands free rein, letting them move over his strong back and down to his flexed buttocks, clutching at his powerful arms. One hand between us, I cupped his balls, feeling their heft and soft weight in my palm, a gasp squeaking out of me as he touched my clit in a way that left my lungs spasming and a climax seconds from slamming through me. The closer I got to orgasm, the more I needed him, the more I needed more of him—all of him.

It didn't hurt anymore—the stretch felt amazing, the ache of his huge cock inside me felt perfect.

And then, with a hard suckle around one nipple and a sudden pinch of the other, I felt my climax breaking through me, a swelling, crackling of pressure and heat that stole my breath and pushed me to gasping, shrieking, clawing at his ass.

In the moment of my climax, he pushed into me, and with the climax still shearing through me, the massive weight of his body against me and the spearing stretch of his cock sliding all the way into me, I was sent tumbling into another orgasm, this one harder than the last. His cock stroked into me, withdrew slowly, and that withdrawal dragged his thick shaft stuttering against me—the next stroke in made me scream. The head of him scraped inside me, the slight curve angling him so he drilled against that spot inside me that left me gibbering and frantic with agonizing ecstasy too intense to even comprehend.

All semblance of restraint left me, then.

I writhed against him, gasping, whimpering. Clawed at his butt, clutching him harder against me. Thrusting, questing, needing him to move, to *move*. More of him, all of him, harder, faster—*more*.

"Roman—" I gasped.

He slid slowly into my stretched and trembling channel, unhurried and lazy. "What do you need, Kitty?"

I clawed at his buttocks, writhing my hips. "*More*."

He rumbled a laugh, resisting my efforts to make him go faster. "What, this isn't enough for you?"

"No," I groaned, the admission torn from me. "I don't know what I want, I just want more."

He wrapped his arms around me and rolled, bringing me on top. I groaned breathlessly at the depth of his penetration, like this; I tucked my shins under my thighs and pushed up, bracing my hands on his chest. He gripped my hips and pulled me down as he thrust into me—if I'd been under the impression being on top would give me control, I was wrong.

Did I even want control?

I didn't, I realized.

I wanted…

His control.

His arrogant way of just taking me, giving me what I wanted even when I didn't know what I wanted.

I rested my head on his chest and pulled forward, drawing him out of me, and then slowly sank back down, impaling myself on him. He let me do this for several long minutes, and each time I adjusted the angle of my hips to find where it felt best, where he hit me just right with each thrust in.

"How's that, Kitten?" he asked, crooning in my ear. "Is that enough for you?"

"No," I cried, a helpless whimper. "No. I need more of you."

Without warning, he gripped my butt cheeks in each of his huge hands, pulled them apart as he lifted me up, clutching me in a tight, unforgiving grip, my body a prisoner to his desires. He slammed me down onto him, my ass slapping against his thighs, his cock driving into me with an abrupt, racking force. I screamed in surprise, and then my lungs seized and my next scream caught in my throat as he did it again, using his grip on my buttocks to jerk me down while meeting me with a driving upward thrust.

Lightning crackled inside me, searing through my core with each thrust. Harder, then, until my boobs ached from the way they bounced forcefully up and down with his thrusts—I sank into his grip, into his control, cupping my breasts to keep them from slapping painfully as he moved into me harder and harder, trusting him to hold me in place, to guide me.

"Fuck, you're beautiful," he growled. "So fucking perfect, Kitty. Fucking incredible."

I snapped my eyes open to meet his, and my heart cracked and swelled in my chest at the raw, open vulnerability in his gaze, in the unashamed emotion in his eyes—he was overwhelmed, awed, worshipful of *me*, unable to contain the way our union made him feel.

I held his gaze as I rode him to my third climax—or was it my fourth? Fifth? I'd lost count. He drove it out of me, guided me to it, each thrust driving me closer and closer, his cock hitting me where it made me lose all control, dragging against my throbbing clit on the way out and the way in. I writhed, thrashed on him, riding him with my hands on my breasts, our eyes locked, until I came with a ragged cry.

"Is that enough for you, Kitty?" he asked.

I shook my head, letting go of my breasts as I fell forward to brace on his chest, still writhing, drawing him out and sinking onto him. "I don't want it to ever stop," I breathed. "Don't stop. Give me more, Roman. Give me everything—*everything*."

He sat up, taking me with him. Lifted me away, set me on the couch. "I need you in a bed for what I want next."

I stared down at his massive, latex-sheathed cock, the rubber slippery and dripping with my desire. "You still haven't come?"

"You'll know when I do, Kitten, trust me on that," he murmured. "Now, the bedroom." He stood up, gesturing at a doorway I'd not even really noticed.

I bit my lip at the primal intensity of the man as he stood over me, naked, his condom-wrapped cock swaying in front of me, the room smelling of our sex, my core and thighs trembling with the aftershocks of repeated orgasms. I slid my legs out from under me and got to my feet, swaying, my legs wanting to give out.

He grinned as he caught me, scooped me up in his arms. "I'll carry you."

"Good, because I don't think I can walk."

He covered my mouth with his in a slantwise kiss. "And I'm not done with you yet."

"Oh god," I whimpered. I gazed up at him. "Please don't ever be done with me. I need so much more of you."

"You kill me when you say shit like that," he growled. "Makes my chest ache and my head spin."

"That's called emotion," I told him, palming his stubbly cheek.

He kicked open the door, twisted to slide through

it with me in his arms, kicked it close behind us. The room was small, big enough to hold the mammoth California King bed and nothing else, which was covered in a smooth white duvet, with plumped-up pillows and a sprinkle of rose petals across the foot end of the bed.

He stood at the foot, still holding me in his tireless arms. His eyes burned into mine. "You make me want things I didn't know I could ever want," he said, his voice pitched so low I could barely hear him.

"Like what?"

"To make you mine."

I rubbed my thumb over his cheekbone, and then his lips. "That's exactly what you're doing, Roman."

He set me on the bed on my back, his eyes blazing; he knelt over me, cock ramrod stiff against his belly. "I need you, Kitty. Need to feel you again. I need—"

For once, he seemed at a loss for words. "What, Roman? What do you need?" My turn to draw the admission out of him.

"Just...*you*. Until we're both so far gone neither of us can move."

I slid my thighs apart, cupping my breasts to present them to him—another quaking aftershock rippled through me, serving only to make me want another one, want more of what he could give me in the way only he could give it.

Instead of taking my offering, he gripped me by the hips and pulled me toward him, until my butt slid up the slope of his pressed-together knees.

I expected him, then, to slide into me, to take me like that. I trembled with the anticipation of it, core clenching with the need to feel him inside me again.

Instead, he reached down, cupped me by the back of the neck, and lifted me up so I was sitting on his thighs. "Know what I want right now, Kitty?"

TWELVE

Roman

S HE GAZED UP AT ME WITH THOSE WIDE BROWN EYES FULL of heat and wonder and need. "What, Roman?"

I should gentle it, go slow, make it last, make it...romantic, or something. But I couldn't. I'd been holding back for so long it hurt; so long my balls ached with the need to release. I just couldn't hang on any longer. I needed her, and I was going to take her—it wouldn't be soft, and it wouldn't be gentle. It wouldn't be for her.

Her eyes widened further at what I assumed was a feral glare of my raw, threatening lust. "Roman?"

I tried to be gentle, I really did. But my restraint was shot—just *gone*. She'd eradicated every last shred of self-control I had, and now all I could do was just *take* her.

I tossed her onto her belly on the bed, and she crawled away from me toward the headboard and the pillows; crawling away, but not to escape. Her eyes were fiery, demanding, eager.

"You like that?" I growled. "You like being tossed around?"

She whimpered, not quite an affirmative but as much of one as she was capable of, it seemed. I grabbed her ankle and dragged her back to me, making her whine in her throat and stare at me over her shoulder. I snagged her by the hips and yanked her beautiful round ass in the air, caressing it as it was presented to me. I groaned at the beauty of it, the glorious perfection of her curves—the spread of her hips and flare of her ass, the tight slit of her pussy peeking out between her thighs, her narrow waist and heavy breasts hanging and swaying as she knelt in front of me.

"So fuckin' perfect," I murmured, giving her ass a not entirely gentle smack.

She squeaked at the little slap. "Roman!"

"Think I could have that ass of yours all spread out for me like this and not spank it? Think again, princess." I smacked the other cheek as I nestled my hips against her. "And that's just the beginning of what I'm gonna do to you now."

She moaned. "Oh…oh god, oh god."

I spanked her again. "Can you tell me you don't like that, Kitty?"

She shook her head, writhing away from me even as her eyes darted to find mine over her shoulder telling me to do it again.

"Can you?" I demanded, needing her voice.

"No!" she cried. "No…I like it, okay? You want to hear me say it?"

"Yeah, I do."

"I like it, Roman. I like everything you do. I like it when you're rough. I like it when you toss me around."

I palmed both cheeks, caressing them, kneeling behind her and nestling my cock between them. "You like it when I'm rough?"

"Yes—yes, god…yes, Roman, I do. Okay? I like it when you're rough. So you wanna be rough? Go ahead!" She writhed, reaching a hand between her thighs. "Give me all you've got, Roman. Give me you, all of you, any way you want to give it to me."

"Kitty—fuck." I gripped my cock and angled it to nudge against her slit. "This is what I need."

She moaned, a drawn-out whimper of need. "Me too—that's exactly what I need."

"Touch yourself, Kitty. Make it feel as good for

you as it will for me."

"I am."

I flexed my hips, teasing her seam, feeling with my fingers to find her opening. "It won't be gentle, and I won't last long."

"I can take everything you can give me, Roman. I can handle it." She reached between her thighs and grasped me, guided me to her entrance and sank against me without warning, taking me inside her. "Go, Roman. Show me."

"Ohhh fuck, Kitty. God, you're perfect."

"I'm not perfect."

"You are to me." I pushed against her, the generous mounds of her ass taking my thrust. "You're perfect. To me, and for me."

"I'm perfect for you?" She gasped.

I slicked out of her, paused, and then thrust in, harder, rocking her forward. "Yes, Kitty. You are."

She let me rock her forward, and then on my next thrust she sank back against me, taking my thrust with a slapping of my hips against her ass. *Ohhhh* god—oh *god* oh *god* oh *god*, Roman—"

Each emphasized word was ripped out of her as I thrust in. She clawed one hand into the duvet, letting her upper body sink against the bed while keeping her ass high in the air, her other hand thrust between her thighs, fingers moving against her clit. I cupped her ass as I thrust into her, palming it, caressing it, still trying to hold back just a little longer.

I couldn't. When I felt her pussy start to clamp around me with the precursor of her climax, I growled as I gave in to the need to just fuck her to my own orgasm. But it wasn't fucking—I knew that. It was the act of fucking—hard and rough and primal—but it was fraught with a complex tangle of intensity and emotion I knew the name of but didn't dare speak out loud, or even admit in my own head. It was so much more.

I let myself go, then. "Kitty, Kitty, Jesus—you feel so incredible…god, I can't stop myself."

"Don't stop! Just like that, Roman, please, god, please don't stop."

"Never, I'll never stop, Kitty."

She was grinding into my thrusts, her fingers flying against her clit—her ass slapped against my hips, her core taking my cock in slick, loud slurps, our voices raised in unison, in wordless cries of abandon. I spanked her again as I thrust, and she screamed, ground against me harder, so I spanked her harder, one side and then the other until her ass was pink all over and she was screaming nonstop and I was fucking with everything I was, my voice roaring, my body clenching, clamping, spasming. Heat blasted through me and pressure subsumed me, dizziness washed over me and I lost myself in a white wave as I emptied myself into her.

"Roman!" Her sweet musical voice crying my name was what brought me back.

I was still moving, still thrusting against her lovely round ass, now pink from being spanked. I smoothed my hands over it, bent, kissed it here and there and everywhere, soothing the pink as I finally stopped moving. And still I kissed the curves of her ass, and then to her hips, which sank down against the bed as she collapsed onto her belly. I knelt above her, overcome by emotion I couldn't fight anymore—it had me in its raw, possessive intense grip.

This woman was *mine*.

I kissed her from her ass to the small of her back, up the center of her spine, over her shoulders. I rolled her, gently this time, to her back. Kissed her clavicle. Her forehead. Her breastbone. Her belly. Each hip, where my fingers had left bruises on the pale skin.

I saw those bruises and winced. "Shit." I kissed them again, as if I could erase them. "I didn't mean to grip you that hard. I'm sorry, Kitty."

Kitty lifted, curling to look, and then met my eyes with a tender smile that shot straight to my heart. "Don't be. I bruise easily, for one thing, and I *really* like how I got them, for another." She curled her hand around the back of my neck, drawing me back down to her body. "Keep kissing me. That'll make it all better."

So, I kept kissing. Not erotically, this time, but... something else. A drive to show her how I felt in a way I could never encapsulate with words. I knew what it was, and I couldn't say it. Not even to myself. But I could try to show her—I was desperate to show her, so she would understand it, so she wouldn't let me go. So we could do this, what we just did—what we were still doing—again and again, and again, until we'd erased every memory of everyone else, every other experience. Until this, with us, was all there was.

Kissing her beautiful body over every inch of creamy flesh was all I could think of to show her all of this.

She was ticklish on her sides, giggling as I kissed there.

And on the backs of her knees, too.

Her toes weren't ticklish at all, which I discovered when I kissed them, each one in turn. The bottoms of her feet were, though.

I ended my kissing exploration of her body with my face framed between the V of her thighs, intending to continue by making her scream all over again.

She caught me, stopped me. "No, no. I can't. Not again, not yet."

Instead, she pushed me to my back. "My turn."

"For what?"

She shrugged, a movement which left her gorgeous tits swaying in a way that had my cock throbbing in the condom I hadn't discarded yet. "To do something for you."

"You've already done everything," I said.

She only smiled, and left the bed. She found the bathroom, and I heard water running; she returned with a washcloth, which she lay across my belly. Her eyes soft and warm and full of that same complex tangle of emotion and intensity I still didn't dare name, she held my limp cock by the base and tugged the condom off of me. She knotted the end of it and tossed it into the nearby waste can. With exquisite tenderness and gentility, she used the warm washcloth to wipe me clean, handling me this way and that, wiping, dabbing, wrapping the warm wet cloth around me, cleaning me until I showed no trace of anything. She tossed the washcloth aside and sat on the bed next to me. Her eyes were on mine, and I know we were both thinking similar thoughts.

"What we just shared, Roman—" Her voice and eyes were both hesitant, but still open. Determined, intentionally vulnerable. "That was more than just sex."

"I know."

"A lot more."

"I *know*, Kitty."

Her eyes searched me, and I let everything I was feeling show through—the confusion at the intensity of it all, the fear the feelings engendered in me.

"Do you trust me, Roman?" she asked.

I nodded without hesitation. "Yes."

"If I tell you I think I'm falling in love—what will you do?" She bit her lip, hard, fear in her eyes. "I didn't mean to. I didn't want to, honestly. But I am."

I wanted to tense up, to shut down. I wanted to walk out—Love; she'd said it. "We just met. We barely know each other."

She just shrugged again. "I know what I need to know. And I knew it was happening before I came onto this boat. I knew doing this with you would end up like this. I felt it happening and I still came."

"What if I can't do that?"

"Fall in love?" She pierced me with her eyes, those brown orbs now fierce and strong and confident. "Or admit that you already are?"

I swallowed hard. "The second one."

She twisted to sit cross-legged, facing me, resting her hands on my stomach. Her smile was gentle but contained a hint of teasing. "You big sissy. You can't even say that much?"

I just shook my head, lying on my back, staring at the woman on the bed with me, amazed at her confidence, at her strength, the way she knew who she was and what she wanted and was willing to risk getting hurt to get it.

"Well, that's okay. You will."

I smirked. "You think so?"

She nodded, grinning. "I know so. It won't take long and I'll have you wrapped around my little finger."

"Don't count on it, babe."

She traced my abs. "Roman, look—this doesn't have to be complicated or scary. You just have to keep showing me how you feel. I don't need you to be able to verbalize it all the time—you're not like that, and I get it. But if you can show me, that'll be enough."

"How did this happen?" I asked, shaking my head.

She just laughed. "Love happens, Roman. Even to guys like you." She smirked. "Look at your cousins. I don't think any of them expected to find the partners they have."

"Yeah, you're right about that. I talked to Bax a little bit a few days ago."

"And? What'd he say?"

I shook my head. "A lot of stuff. I was kind of hammered when we talked, but the upshot of it was that I think he knew this would happen, and was warning me to not be an asshole if and when it did."

I sighed. "So here it is, happening. And I'm trying not to be an asshole about it."

"So you admit you're falling for me?" Her eyes danced with humor, but the question wasn't a joke.

I clenched my fists, arms crossed behind my head, chest rising and falling with deep, fast, panic-laced breaths. I forced my eyes to hers. "I can admit I have feelings I'm sure as fuck not familiar with."

"It's a start." Her eyes roamed my body, tracing and dancing down from my eyes to my chest to my abs, to my cock. "I have an idea."

"Uh-oh," I laughed. "Why do I have a feeling this is going to get tricky?"

She ran her palms over my abs, caressing them in a slow exploration that dared lower inch by inch. "It's a reward system, Roman."

"Reward?" I sucked in a breath, eyes narrowing at her as she teased her touch lower. "What do I have to do for the reward, and what is the reward?"

She bit her lip, her eyes sultry, a smirk curving her mouth even as she gnawed on that lip. "Well, you put your feelings for me and this whole situation into words, and I'll do things you'll enjoy."

"I enjoy a lot of things, Kitty."

She licked her lips. "Um…things to your—your cock. With my hands…and mouth."

"I could probably play this game."

"I thought you might." She traced the length of my cock with a fingertip, and it twitched on its way to hardness. "Let's start with a question."

"Okay—shoot."

She stared at me, thinking hard. "Would you consider a monogamous, committed, long-term relationship with me?"

"Can I just give you a yes or no answer, or do I have to elaborate?"

She shrugged. "The better your answer, the better the reward."

Maybe I should explore this a little. "Short answer, then: yes."

She slid her fingers under my hardening cock, lifting it away from my body, leaned over me so her breasts brushed against me and draped onto my belly. Then she wrapped her lips around the head, suckling once, a brief *pop* of her lips around me and a flick of her tongue. And then she backed away, releasing me.

"And the long answer?" she queried, tracing the lines of my abs with her finger again.

"The long answer? You specified three elements to a relationship: monogamous, committed, and long-term. The monogamy part isn't hard for me— I've never cheated because I've never been in a real relationship, and never been the other guy, either. The one time a girl tried to hook up with me and I found out she had a boyfriend, I left before it could go any-where. I told her I'd never want to be cheated on, so I won't be the other guy. I'm nothing if not loyal."

I realized this game was dangerous—I was giving her truths I'd barely thought about myself in so many words...and I wasn't just doing it for the reward, ei-ther. Which was the most dangerous part of it all.

"Committed? I guess I don't think I have a prob-lem with that—it goes with monogamy, right? It just means I'd be dedicated to making sure the relation-ship works and is healthy and whatever. So, why would I get into a relationship if I wasn't committed to it? I've gone my whole life without bothering with a relationship—if I'm going to start one, I'm sure as fuck going to commit to it. I finish what I start, Kitty. Goes hand in hand with I said about being loyal."

She nodded, her eyes serious on mine. "So what about the long-term part? Is that an issue?"

"That's the variable. Just giving you the truth, Kitty." I let out a breath. "I don't know what this is or how it happened or why it's happening, or why to me, but it is, and I can't deny it. I won't make any promises about a length of time. I just know I could see myself committing, and being loyal for as long as it works between us."

"That's a really good answer, Roman." Her eyes twinkled, sparkling with humor and with lust.

She lifted my cock again—it was rock hard now, and burgeoning to its full length. I kept my fists clenched behind my head, watching in rapture as she took me into her mouth, more of me now. Her fist was wrapped around my base, pumping gently, and her lips slid down past the rim of the head, and then she backed away slowly, extending her tongue to lick the tip as I left her mouth.

"Holy fuck, Kitty," I snarled. "Playin' a dangerous game, honey."

She shrugged. "I told you—the better the answer, the better the reward."

"So you liked that answer even though I can't make any promises about it being long-term?"

She nodded. "Yes, because you were honest. I appreciate honesty over you saying something just to sound good, or what you think I want to hear."

"You'd have seen right through me if I'd tried to make up some bullshit about promising you forever."

"Exactly. I have a really sensitive BS detector, you should know." She cupped my balls in one hand, massaging them. "Next question—and this one isn't a yes or no, so it won't be quite as simple to answer…when you consider a relationship with me, how do you feel about that?"

I took a moment to think—which was tricky considering the euphoria of her touch. "Hmmm.

That's complicated. I feel nervous, because I've never been anyone's boyfriend. I'm a selfish dick, Kitty. I feel like I'd be a shitty boyfriend because I'd only ever be thinking about how I can get you to have sex with me. I just don't know how to not be selfish. I'm not saying I can't learn or that I won't try, but that's my concern. I'm also concerned you'll try to change me. Emasculate me or some shit. Make me carry your purse or watch those bullshit reality shows or have conversations about our feelings all the time, or try to get me to stop swearing or be less macho or whatever you want to call it. I watched my buddy Peterson get into a relationship with a girl—she was hot, but high-maintenance. Before he broke up with her, she had him dressing like some preppy Ivy League twerp, never let him go out with us, wanted him to quit jumping and get a safer job—which was what prompted him to break up with her." I met her gaze steadily. "So, if this turns into a thing between us, don't think that just because we're dating that I'll suddenly become someone I'm not. I'll try to be less of a self-centered asshole, but don't think you can change me." I thought some more. "But on the other hand, I also feel like getting into a relationship with you could be really cool. I like who you are as a person, which I honestly can't say about many people. I like being around you. It's easy to talk to you, to spend time around you. And again, just being honest, here, I like the idea of trying a long-term relationship with you, because the idea of getting to have sex with you every day makes me feel a little giddy. I've never wanted that with anyone, but I do with you."

Kitty just stared at me for a moment, considering her response. "Okay, first of all, I don't *want* to change you. At least, not in a way that would take away from who you are. Add to, maybe, but not change the fundamental nature of who Roman Badd is as a person. I would want you to learn to think about me, put me first in the way I'd put you first, consider how your actions and decisions will affect me, how your words might make me feel. But I'd never ask you to leave a job or abandon your friends or be some guy you're not. And second, when you talk about getting into a relationship with me for the sex, is that the only reason you're interested in it? Or in me?"

"Is this another question, or a follow-up to the first?"

"A little of both, I guess."

I knew this was a make it or break it question. But fortunately, I also knew my answer would make her happy. "No, Kitty. It's not just about sex. It's about the idea of a sexual relationship. Developing a complex and deep relationship sexually as we develop a relationship emotionally." I watched her melt a little, and knew I'd gotten that one right. "It's also about just getting to have someone around day in and day out that's not my brothers. I love them, don't get me wrong, but sometimes a guy just gets lonely, you know? I never realized that until I met you and started feeling it when I wasn't with you."

"Ohhhh, Roman, you really got that one right."

"Do I get a *really* good reward?" I grinned at her, one eyebrow quirked.

"Oh, do you *ever*."

She wrapped both hands around my cock, sliding them down and then up, slicking one palm over the head and then the other. She did this for a few seconds, enough to make me suck in a deep breath and hold it, letting it out slowly as Kitty bent over me, her eyes on mine as she filled her mouth with me, slowly, her tongue fluttering against my shaft as I entered her warm wet mouth. I couldn't help a groan, and felt myself already rising—I prided myself on nearly endless restraint, being able to hold off almost at will, indefinitely. But something about Kitty, her touch, her mouth, her body, those wide, brown, innocent, sultry eyes just stripped away all my self-control. Instead of backing away and asking another question, she fucked me with her mouth again, and again, each slow slide of her lips around my cock taking me higher, closer to release. My belly tightened and my cock throbbed and my jaw clenched, and her eyes watched me all the while, through every sensuous glide of her mouth around me.

"Kitty—god…" I groaned, eyes shutting involuntarily. "Careful."

She laughed, backing away. "Careful? Why are you warning me? Do you think I don't know what will happen if I keep doing that? Just because I'm a good girl who doesn't swear doesn't mean I'm totally innocent, Roman." She bit her lip, stroking me with her fists again. "I happen to know *exactly* what will happen and I'm taking you there on purpose."

I had no answer for that, so I just watched her continue to slick her fists down my length in a slow, hand-over-hand motion.

She didn't stop her stroking, this time. "How do you feel about me, Roman?"

"Ah, the hard one."

She laughed. "Are you talking about *this*," she squeezed my cock, "or the question?"

"Both."

"Doesn't have to be a hard question, Roman. Just answer it honestly. I'm not after the *right* answer, just an honest one, as fully articulated as you can manage."

"How do I feel about you?" I closed my eyes to try and think, but her slow, sliding hands made it difficult. "I really like you. I don't mean that as a cop-out—I honestly just don't *like* most people. The big reason I've never had a relationship is because I've never come across a woman I genuinely liked enough to want to spend that much time with her. Meaning, I'm genuinely interested in who you are as a person." I paused again to think, focusing on my next words instead of the feel of her hands gliding up and down, up and down, so slowly it was maddening. "I respect the fact that you held your ground with me, that you stood up to me being a dick. I appreciate that you weren't just playing hard to get as a game, but that you refuse to compromise what you want. I respect the fact that you know what you want with me, and that you're not shy about it—and I'm talking about the emotional component of this thing. You were honest about what you want, physically, and what you need emotionally, and you're not afraid of getting hurt."

"I'm terrified of getting hurt, as a matter of fact" she corrected. "What happened with my ex hurt. And I already feel more and more deeply for you than I ever did him, and this thing with you and me is barely even a thing." Her eyes met mine, and she paused the moment of her hands. "You have the capacity to really wreck me, Roman. You should probably understand that."

"So, no pressure," I laughed.

"Right, no pressure," she said, laughing with me. "Glad we're on the same page. So. What else?"

"What, you want more?"

She smirked, one eyebrow popped, an amused but also somehow erotic expression. "Always."

"Well, in that case, I've got plenty more."

She leaned down, tits brushing my belly again, fitting her lips around the head of my cock, mouthing it like she would the tip of an ice cream cone. "Is that right? How much more have you got for me?"

"More than you could handle, babe," I growled.

"You think so? You think I couldn't handle all you can give me?" she asked, stroking me, plumping and pumping. "I think I can take everything you have to give and still want more."

"Is that a challenge?" I asked, breathing raggedly, now.

"You bet it is. Give me all you've got, Roman. No holding back, no protecting me from yourself."

"You sure you know what you're taking on, Kitty?"

Her eyes blazed—the sweet, innocent little Kitty had a core of steel to go with her heart of gold. "Try me."

"Fine, as long as you're sure you know what you're getting yourself into." I sucked in a breath, going for broke. "How, I don't know—I barely know you, we just met, this our first real date outside of your apartment…but I'm absolutely falling for you, Kitty Quinn. I don't even know if Kitty is your real name or a nickname. I don't know your middle name, or your parents' names, or if you're an only child." I held her gaze, let her see that I couldn't possibly get more vulnerable than this. "But I'm falling for you. I want to be with you all the time. I want to know everything about you. I feel like a fuckin' sappy-ass pussy saying all this, but somehow it's all fuckin' true."

"I don't think there could possibly be anything more macho or sexy or a turn-on than a big, gorgeous, muscular man like you being strong enough to articulate your feelings."

"Well, regardless of how either of us feel about it, there it is—my feelings for you, put out there, come what may." I growled wordlessly as she sped up the pumping strokes of her fists around my cock. "And now you better quit teasing me and get on your hands and knees so I can finish what you've been starting for the last twenty minutes."

"I had a different idea, actually," she said, her smile sweet and sultry at the same time. "How about you just lay there, keep still, and trust me?"

"I don't hold still well, and I've been laying here giving you time to do what you want without moving for a long fucking time. I'm about done with waiting, Kitty."

"Just trust me a little longer?" She bit her lip, smiling, draping her breasts against my chest in a sinuous dance of her upper body. "Just let me have my way for a few more minutes? Please?"

I grunted in frustration. "You're killin' me, Kitty."

"You're not the only one who finishes what you start, Roman."

Oh shit. This girl is killing me.

THIRTEEN

Kitty

I LOVE THE TASTE OF ROMAN'S COCK IN MY MOUTH AND the feel of him leaking against my tongue. So soft, yet so hard. Velvety. Salty, smoky on my tongue. Warm against my lips. This was the most incredible sensation I've ever felt.

He groaned as I cupped his heavy yet delicate balls in my hands, massaging them while I gently sucked the end of his cock. The look in his eyes was unforgettable.

I'm going to make him come, and he won't be able to stop. This female power is unlike anything I have ever experienced in my life; my heart is pounding, but my nerves are settling and now I feel two things above all else: excitement, and wanting to please Roman in a way he's never felt before.

With his hands behind his head, teeth clenched and jaw grinding, I can tell he was already affected, and was struggling to hold back. I was gambling on being able to break through that control and get him to let loose. Primal Roman is scary, but also makes me so horny I can barely breathe.

I took him into my mouth, tasting his flesh, my jaw stretching to accommodate him—he sucked in a breath and held it, curling forward, abs tensing, to watch me slide my lips further down his erection. I came back up, fluttering my tongue against the side of his cock, licking the top. I did it again, going down, slowly, trying to take more of him. As I felt him at the back of my throat, I couldn't stop a gagging sound.

"Don't, Kitty. Not that far."

I keep my eyes on his, draping my hair to one side to give him a full view of my mouth as I take him even deeper, gagging once more.

"Kitty, I said *don't*," he growled. I did it again, just to provoke him, and he snarled in frustration, pulling away and pushing me off him. "You're not listening, goddammit."

I shook my head, not letting him get too far away, or out of my grip. "No, I'm not. What if I like it?"

"Bullshit."

I laughed, not willing to argue that point, because he was right. "Maybe I just like pissing you off."

"Well, not listening to me is a quick way to do that." He was sitting up, further toward the middle of the bed.

I crawled onto the bed, kneeling over him, pressing my palms against his chest. "Lay down, Roman."

"Don't do that again. I don't like it. You gagging yourself isn't sexy to me."

"It's not? I thought all guys liked that?"

He shook his head. "Just 'cause it's in stupid porn flicks doesn't mean all guys like it. I get off on you feeling good. You doing something to make yourself uncomfortable or whatever because you think I'll like it is stupid."

He was still sitting upright on the bed, ignoring my efforts to push him onto his back. I tried a different tactic. I crawled onto his lap, straddling him, my hand reaching between us to caress his length, pressing my breasts against his chest, kissing him all over—chest, neck, chin, forehead, cheeks, lips, shoulders.

"Lay down, Roman. Please?"

"No more of the gagging bullshit."

"I promise."

He slowly lowered himself onto his back, arms behind his head again. I grasped his forearms, bringing his hands forward, guiding them to my hair. I

smiled at him, licking my lips, and then bit my lip,
just for him.

He snarled. "Dammit, woman. You know what
happens when you do that."

I nodded, my lip between my teeth. It felt totally
natural to me to cup my breasts, framing them for
him, dancing, swaying, undulating as I lowered myself over him again. He groaned, a long, drawn-out
moan as I wrapped my lips around him, kneeling
between his thighs. I curled my fingers around him,
tilting him away from his body. He brushed my hair
away from my eyes, out of my face, and then caught
the mass of it in his fists and piled it on my head, holding it in place with both hands.

I glanced up at him through lowered lashes, and
his expression was fraught, frightening in its intensity. His muscles were swollen and heavy, tense. His
breathing was fast and deep, and he was sucking in
great lungfuls of oxygen, as if barely able to breathe.
His fingers dug into my scalp, and with each successive
stroke of my lips and tongue over his cock, he gradually began encouraging me more and more, faster
and faster, with the gentle guidance of his hands.

Now his breathing was ragged, and it was easy to
see that he was beginning to lose control.

"Fuck, Kitty."

I fisted one hand around the root of him,

pumping him, using my other to cup his balls, massaging them. "I really like it when you talk about your feelings, Roman."

He laughed. "This feels like blatant manipulation, Kitty."

"It is. I'm okay with that, if it gets you to talk to me."

"You really gonna do this?" he growled.

"You have a problem with that?"

"Fuck no." He palmed my cheek. "But I need to be inside you again, Kitty. I need to feel your pussy clenching around my cock. I need to get you screaming again. But if you want to do this right now, then I'll let you."

"You'll let me?" I laughed. "How generous."

"Yeah, I'll *let* you."

"I'd like to see you stop me." I bent over him. "You know you can't handle it when I do this."

I took him into my mouth, tonguing him all the way, stroking, pumping him faster and faster.

"Dammit—goddammit." He buried his fingers in my hair, tangling, pulling me down onto him. "Think I can't stop you if I want to?"

I just made a face at him as I continued to bury him in my mouth.

"I'll stop you."

I was using both hands now, one fist above the

other, with just the head of his cock in my mouth, sucking in short, fast, shallow strokes. He was groaning, eyes closed, head thrown back, every muscle rock hard, hips flexing upward, every inch of his gorgeous, perfect body attuned to me, responding to my ministrations.

No, he couldn't stop. He was mine—*I* was in control. If I stopped now, he'd beg me to keep going. If the situations were reversed, he'd make me beg just to prove the point, but that was his thing, not mine. I just wanted to see how good I could make him feel. I wanted him to lack all ability to breathe, to think, to move. I wanted to give him all the pleasure I could. No games, just pleasure.

He moaned, a surprisingly soft, quiet sound. Not at all macho or gruff. Just a raw, unfiltered response.

Such a turn-on. The sound made me shiver, made my core flutter, my center—my pussy—go hot and damp with desire.

I moved faster, using more of my mouth and deeper slides of my fists.

His next sound was…broken. A raw, ragged gasp as he thrust his hips upward, completely helpless now.

He was on the edge, undeniably. His fists bunched in my hair, tightening their grip so it was almost painful, guiding my bobbing movements in a way that told me he wasn't even aware of what he was doing. I used my tongue, flicking and licking with each stroke, twisting my hands on the way up and plunging them down, faster and faster.

His eyes flew open and met mine. "Kitty—*fuck*—fuck, fuck. You don't want this, stop now. I'm ridin' the edge, sweetheart." He flexed his hips, pumping into my mouth. "Ohhh fuck. Gonna come, now, Kitty. Right now."

I tasted essence, a leaking tease of what was about to happen. I didn't stop. God, no. I kept going. I wanted this, wanted him beyond all ability to hold back.

"Fuckin' hell, Kitty. Fuck!"

He really liked that word, I noticed. Especially as he got closer to letting go.

"Fuckin'—fuck! Kitty—I'm coming—" He tugged my hair twice, but didn't let go, not forcing me on him, but encouraging. Helping me. "Ohhh—*ohhhh* fuck, Kitty! Kitty, Jesus, Kitty."

I tasted him, then, in a blast of hot salty warmth filling my mouth, flooding my taste buds, and I had to swallow hard and fast, gulping loudly, but I kept going, kept taking him, kept taking his pleasure for myself. His groans were primal and helpless, and his fingers in my hair were strong but gentle. More and more, he came and he came, filling my mouth again and again, the taste overwhelming but not unpleasant—it was the texture more than anything that I didn't love. But nothing could stop me from bringing him to the furthest boundary of his ecstasy, my fists pumping in a blur, mouth plunging downward in loud wet slurps. I didn't stop even when he did, but he pulled me away, lifting me bodily off of him and tucking me into his chest, wrapping his arm around me.

He was trembling all over and his heart was pounding in his chest.

"Good and holy motherfucking god*damn*, Kitty," he gasped, after a long helpless moment of panting. "You—that was—holy *fuck*."

I kissed his chest, resting my chin on his pec and gazing at him. "I'm glad you enjoyed it."

He laughed. "Enjoyed? Hell, woman—I *enjoy* burgers and beers and seeing the sunrise from twenty thousand feet in the back of a noisy-ass cargo plane. I *enjoy* watching action flicks and eating popcorn. That, what you just did? There ain't words for it."

Giddiness flooded me, along with pride and satisfaction and sensual enjoyment in my ability to give him that. After a few moments of comfortable silence, our eyes locked, and silently we exchanged ideas and thoughts and emotions neither of us had the words for. Something amazing had just happened for both of us, and we were content to drift among our own thoughts, thinking about what it all meant.

After several minutes, my chin still on his chest, I told him the things he said he didn't know about me. "My full name is Katerina Maureen Quinn; my parents called me Kat until I was six, and then one day my dad called me Kitty as a term of endearment, and it just stuck, and I've been Kitty ever since. My best friend and roommate Izzy calls me Kit-Kat sometimes. My parents are John Albert and Maureen Tisdale Quinn—my mom goes by Mo."

"Tisdale?"

"It's a family name, and she hates it. She'd actually be pissed at me for telling you. She made a game out of making my dad try to guess her middle name for the first six months they dated. They've been married thirty-nine years. My dad is a philosophy professor at UAA, and my mom is a kindergarten teacher at the same elementary school she and I both went to. I'm an only child, but I have three cousins—Alex and Ginger on my mom's side, and they live in Fairbanks, and Riley on my dad's, and she lives in LA."

He nodded, absorbing the information. His hand was resting on my back and smoothing in slow, caressing circles. He smiled at me. "Tell me something you think would scare me."

I stared at him; surprised he'd ask that. "Wow. Going for the deep stuff, huh?"

"You pulled me into this, Kitten, so now I'm in it.

No backing down now."

I frowned. "You think I pulled you into it?"

He shrugged. "Not in a bad way. And it honestly wouldn't have happened if you hadn't encouraged me. I'd'a been too pussy."

"Fair enough," I laughed. "So, something I think would scare you." I thought for a moment. "Okay. I want to get married, and I want to have kids. Not soon, necessarily, but I do. And I want it in that order—get married, and *then* have kids." I ran my hand over his chest, enjoying the feel of his huge, hard muscles under my palm. "I don't want a big, elaborate wedding. Mom, Dad, Aunt Leah and Uncle Drew, Aunt Mackenzie and Uncle Kevin, my cousins, and the Badd clan."

"You've thought about it? Your wedding?"

I laughed. "Well, yeah. Just about every girl does, I think. When I was a little girl, of course, I wanted a big dramatic fairy-tale wedding with swans and paper snowflakes and glitter. But now, I just want it to be… meaningful. Sweet, sincere, and simple."

"Swans are mean," Roman grunted. His eyes twinkled, though. "Simple sounds good."

I watched him for signs of panic. "So…does that scare you?"

"You expecting me to propose, like, next month?"

I laughed. "God, no."

"Then, no. I knew you wanted a ring and kids—you said that was part of why you and your dumbass ex split up."

"He wasn't a dumbass."

"He was if he had you for eight years and couldn't decide if he wanted to marry you."

"It's okay, Roman. You don't have to butter me up anymore." I said it with a grin that told him I was kidding.

"I'm not buttering you up, goddammit. Just telling you the truth as I see it."

I reached up and palmed his cheek. "Roman, calm down, jeez. I was kidding."

He cracked a grin and I realized he'd been having me on. "Got you."

I smacked his chest, cackling. "You *do* have a sense of humor! I was starting to think you didn't."

"I've got one, it just tends to make use of curse words and insults."

"I've noticed," I said, dryly.

He reached low, grabbed my backside, and pulled me up onto him, cupping a double handful of my butt as he lay me on his body. "Now. How about you scoot up here and sit on my face so I can see how loud I can make you scream."

"Sit on your face?"

He smirked. "Yes ma'am. Just hold on to the

headboard and ride my face until you can't stay upright no more."

Slowly, hesitantly, feeling supremely awkward, I grabbed the headboard for balance and climbed up his body, straddling his chest, and then centered my core over his mouth. His thumbs brushed over my seam, sending heat sizzling through me, and then he gently pulled my lips apart and flicked his tongue over my clit—I whimpered.

"One…" he muttered.

Another lick, and I gasped.

"Two…"

A slow fluttering, a swiping, a circle, a patternless, rhythmless assault, and I lost myself in screams. "Three," he said, rolling his R, making me realize with a laugh that he was referencing the Tootsie Pop commercial with Mr. Owl.

"Don't—oh, oh god, oh god—you can't make me laugh while you're doing that," I protested.

"No?" He only pulled away to murmur the word.

"No, it's not fair."

"I don't play fair, Kitten. Never have, never will."

No fingers, just his tongue, and I was screaming in seconds, coming in under two minutes. Writhing, grinding shamelessly against him, doing exactly what he told me to do—riding his face.

The second I was finished with my orgasm, he

picked me up, flipped me forward onto my back, and levered himself over me. Impossibly, he was hard again. I reached for him, brought him to me, and thought of nothing except the anticipation of the ache of him inside me, the beautiful burn of stretching around him.

He was nudged against my opening, and I was writhing against him, still shuddering from my climax, and I knew nothing except my need for him, and a sudden, blinding wildness.

At that moment, a fist pounded on the door. "Mr. Badd—it's Captain Martin, sir. I'm terribly sorry to disturb you, but I've been hailed by the Coast Guard. You're needed in Ketchikan, Mr. Badd. It's an emergency."

Ducking his head and snarling, he spoke with his lips against my breastbone. "What's the emergency?"

"It's your father, Mr. Badd. There's been an accident."

"Fuck." He rolled off me, flopping onto his back. "Fuck! Do you have any other information?"

"I was not told anything beyond that you are needed back in Ketchikan, and that there'd been an accident involving your father." A pause. "I'm very sorry to have had to intrude upon your privacy."

"So we're heading back?"

"Actually, I believe your cousin, a Mr. Brock Badd,

is coming to get you in a seaplane."

"Fine. Thank you." He had his arm over his eyes, shielding me from seeing his reaction. "Do you have an ETA?"

"About fifteen minutes, sir."

Silence, then. What was I supposed to say? I reached for him, touched his arm. "Roman, how can I help?"

He didn't answer for a long moment. "Fuck if I know." Silence. "Fucker probably relapsed."

"I'm sorry this is happening." I wanted to stop it, to stop the pain I saw him hiding. "It'll be okay, Roman. It's okay."

"You don't know that. Nobody knows that." He rolled forward and off the bed, jerking open the bedroom door and vanishing through it, still naked, his massive cock swaying between his thighs.

He left the door partly open, and I watched him stalk around the saloon and rear deck, shoving his legs into his underwear and suit pants, then the undershirt, fingers nimbly doing the buttons of his button-down. Leaning against the railing, he made quick work of his socks and shoes. I went out after him, stepping into my dress. The tape wouldn't stick right anymore, but it mostly kept me in place. Without a word, I found my shoes, and my purse. I heard an engine in the distance, swiftly approaching, the loud roar of twin propellers—Brock's air taxi. I dug a hair tie out of my purse and tied my hair back, wiggling my feet into the sandals.

Roman eyed me. "What're you doin'?" His accent was back, and thick.

I blinked at him. "Getting ready to go."

"Boat won't be back to Ketchikan for a while yet."

I stared back. "I'm coming with you."

Another silence, except for the sound of Brock's plane getting closer. "No."

I sucked in a breath; a sharp hurt slicing into me at his rejection. "Why not?"

"Don't know what I'm walking into. This is messy-ass family shit."

"I'm not afraid of messy family stuff, Roman. I want to go with you."

"No, you don't." He glanced over to watch as Brock landed the plane and coasted up behind the yacht, which was now at anchor. "This shit with us is so new there ain't even paint on it—shit, there ain't even drywall. Just studs and subfloor. You don't need any of this."

"Roman, come on. I know things are new between us, but I can still be there for you."

Roman shook his head. "Nah. I appreciate the thought. I'll call you and let you know what's up. But right now I want you to call up to Captain Martin and let him know what you want to do. You can get some rest and he'll take you back to Ketchikan in the morning, or you can go now. Whatever you want. He'll arrange for Tony to meet you at the dock and run you home." He didn't look at me. "I'll call you, promise."

Brock had positioned the floatplane so it was perpendicular to the yacht, the wingtip facing the stern. With an agility belied by his size and bulk, Roman hopped down onto the swim platform at the rear of the yacht, balanced, and then leapt out, caught the strut, and threw himself onto the float, hauling himself aboard. The entire maneuver took less than ten seconds, and he'd made it seem easy, effortless, even though the initial leap had been several feet from boat to plane.

"Roman!" I called, eyes stinging.

He waved. "I'll call you!"

And then, with a slam of the door and a roar of the propellers, he was gone.

"Dammit," I said, slapping my hand on the stern. "*Dammit*, Roman."

FOURTEEN

Roman

I KNEW I WAS BROODING, BEYOND EVEN THE STRESS AND worry of not knowing what had happened with Dad. Brock had, so far, seemed okay giving me the silence to deal with my own thoughts as we flew back to Ketchikan. About ten minutes into the flight I realized we weren't heading to Ketchikan.

"The fuck are we going, Brock?" I growled through the headset.

"Seattle. Northwest Hospital."

"Why?"

"That's where your dad is, I guess."

"What about Rem and Ram?"

"Already on their way." He glanced at me. "Your

phone is off, and nobody could get hold of you. Took an act of Congress to get in touch with Captain Martin, and make him understand it was a life-and-death emergency, and to get your position."

"Thanks for coming to get me."

Silence. "Kitty didn't seem happy to be left behind."

I stewed, only answering after a long tense pause. "Didn't make sense to bring her along. Not even sure myself what's happening."

"Sure that's your call to make?"

"We're still—it's not…" I groaned, rubbing my face. "It's complicated."

"That's a puss-out if I've ever heard one." He took one hand off the yoke and adjusted something.

"The fuck do you know about it?" I snapped.

"Not a damn thing. But I know a puss-out answer when I hear one." He eyed me, not wary, just… watchful.

"I don't know what it is, Brock. We were still figuring it out when Captain Martin came to our room."

"So you're not just hooking up?"

I shrugged. "I…I guess I thought that's what it would be. But it's not turning out that way." I shook my head, scrubbing my hands through my hair. "Fuck."

"'Sup?"

I shifted in my seat, growling. "Everything. Dad. Kitty…the timing is just shitty."

"You were a dick just then, weren't you?"

"We may be family, but we ain't that close, Brock."

"Just asking."

"Mind your own fuckin' business."

"You're on my plane, bro. Means I get to make your shit my shit." He grinned at me, elbowing me. "So…you were a dick to her, weren't you?"

"She wanted to come and I said no. Then I left." I thought about it, and groaned. "Fuck."

"You were a dick?"

"I was a dick." I sighed. "I just—we talked about it being a thing, but…" I shrugged.

"A thing?" He quirked an eyebrow at me, looking so much like my brothers and me that it was disorienting.

"Yeah, it's definitely a thing…" I rubbed a piece of plastic facing on the plane's dashboard. "…With me and Kitty."

Brock shook his head. "And then you literally leapt off the ship to get away?"

"It wasn't that, it was…" I tried to formulate a way to put it that didn't leave me looking like a douchebag. "My dad is hurt, man. I don't know how bad, or if he's even alive. I don't fuckin' know. I don't know what happened. I don't know shit. And I didn't want to bring her into that. It's messy, man. My dad is a fuckin' disaster. I thought he was doin' better, which was why we moved up here to do this whole stupid fuckin' bar bullshit, but now he gets into an accident? He was drinkin' again—I'm fuckin' sure of it."

"I got a million questions about your family, but I'll save 'em."

"Since we're stuck on a plane for another hour—you might as well ask."

"First, you don't know he was drinking—just pointing out the facts as we know them right now. And, if she wants to jump into your messy family bullshit headfirst, that's her choice, not yours, right? I mean, god knows my brothers and I know all about messy family business, and we learned quick that when a woman wants in, she'll get in, man. If you don't want that, you gotta tell her. But if you want it to be a 'thing' you can't shut her out."

"Sounds like you're lecturing, not asking."

He grinned, shrugging. "Yeah, well…" Brock glanced at me. "On another topic, you seem pissy about that bar you are opening."

"We're not talking about that."

He chuckled. "Not going well, I take it?"

"I said we're not talking about it. For real, man." I poked a switch on the dashboard. "Leave it alone. I can't handle that on top of everything else right now."

"Don't touch that," Brock said, smacking my hand away. "You know, you *do* have family that's sort of in the biz, if you know what I mean."

I punched his shoulder, and not gently. "I jump out of airplanes for a living, asshat, you think I don't know not to flip switches? I ain't stupid, bro." I leaned back, crossing my arms over my chest. "And for the last time, I'm not talking about the bar right now. Let me get through this shit with Dad first."

"Fair enough."

We didn't talk much the rest of the way to Seattle—I was stewing about Dad, mostly. Well, that and Kitty. It was dawning on me now just how shitty I'd left things.

Fuck, I'd messed up.

Dad, though—he fucked with my head. I just *knew* he'd relapsed. I'd really hoped the changes we'd made would push him into a better place...and for a while, it seemed like it had. He had called us a few times over the last few months, given us updates on his travels, and he'd always seemed great. We'd ask him if he'd been drinking, and he'd just say no, he was done with that shit. Not defensive, not shutting it down, just matter of fact. I'd hoped he was getting better. Not fixed, I knew that wasn't a thing, would never be a thing. But maybe he wouldn't need us to babysit him just to keep him alive.

An accident? That smacked of a relapse. Made me sick to my stomach, honestly. How bad would it be? Would he be paralyzed? In ICU for months? Was he in trouble with the law?

No way to know until I got there, but I just had a gut feeling it wasn't some random accident.

Which, somehow, led me to thinking about Kitty. I kept seeing her at the stern of the yacht, calling after me, looking so hurt. Like I'd stabbed her in the heart. Which, I suppose, I kind of had. We'd just had this amazing evening and a heart-to-heart talk about wanting it to be a thing with us, and then I'd bolted and left her in the lurch.

What a puss-out.

We had talked about starting a relationship. Which was fucking scary as hell for me.

A relationship? Me? Crazy talk.

But it wasn't.

It was, but it wasn't. I mean, it was totally nuts, because I barely knew the girl, had only met her a few weeks ago. But it wasn't crazy, because some drive, some instinct deep inside told me this made sense. I wanted this. I wanted this girl.

So why the hell had I been such a dick?

Letting her into my actual life when it really counted, letting her support me during a hard, shitty, scary situation? That was different than admitting I liked her and was falling for her and wanted a relationship with her.

I was so lost in my thoughts that I didn't even notice that we'd landed in Seattle. Brock elbowed me. "You better go, man."

I started, glancing around. "Shit, we're here."

"Yeah. I told your brothers our ETA and they have a cab waiting up at the curb." He flicked a few switches, shutting down the engines. "I have some business here, so I'll be around. You've got my number?"

I shook my head. "Nah, I don't have anyone's number."

"Gimme your phone, I'll program my number into it."

I powered my phone on, unlocked it, and gave it to him and as he was typing, it started blowing up, notification after notification bleeping and dinging. When he finished, Brock handed it back to me, laughing.

"I couldn't help noticing the amount of notifications you have."

"Yeah, well I had it turned off."

"Got a message from Kitty." He eyed me. "Call her, man."

"Yeah, I will. Thanks again."

He hesitated. "Hope your dad is okay."

"You wanna come?"

He shrugged. "I…nah. Not right now. You need to figure your shit out with him. If you need help, I'm here. We're all here."

"He's your uncle, Brock."

He tapped the yoke with his fists, not looking at me. "It'd be weird. I've never met him, and he's my dad's twin. That'd be…hard."

"Oh, I hadn't thought about that." I held out my fist, and he bumped it with his. "I'll get hold of you."

I left the plane and jogged up to the curb, where a cab was waiting to take me to the hospital. My cell phone was burning a hole in my pocket—more specifically, the message from Kitty, but I ignored it. I couldn't think about her right now. I just couldn't. The closer to the hospital I got, the more my nerves started to jangle.

I entered the hospital, signed in, got directions to the room. Jogged up, heart pounding. My shoes squeaked on the floor tiles, and the only other sound was the hum of the fluorescent lights overhead; the antiseptic smell assaulted my nostrils, and I forced myself to shake my fisted hands loose. I found my dad's room—heard Rem and Ram, and Dad's deep voice rasping angrily.

I hesitated outside the door, knowing I needed to go in, but not wanting to. I didn't want to deal with

Dad. I didn't want to know what had happened.

I wanted to be back on the boat with Kitty.

I sucked in a breath, clenched my hands into fists and shook them out, and then entered the room. Remington was on the window side of the bed, Ramsey on the door side, and they and Dad all looked at me as I entered.

"Look who finally shows up," Dad rasped. "And all dressed up, too. You shouldn't have bothered, son."

He was beat up, bad. Broken left arm, the cast up to his shoulder and down to his fingertips, a broken right leg, bandage on his head, a black eye.

I didn't say anything as I stalked in, seeing my dad in a hospital yet again—the last time, after his heart attack, I'd sworn I'd never set foot in another fucking hospital. Yet, there I was.

I leaned against the wall near the foot of the bed, arms crossed over my chest. "What happened, Dad?"

He plucked at the blanket next to his thigh. "Right into it, huh?"

"Yeah, right into it. I got called away from something important, and didn't know whether you were alive or dead, or what. So yeah, I'm gonna skip the goddamn pleasantries."

"Well, obviously I'm not dead. And if you were coming to a hospital, obviously I wasn't dead."

"No shit. Point is, I had no information about

what happened or how bad off you were."

"Something important, huh?" Ram said, grinning at me. "Meaning Kitty. Your new girlfriend."

"What happened, Dad?" I asked, ignoring Ram.

"Car accident. Wrecked the trailer." He gestured at his arm and leg. "And myself, obviously."

"I notice you're not denying what I said," Ramsey pressed.

"I'll throw you through the fuckin' window if you don't shut the fuck up, Ramsey," I snarled. Turning back to Dad, then. "You were drinking."

He didn't answer, didn't look at me. For a long, long time, he remained silent. "Yes. I was drinking."

"So, you are dating her?" Ramsey said, smirking.

I stomped over to him, fisted his shirt and lifted him up, my face in his. "Shut—the *fuck*—up."

He raised his eyebrows, unafraid. "Whoa, touching buttons, huh?" He knocked my hands away, shoving me hard. "Shit is serious, then."

I was suddenly sapped of all energy. I sank down to sit on the edge of Dad's bed. "What *happened*, Dad?" I rubbed my face with both hands and then met his bloodshot eyes.

He rested his head backward on the pillows, staring at the ceiling. "I ain't been this far north since I left Alaska forty-some years ago." He rolled his head side to side. "It fucked me up."

A long silence indicated that he wasn't planning on saying any more. I took exception to that. "Care to elaborate?"

"Nope."

"Too fucking bad." I glanced at Rem and then Ram. "You hear anything I haven't?"

They both shook their heads. "No, he wouldn't talk about it till you got here," Rem said.

"Well, I'm here, so talk."

"We were nineteen when we all thought we'd come down to Seattle and live it up. Till then, our idea of the big city was Anchorage or Fairbanks. Seattle was…big time, you know? Me, Liam, Lena, and Caitlin."

"Caitlin?" Rem asked.

"My girlfriend at the time." He scratched his head. "She was—I liked her. A lot. But she was camouflage, you know?"

"Because you were in love with Lena?" Ram asked.

He nodded. "Bad. But she was with Liam. I thought I could handle it, I thought I was hiding it."

I sighed. "Not so much, huh?"

"Nope. We all got kinda trashed over at a park on the sound. I ended up talking to Lena, and Liam was talking to Caitlin. Not *doin'* nothing, just talking. And she just, outta the blue she looked at me and said,

'Lucas, I know you're in love with me.'" He paused a moment. "I didn't even bother denying it. Didn't know what to say. What was there *to* say? That was... that was the start of everything blowing up between Liam and me."

"So you went back to the park?" I guessed.

He nodded. "Yep. Felt like the day it happened." Dad's voice was tight, thick. "It's been forty years since I've seen her. She's been in her grave almost fifteen. But it still fuckin' hurts as bad as ever."

I stared at him. "Jesus, Dad. You really had it bad for her."

"You don't know what Lena was like." He ducked his head. "Liam deserved her, though. He was...well, he was always getting me outta trouble." He grinned at me. "Like Rem and Ram are always getting you outta trouble. You're too much like me."

"'The hell I am." But I grinned when I said it.

"Yeah, Lena was...one of a kind. I tried like hell to get over her. Tried everything. Nothing worked. Spent my whole goddamn life trying to outrun and outdrink the ghost of that woman. Never could. I sat in that park and heard her telling me I was her best friend, and she'd always love me like a best friend, but she'd always love Liam as more than a friend in a way she couldn't with me. And that she was sorry, and she didn't want to hurt me."

"Ouch," Rem said, wincing.

"Yeah, fuckin' ouch." Dad was lost in the pain. "I went out, bought a half gallon of my ol' buddy Jim Beam, and got fucked."

I stared at him. "Jesus, Dad. A half gallon?"

He stared at me hard. "Don't tell me you've never done it."

I winced, thinking back to Ketchikan. "No, I have. But I'm not an alcoholic."

"And you've never lived your entire goddamn life with your fuckin' heart torn to shreds without hope of it ever gettin' fixed."

"I'm sorry you've gone through that, Dad," I said. "I had no idea."

"None of us did," Ram said.

"No shit—I wanted it that way. I was a shitty dad to you three, but I've always loved you." He seemed embarrassingly close to tears, and none of us knew how to handle it. "I just been shitty at it."

"Dad, goddammit," I rubbed my face again. "Did you hurt anyone else, or just yourself?"

He swelled with anger at the accusation, but quickly deflated. "No. Just myself. Going around a curve in the middle of nowhere, lost control, jack-knifed, rolled the whole business down a ditch. Woke up here."

"What were you doing up here?" Rem asked.

He shrugged, picking at the blanket again. "I was thinking of trying to make my way north."

The boys and I traded glances. "How far north?" I asked.

He shrugged again. "I dunno. Hadn't thought about it. Just…north. Facing my demons, you know? Clearly, that wasn't a good plan." He glared at us each in turn. "Woulda been fine if you'd left me well enough alone in Oklahoma."

"You'd be dead of another heart attack, or cirrhosis, or some other shit," Ram said. "And you fuckin' know it."

He growled. "The fuck you know about it?"

I glanced at my brothers, and then at Dad. "I think you should come up to Ketchikan with us. You'll need time to heal, and you can't do it alone, and we sure as fuck aren't living in Seattle."

"Rome?" Ram asked. "We don't really even have our own shit straightened in Ketchikan."

"We'll figure it out," I snapped.

Dad looked about ready to pop. "I ain't goin' back there. No fuckin' way."

"Dad—there's no real choice." Remington was trying to play peacemaker. "We own property up there now, and you're a mess and you need help."

"All'a you get the fuck out." Dad picked a cup of ice off the table and threw it at me, bonking the cup off my head and spraying ice everywhere. "Get the fuck out. I gotta think and I can't do it with you assholes using all the oxygen."

Remington was the first to leave, followed by Ramsey. I hesitated, halfway out the door. "Dad—"

He threw an entire tray of half-eaten food at me. "Fuck off, boy, if you know what's good for you."

I dodged the tray and ducked out, leaving the mess for someone else to clean up. Ramsey and Remington were halfway down the hallway toward the waiting room, and I followed them.

Upset, pissed, and all over the place, I barely saw the waiting room. I just plopped into the nearest empty chair and bent forward, burying my face in my hands. It was the middle of the night and there was no one around. I was glad for the quiet; I needed to get my shit together and process everything that had happened in the last twelve hours.

Seeing that I was ignoring them, Rem and Ramsay mumbled something about going to find a coffee and left me alone with my thoughts.

I didn't see her, hear her, or even smell her—all I knew was one second I was wallowing in my own issues, and the next I was being pushed upright by soft, warm hands. Those same hands threaded fingers through mine, and then her weight was settling onto my lap and her face was burying into my throat.

Her presence was all around, everywhere. She was everything.

I could only breathe in her scent and absorb her warmth, and wonder at my good fortune. She was exactly who I needed in this moment.

"What the fuck are you doing here, Kitten?"

"I'm your girlfriend, you big dummy." She reared back and gazed up at me with her big brown eyes. "Just because you freaked out and acted like an idiot doesn't mean I'm not going to come support you."

I blinked hard. "Jesus. After that way I left I don't deserve this kinda treatment, sweetheart."

She patted my cheek, nuzzling into my neck. "That's the thing about relationships, Rome—what we deserve doesn't enter into it. I decide what you deserve, not you."

"I was an asshole."

"Yes, you were. Kind of your thing."

Kitty tugged on my hair. "But maybe I can help you with that. And you don't have to sprinkle every sentence with half a dozen curse words, either."

She giggled in my ear, and that giggle went straight to my cock for some reason. "Remember how I reward you when you're nice, Roman?"

"Better be careful, Kitten, or you'll find yourself bent over a hospital bed."

She gazed up at me, bold, meeting my challenge.

"You make these threats like you think it's not exactly what I want, Roman."

I glanced down at Kitty. "Be honest for a minute. Why are you here after the way I left?"

She smiled. "Roman, you don't get it? This is how it works. This is what it means to be in a relationship. I knew why you left the way you did. You're worried about your dad and don't know how to show it, and you're afraid of messing up being in a relationship with me, so you just say screw it and sabotage yourself by being a butthead."

"You barely know me, Kitten. How do you know that much about me?"

She nuzzled me again. "We haven't been with each other long, but that doesn't mean we don't *know* each other. I get you, Roman. How, I don't know, but I do."

"So...you're my girlfriend?"

She nodded. "Unless you changed your mind?" Her eyes told me she was not entirely kidding.

"No," I whispered. "I haven't changed my mind."

"Good." She snuggled close, gazing up at me. "So. Tell me about your dad's accident."

"Before I do that can you tell me how you managed to get home, get changed, and get down here so fast?"

"It turned out to be pretty easy. Captain Martin went full speed ahead to the dock nearest the airport. I called Izzy and she met me there with a change of clothes and some toiletries. I booked a ticket on the first flight out to Seattle from the boat, so we Ubered it over there, I caught the flight, and now I'm here. Simple." She rubbed my shoulder. "So now, tell me about what happened to your dad."

"He got drunk and rolled his trailer off a ditch." I sighed. "There's a lot more to it, though. He was in love with his twin brother's girlfriend, and never got over her. They fought over it, and ended up never speaking again because of it. I grew up not even knowing I had cousins. Now Dad is fucked up and we have to take care of him, but he's being a bastard about moving back to Ketchikan because it'll open up all the old hurts from way back. So it's a mess."

She winced. "Sounds like it. What will you do?"

"Hell if I know. I suggested Dad come to Ketchikan with us and he threw a tray at my head." I shook my head, sighing. "I don't know. Plus, there's the bar to think about."

She hesitated, clearly not wanting to piss me off. "What's the deal there?"

"It's not as easy as we thought," I admit.

She laughed—she actually laughed. "So you admit it?"

I growl. "Don't push my buttons right now, babe."

Rem and Ram returned to the waiting room just then, coffee cups in hand, looking surprised at how cozy Kitty and I were.

"I don't think you guys have met properly, yet," I said. "Kitty—these are my brothers Remington and Ramsey. Guys, this is Kitty."

For once, my brothers managed to behave, and if they had any questions about why she was here they kept them to themselves.

Instead, Ramsey said, "Did he just admit that the bar was a fuckin' mistake?"

"No," Kitty said, "but he did admit it was harder to get it going than you guys first thought," Kitty said.

"*We* didn't think it would be," Remington said. "I told his ass it wouldn't be easy."

She frowned. "So why'd you go along with it?"

Ramsey laughed. "He's our brother, for one thing, and he's gone along with plenty of our stupid ideas."

"But mainly we didn't have any better ideas," Remington added.

She shook her head. "I can't believe you guys thought you could just buy a place and open a bar without knowing the first thing about it. I'm honestly surprised you're as far along as you are."

Ramsey laughed again. "We have the place reno-
vated, because we're good at that shit. But we got no
fucking clue what to do next. We're blowing money left and right. I think we have like a hundred bottles of whiskey, maybe ten cases of pint glasses and
whatever, and no clue what else we need. This idiot
is googling like a nutcase, but he's no closer to have
a fucking clue than when we were in Oklahoma. But
his ass is too stubborn to ask for help, so we're just
letting him do his thing."

Kitty just laughed. "And here you three lunk-
heads are with eight cousins who own one of the
most successful bars in Alaska." She patted me on the
cheek, rolling her eyes. "You can lead a horse to water, Roman, but you can't make him drink."

"Seems to be the theme right now, huh?" I asked.

She nodded, and then stared up at me. "Take me
to meet your dad."

I stared back. "You sure?"

She nodded. So, I stood up, setting her on the
floor, and glanced at my brothers—their eyes were
wide, shocked. "Let's go introduce Dad to my
girlfriend."

EPILOGUE

Juneau

"WHY ARE WE HERE AGAIN?" I ASKED IZZY AS WE rode the hospital elevator up to whichever floor we were going to.

"Because she's our best friend, and this is her boyfriend's dad. Besides, it's the right thing to do." Izzy touched up her lipstick, using the reflecting surface of the elevator button console as a mirror.

"How do we even know it's a boyfriend-girlfriend thing? She hasn't told us much." I looked at Izzy, thinking I should spruce up a bit in case these purported hot-as-hell triplets were all in attendance. I didn't, though, because why should I?

"The fact that she wouldn't tell us what happened

with her and Roman tells us all we need to know." Izzy handed me her lipstick and pulled out her eyeshadow.

Just then the elevator doors opened and we headed to the nearest ladies' washroom so Izzy could finish her makeup.

By then I'd decided to play along. I put on the lipstick, and then plumped up my cleavage, tugging the bra and shirt down and pushing the girls up, following it with some eyeshadow and mascara.

"She could just be waiting until we actually see her," I said, resuming our conversation. "We only talked on the phone for like ten minutes."

"And she said that night on the boat was the best night of her life. But she also said his dad is in the hospital, so she's keeping Roman company at the hospital."

"Why are we here? Isn't this kind of private family business?"

Izzy stared at me. "Which one of us is supposed to be the nice one, again?"

"You're super nice."

"No, I'm not. I'm an ice-cold skank."

I rolled my eyes. "Oh stop. Don't be dumb. You're neither ice-cold, nor a skank, nor a bitch."

"I'm all three, and more besides." She smacked my butt as we walked out the door. "Showtime."

Realization dawned on me as we left the

washroom. "Hold up. Wait, wait, wait—hold up."

She stopped, popping a piece of gum in her mouth. "Yes, Juneau?"

"This is about Roman's brothers, isn't it?" I asked, gesturing at her appearance.

Izzy hiked her miniskirt a little higher, so the hem came to just above mid-thigh. "It's about supporting our friend." She winked at me as she pivoted. "And if her boyfriend's brothers, who are single as far as I'm given to understand, happen to be there, then so be it."

I huffed. "You're absolutely shameless!"

She popped her gum. "Yup!"

"But you've dragged me into this!"

She caught at my arm and pulled me beside her. "Are you single?"

"Yes, but—"

"And do you like hot guys?"

"Well, yeah, but—"

"You saw Roman outside our apartment. He's hot—am I right?"

"Yes, Isadora, but—"

"Thus it stands to reason his identical triplet brothers are also hot. And when was the last time you got laid?"

"Last month, but that doesn't have anything to do with—"

She popped me on the butt again. "So? Let's go! Worst-case scenario is we're there to support our friend. Best-case scenario is we meet some hot guys, and possibly arrange a little hookup scenario."

"You are shameless!"

"You said that already." She winked at me. "And that's why you love me."

I huffed again as we headed toward the appropriate room number. We heard voices, loud ones, raised behind the door. We'd been told Roman's dad was a bit rough around the edges, and we could hear him now.

"I swore I'd never return, and I don't want to be here, goddammit!" His voice was deep, rough, old, and raspy.

"But, Mr. Badd—" I recognized Kitty's voice immediately.

Izzy and I just looked at one another and listened in.

"Name's Lucas, girl. Use it. Don't much stand on formality."

"Okay, Lucas, then. You swore, how long ago? Forty years ago? Thirty? More years ago than I've been alive. A lot has changed. *You've* changed." I heard her voice hesitate. "And, to be honest, none of the people involved are...are..."

"They're all dead." His voice was blunt and

almost rude. "Don't make it easier. And seeing my nephews would be…" His voice trailed off in that way that men often do.

"It would be good for you. You have family. Your sons have started connecting with them. Maybe you can, too."

"I don't wanna."

"You're being petulant, Lucas."

"Kitty, you're using ten-dollar words on a ten-cent fella, sweetheart."

"You're way smarter than you give yourself credit for."

"Don't count on it," he grumbled.

There was a pause and then we heard, "And I don't appreciate you using my weakness for pretty women against me, Roman."

"I see where Roman gets his talent for flattery," Kitty said.

"I'm gonna go get more coffee," I heard a voice say.

Izzy moved out of the way as the door to the hospital room opened, but I was not fast enough.

The door swung open, and a huge male body swaggered out and slammed into me, knocking me backward.

I staggered backward, but my feet wouldn't co-operate, and I found myself falling. Things happened in slow motion as sometimes happens, and I knew I wouldn't be recovering from this one.

But, instead of hitting the floor, I felt a pair of hands grab me by the waist. Well... "waist" is not exactly accurate.

My ass, is what he grabbed. It was just one hand, though, because the other was wrapped around my shoulders. I was hovering inches above the floor with a powerful, massive hand on my ass and another around my shoulders, and the most vivid blue pair of eyes I'd ever seen were staring down at me.

"Hi," I breathed. "Thanks. I'm Juneau."

His laugh was a rumble I felt in my chest...and my gut.

And further south.

"I'm Remington."

Oh boy.

Ohhhhhhhh boy.

I now understood why Kitty was so hung up on Roman Badd.

Jasinda Wilder

Visit me at my website: **www.jasindawilder.com**
Email me: **jasindawilder@gmail.com**

If you enjoyed this book, you can help others enjoy it as well by recommending it to friends and family, or by mentioning it in reading and discussion groups and online forums. You can also review it on the site from which you purchased it. But, whether you recommend it to anyone else or not, thank you *so much* for taking the time to read my book! Your support means the world to me!

My other titles:

The Preacher's Son:
Unbound
Unleashed
Unbroken

Biker Billionaire:
Wild Ride

Big Girls Do It:

Better (#1), Wetter (#2), Wilder (#3), On Top (#4)
Married (#5)
On Christmas (#5.5)
Pregnant (#6)
Boxed Set

Rock Stars Do It:

Harder
Dirty
Forever
Boxed Set

From the world of *Big Girls* and *Rock Stars*:

Big Love Abroad

Delilah's Diary:

A Sexy Journey
La Vita Sexy
A Sexy Surrender

The Falling Series:

Falling Into You
Falling Into Us
Falling Under
Falling Away
Falling for Colton

The Ever Trilogy:
Forever & Always
After Forever
Saving Forever

The world of *Alpha*:
Alpha
Beta
Omega
Harris: Alpha One Security Book 1
Thresh: Alpha One Security Book 2
Duke: Alpha One Security Book 3
Puck: Alpha One Security Book 4

The world of Stripped:
Stripped
Trashed

The world of *Wounded*:
Wounded
Captured

The Houri Legends:
Jack and Djinn
Djinn and Tonic

The Madame X Series:

Madame X

Exposed

Exiled

The One Series

The Long Way Home

Where the Heart Is

There's No Place Like Home

Badd Brothers:

Badd Motherf*cker

Badd Ass

Badd to the Bone

Good Girl Gone Badd

Badd Luck

Badd Mojo

Big Badd Wolf

Badd Boy

Dad Bod Contracting

Hammered

**The Black Room
(With Jade London):**

Door One

Door Two

Door Three

Door Four

Door Five

Door Six

Door Seven

Door Eight

Deleted Door

Standalone titles:

Yours

Non-Fiction titles:

You Can Do It

You Can Do It: Strength

You Can Do It: Fasting

Jack Wilder Titles:

The Missionary

To be informed of new releases and special offers,
sign up for
Jasinda's email newsletter.

Made in United States
North Haven, CT
20 October 2021

10460061R00208